CW01095216

About the author

Susan Parry began writing when she was a university professor at Imperial College. Her work included forensic studies and archaeological investigations that form the basis for her writing. She lives with her husband in Swaledale, where the views from her house provide inspiration.

Acknowledgement

Special thanks go to Sonia Marshall of the United Kingdom Accreditation Service for her invaluable advice regarding regulation of forensic laboratories.

website: www.susanparry.co.uk
facebook/instagram: susanparryauthor
twitter: @susan_parry

DEADLY EMBERS

A YORKSHIRE DALES MYSTERY

SUSAN PARRY

Viridian Publishing

First published in the United Kingdom in 2019 by
Viridian Publishing

Viridian Publishing
PO Box 594
Dorking
Surrey
RH4 9HU

www.viridian-publishing.co.uk
e-mail: enquiries@viridian-publishing.co.uk

ISBN 978-0-9567891-7-4

For Phoebe

Chapter 1

Blue flashing lights illuminated the blackness of the car park as Mills approached the entrance to the industrial estate. Abandoning her car in the street, she ran to where Brenda was standing alone in the thick smoke. They huddled together as the flames whipped wildly out of the top window of the burning building. Firemen were calling to each other, dragging hoses, running and shouting.

'Well, that's the end of Yardley Forensics,' declared Brenda.

Her harsh tone surprised Mills. She sounded completely resigned to losing her business. It was unlike her boss to give in so readily.

'Don't be silly,' Mills said, trying to sound positive although she didn't feel it. The place was ruined. How long would it take to reconstruct and install new labs? She didn't even know if Brenda owned the building and now wasn't the time to ask. She could sense her boss shaking beside her and took her icy hand. 'Don't worry, it'll be all right.'

Only then did she notice that Brenda was wearing what looked like pyjama bottoms under her coat and her feet were bare except for sheepskin slippers.

'How did you hear about the fire?' Mills asked.

'The police called. I was already half-asleep. Did I wake you when I rang?'

'Wake me? I'm not in bed at eight-thirty.'

Mills watched the fire crew aim jets of water through the burnt out windows and imagined the damage inside.

She asked, 'Has anyone gone in?'

Brenda shook her head. 'No, they won't risk it with the gas cylinders and solvents, not until they're safe. I'm glad. I wouldn't want them risking their lives over this.'

'I suppose there's nothing we can do,' Mills said.

'No. Just watch it burn down,' she replied angrily.

They continued to watch helplessly until a police officer approached them.

'They're beginning to get it under control,' he said. 'They know what they're dealing with and they'll keep going until it's been put out. At that stage they'll want to investigate the cause of the fire and I'll need a statement from you. I understand it's a forensic laboratory?'

Brenda coughed. 'Yes.'

'In that case we'll keep it safe until you can get proper security put in. We'll send a specialist round to see you about that.'

'I can't imagine there will be anything left worth saving,' replied Brenda.

He gave her a sympathetic smile and headed towards the road. As he reached the entrance gate, a car came round the corner and screeched to a halt a few yards in front of him. They watched him direct the driver to the far corner of the car park then open the door for a young woman to climb out. She was dressed in leggings and a thick sweater and it was obvious that she was very pregnant.

'What's Chloe doing here?' Brenda asked.

'Is that Tim's girlfriend?' She'd heard a lot about Chloe and knew they were due to be married soon but Mills had never met her.

The policeman was ushering the girl towards them looking very anxious. She was staring at the smouldering building.

'This young lady says she's here to pick up her fiancé,' he said, looking anxiously at each of them in turn.

'Tim isn't here, love,' said Brenda. 'I didn't call him – there seemed no point.'

The girl appeared confused and kept glancing up at the building.

'How did you hear about the fire?' asked Mills.

Chloe looked at her wild-eyed. 'Where's Tim? Is he safe?'

'He's not here, Chloe. Brenda didn't contact him.'

The policeman took the girl's arm and looked directly at her. 'Why do you think your boyfriend is here?' he asked, emphasising each word as if she was deaf or stupid.

'Because I dropped him off this evening and he said to pick him up at ten!' she shouted. 'Is he still in there?'

She pulled away from the constable and ran over to the fireman in a white helmet. They talked animatedly before she began to move towards the building. He followed but her way was barred by the fireman at the entrance and after a brief struggle she collapsed.

'Oh no! No, no, no!' Brenda shouted as she ran over to the prone figure.

'Our technician,' Mills explained to the police officer as they followed. 'He must've been working on something.'

She pulled out her phone and tried calling him, praying he'd answer from a pub in the town or at home, hoping there had been a huge mistake and he was fine. It rang and finally went to voicemail. She left a message saying they were worried about him and to ring her.

An ambulance was called and they tried to make the girl comfortable on the cold ground. She came round but was hysterical, calling Tim's name and crying out. She struggled to get up but collapsed back, too overwrought to do anything but sit supported by a policewoman. When the paramedics arrived Chloe refused to leave until there had been a search for Tim in the building. They insisted she had to go to hospital to make sure baby was all right. Brenda was in an equally bad way and just kept repeating that it was all her fault. Eventually they walked the girl to the ambulance draped in a blanket and helped her up the steps into the back. Mills suggested that Brenda went with her while she stayed with the police to answer any questions about the lab. In reality she was worried about Brenda's health and felt it would be better if she was in the warm. Besides, her boss obviously knew the girl better than she did.

It was another couple of hours before the flames had gone and all that was left was the acrid smoke. By then a journalist had arrived and a small group of on-lookers had gathered in the road. The fire crew agreed they would do a quick search of the areas where it was safe to do so and an officer in breathing apparatus disappeared up a ladder and in through the window. Everyone waited in silence for him to reappear. It was several minutes before he emerged and shouted something down to the leader. The constable went to speak to them and eventually came back over to Mills.

'Unfortunately there appears to be a body in there,' he kept his voice down. 'Obviously they can't approach to identify it with the condition of the building and it will be difficult even once it is recovered. I suppose we can assume it's your colleague if he was working up there?'

'How long will it take to identify him?' Mills asked, still hoping they were mistaken.

'You tell me,' he replied. 'Aren't you lot the forensic experts?'

It was getting on for two o'clock when all but one of the fire engines left. Mills watched from her car as they filed down the road towards town. The journalist had left an hour ago after she refused to be interviewed. She had stayed on to see if the body was removed from the building but nothing had changed. Now she climbed out and walked stiffly to the car park entrance where the police constable remained on duty.

'Is there anything I can do?' It was a stupid question but she needed him to tell her to go home. Of course there was nothing.

'Not now. Not unless you know why your colleague was working on his own so late.'

She shook her head.

'But we will need your help to pull all the information together. The other lady, is she your boss?'

'Brenda? Yes. I'd better see if she's all right – and Chloe.'

'The pregnant lady? They'll have taken her to the District Hospital. It'll have been a shock for her.'

Mills drove through the deserted streets in a daze.

Parking was easy but it took her a while to find out where Tim's fiancée had been taken. She assumed the ambulance had delivered her to the Emergency Department but was told that she'd been sent to the Delivery Suite. Of course – the one place open twenty-four hours a day that could check the baby was all right. Mills was feeling the effect of the long night as she walked through empty corridors to the other end of the hospital. As she approached Strayside Wing she could see Brenda at the end of the corridor slumped awkwardly on a seat, clearly fast asleep. Mills sat down beside her and gently took her hand.

'How are you?' she asked.

Her boss wiped dribble from her chin and sat upright.

'I'm fine.' The tremor in her voice contradicted her.

'And Chloe?'

'They're monitoring the baby. They rang her mother, she's in with her now.'

'Then I'll drive you home.' She looked at her watch. It was already three-thirty.

Brenda asked to be dropped at the lab to pick up her own car but Mills thought it best not to return to the scene.

'Let's go back to your place and get some sleep, Brenda. We'll have a lot to do in the morning.'

They drove in silence. Brenda nodded off, her head plunging forward whenever the car slowed. Mills was trying to work out if Tim could have been in the lab that night and why. He'd sometimes worked for her during a weekend but she'd not given him anything to do recently. Brenda knew of their arrangement – bits of analysis associated with the research Mills was doing at the university. Tim was glad of the extra money because the impending wedding was going to be expensive. But she had never once asked him to work during the night.

At Brenda's she said goodnight to her boss and threw a duvet on the unmade bed in the spare room. They agreed they would set their alarm clocks for eight so they could get to the lab in time to catch staff turning up for work. Mills climbed under the duvet fully clothed and closed her eyes, hoping for a few hours sleep. The next thing she heard was her phone alarm. She rolled onto her back and kicked at the weight on her feet. Pulling herself up to a sitting position she discovered a black cat staring back at her. It jumped off the bed, fleeing through the door as Mills struggled to get her trainers on before making for the bathroom. The mirror was steamed up and she guessed Brenda had washed already.

Her boss was seated at the kitchen table with her head in her hands.

'There's tea in the pot. It's been made a while but it should still be hot.'

'Have you been up long?' Mills asked.

'Couldn't sleep. I've been looking online. There must've been someone from the papers there last night; it's on the local news. One fatality, identity not disclosed but probably an employee.'

'They don't know that yet.'

'Chloe seemed pretty certain, poor girl.'

Brenda looked up at Mills. Her expression was questioning, almost accusatory.

'Did you give him some private work?'

'No!' She regretted shouting and lowered her voice. 'No I didn't. I can't imagine why Tim would be in the building.'

Mills fetched herself a mug of tea. It was tepid but it gave her something to do. She stood by the sink looking at Brenda's hunched back.

'I was wondering, do you think he accidentally started the fire himself?'

Brenda shook her head. 'We don't know what went on up there do we? How were we to know he was in there?' She blew her nose loudly. 'How could we know someone was there?' she muttered to herself. 'It shouldn't have happened. It never should've happened.'

Mills couldn't understand what she meant and went to fetch her phone from the spare room. She wanted to see if the police or Chloe or customers had tried to contact her. So far there were no new messages. When she returned to the kitchen Brenda was sitting upright trying to put on a brave face but her eyes were red and puffy. Mills suggested they go to the lab to pick up Brenda's car and find out what progress had been made in identifying the victim of the fire.

A uniformed officer waved them into the car park. The smell of smoke still hung in the air and the wind was carrying ash across the tarmac. There was broken glass below the holes where the windows had been. A temporary barrier had been put across the entrance to the lab and a policewoman stood to one side, presumably to prevent anyone entering the premises. The members of laboratory staff were huddled together in front of the building.

Glyn, the lab manager, came over. 'I heard what happened on "Stray FM" as I was driving in. What can we be doing, Brenda?'

'Nothing, pet. They won't let us in until they've investigated the cause.'

She had hold of his arm and was steering him away from the group of technicians as she continued to talk. Suddenly they stopped and, although Mills couldn't hear what was being said, she guessed Brenda was telling him about Tim. Glyn was shaking his head. He was looking up at the sky and rubbing his face with his free hand. Brenda moved him towards the group and stood with them for some time. After a while the girls were hugging and comforting one another. Mills watched, unable to contribute.

She took the opportunity to find out if there was any new information by asking the police officer at the gate. He explained they were keeping the site secure now that the body had been recovered. He could give them no further details but suggested they gave statements as soon as possible.

Brenda eventually came back over, leaving the group looking lost.

'I told them to go home and wait to hear what we're to do. It's all I could say.'

Mills didn't trust herself to respond. She was angry with the way she had dismissed her team so readily.

'They want us to go to the police station to give our statements,' she said.

Brenda stopped and turned to face the burnt out building.

'Well, at least we were insured,' she said.

'Do you own the building?' Mills asked.

'Yes. I do.'

'So you'll be able to renovate the labs.'

'I don't think so, pet. I'm getting too old for that. The main thing is to pay off the mortgage.'

Mills didn't know how to respond. She'd assumed that they would spend the next year rebuilding the business. It was a shock to think the lab may no longer exist and she was appalled that Brenda would give up so easily. In fact she would have suspected that Brenda was pleased with the outcome – if it wasn't for Tim's death. Mills thought about some financial problems the lab had been having over the past year and understood that Brenda might feel relieved for them to go away overnight.

'You know it's going to be a huge problem sorting out the work we had going on in the lab,' she told Brenda. 'We'll have to account for every single forensic sample we had stored, including the ongoing work and all the data from previous analyses.'

When there was no response, she continued, 'The investigation into the cause of the fire could go on for months. And the inquest…'

'I don't want to talk about it now,' Brenda said crossly. 'Let's just get the statements over and done with.'

Mills was heading for her Mini but Brenda stopped. 'I'll take my own car, thank you,' she said marching off.

The tears wouldn't stop as Mills drove to the police station. Lack of sleep, the horror of accepting that it would be Tim's body removed from the fire, added to Brenda's desire to walk away from the lab, had finally defeated her. She waited outside the police station and they walked in together in silence. They were kept waiting before staff were available. Brenda remained taciturn, Mills was feeling unsympathetic. She was pleased when finally it was suggested they went into separate rooms to give their written statements.

As it turned out there was little information that Mills could provide apart from routine replies to questions about the lab and the nature of its work. She didn't know why Tim, if it was him, was in the building; she hadn't arrived until after the fire brigade were tackling the blaze and had no idea how it might have started. Yes, it was possible that something Tim was doing could have caught fire but as she didn't know what he was up to she couldn't speculate. Mills wondered how Brenda was getting on and looked for her as soon as the interview was over but there was no sign of her. She had left already.

Someone called out and turning she saw a middle-aged man coming towards her.

'Dr Sanderson?'

'Yes.'

'I'm Richard Stewart. I'm the DI investigating the fire at Yardley Forensics. Have you given your statement?'

'Yes.'

'I'd appreciate any thoughts you may have regarding the unfortunate circumstances of the death of your colleague.'

'We don't know it was Tim,' Mills maintained.

'Ah, I'm afraid we do. Sorry. His fiancée's mother identified him this morning.'

'So he wasn't badly burned then?'

'Parts were, unfortunately, but the cause of death appears to have been asphyxiation. The PM will confirm it. I only mention this because I know you're a forensic scientist. I hope it's not too disturbing?'

'Do they know what caused the fire,' she asked,

ignoring his question.

'No, it's far too early to say. The investigators are starting work tomorrow and it could take days.'

'But they'll find out the cause – whether it was faulty electrics or something Tim was doing?'

'I hope so. We'll need that for the inquest. The only bit of information we have so far is from the fire brigade. They felt that the fire began at ground level and went up but the fire scene investigators will confirm whether that was the case.'

Chapter 2

The lurcher, clearly surprised to see Mills in the middle of the day, bounced around the hall. It was a relief to be home and she bent to give Harris a hug. He responded by jumping up, nearly knocking her over. The answer machine was flashing but she ignored it, determined to have a shower and change her clothes before she did anything. Whoever had called would have to wait.

It wasn't long before she was seated at the kitchen table with a plate of beans on toast in front of her. She'd had nothing to eat since yesterday teatime and she was feeling weak with hunger. It was her comfort food of choice. She followed her meal with two mugs of tea and finally felt ready to face the phone calls, starting with her university colleague.

'Nige, I'm sorry. I should've rung you to say I wouldn't be in.'

'You didn't have lectures today, did you?'

'No but I was supposed to see a second-year tutorial group this morning.'

'What's the problem?'

She told him about the fire and found herself getting very emotional when she talked about Tim.

'What was he doing there?'

It was an obvious question but she hadn't an answer.

'They'll investigate the cause of the fire, won't they?' he asked.

'Of course. If he started it, they'll find out.'

'Is that what you think?'

'I can't imagine any other explanation, unless someone left an oven on overnight and something caught fire.'

It sounded unconvincing as she said it.

'I'm surprised Nina didn't tell me,' he said.

'Nige, your wife may be a member of the North Yorkshire Police but that doesn't mean she'll know about everything that's happened in the county.'

'I suppose not. I'll let her know anyway.'

'I just wanted to let *you* know that I probably won't be in unless it's necessary until I sort Brenda out – she doesn't seem particularly focussed at the moment. I'll cover my lectures but I'll reorganise anything else.'

'OK. Let me know if I can help with any archaeology stuff.'

Mills divided her time as a lecturer between the Archaeology and Forensics Departments. She shared an office with Nige in the Archaeology Department where he was a senior member of staff. Normally she would spend one day a week or even less at Yardley Forensics purely in a consultancy role, helping Brenda with the administration and using her expertise to advise the analysts.

There was a loud tap on the window so she finished the call hurriedly and went to open the front door.

'Muriel!'

'Hello, love. I saw the car so I didn't let myself in. Do you still want me to walk Harris today?'

The dog was already tugging at the lead hanging on a hook in the hall.

'No, not today thanks. I think I'll take him myself.'

Her neighbour was studying her. 'Is everything all right,

dear? Only you look tired. Aren't you feeling well?'

Mills forced a smile. 'No, I'm fine. It's just… there's been… we had a fire, that's all.'

She could tell Muriel wanted to know more. 'I'll come round and explain later but I just need to get Harris out now.'

She put on her jacket and fiddled with the dog's lead until she heard the gate close.

'See you later!' Muriel called from her front step as Harris pulled Mills up the road.

It was cloudy and the sun gave no warmth. In another hour it will have disappeared behind the hills across the dale. Mills pulled the heavy scarf round more tightly against the cold wind, wishing she'd worn a hat. She let Harris off the lead at the top of the track where he ran off, stopping to examine mole hills and rabbit holes before coming back for a treat. Although he'd only left the rehoming centre a few months ago, he'd learned quickly and she assumed he'd been trained well by his previous owner.

He led her along the familiar route following the contour from where the track petered out. Mills looked around, trying to concentrate on the views towards Muker in an attempt to relax with a form of mindfulness. Unfortunately the peace was soon broken by the sound of a quad bike tearing towards her.

'Harris! Harris!' she screamed, uselessly.

It was the one problem she had yet to solve – his reaction to motorbikes and quad bikes. He would bark loudly, chasing the vehicles for some distance before giving up and frightening Mills, who was concerned he might be hurt or, worse still, cause an accident.

On this occasion the lad on the quad bike didn't seem concerned. He flew past without acknowledging her, looking round only once as Harris slowed and gave up the chase. She waited for him to return, praising him for coming back – against her better judgement. Mills wondered if the lad was Justin Price. She'd seen him grow up over the years and reckoned he must be in his twenties now. She knew he'd been to college in Newcastle to study but guessed he was home and helping his dad on the farm a few miles away.

Mills walked on until the cold was making her uncomfortable.

'Come on Harris, let's get back and light a fire, shall we?'

Her plan was to settle down in front of the telly to forget what an awful day it had been.

But when she got back Muriel was lying in wait. 'I've made scones – I thought you might like some to cheer you up. They're cherry and walnut.'

Mills thanked her and explained very quickly about the fire at the lab. She couldn't bring herself to talk about what had happened to Tim but made her excuses and went to go inside.

'What about tomorrow? Will Harris need a walk at dinner-time?'

'Ah, yes I guess so if it's all right?'

Muriel smiled. 'Of course it is. The exercise does me good and the money comes in handy for those little extras for Christmas. It'll be November this week and I like to shop early.'

Inside the answer machine was still blinking. Mills carried on going through the messages. The departmental office in the Forensics Department wanted to know why she'd missed her tutorial that morning – she would send her apologies later. Glyn wanted to talk about the fire; as the lab manager he felt responsible for the staff, or that was his excuse. Donna had been the analyst closest to Tim and she sounded incoherent. The last message was her friend Nina. Nige had told his wife about the fire and if Mills wanted to talk she would be in the office all day. She was surprised there was nothing from Brenda and wondered if she should get in touch to see how she was coping but decided to send her a message instead.

It was tempting to call her friend first but she took a deep breath and rang Glyn. To her relief there was no answer so she wouldn't have to speak to him. Donna answered almost immediately and straight away burst into tears.

'Sorry, sorry, I'll be all right. It's been so shocking to think it might be Tim. I keep ringing but he's not answering his phone.'

Mills realised only then that not everyone would know that the body brought out of the fire had been confirmed as Tim's.

'I'm so sorry, Donna. Chloe's mother identified him this morning.'

There was a long pause before the girl said, 'But I saw him leave after work. He was getting on his bike. I don't understand how he was still in there.'

'I assume Chloe drove him back to the lab later. She arrived at ten to pick him up.'

'But why was he working so late into the night? Was it something he was doing for you?'

'No!' Mills replied angrily, feeling she was being accused

of causing his death. Then, 'Sorry I shouldn't have snapped at you.'

'No, it's my fault.'

'Listen, Donna. It will be a while before the fire investigation team report and the inquest is held but at least we can try to understand what Tim was doing in the lab. You know what he was working on, he talked to you. Can you think of anything that might give us an insight into what was going on?'

'Not immediately but I'll think about it. It's something I can work on. It's better than waiting with nothing to do.'

Mills had another thought. 'How well do you know his girlfriend, Chloe?'

'I've met her a few times. I went to dinner with them and we've been out occasionally in a group.'

'It might be nice if someone from the lab makes contact, if you feel comfortable about it. She might like to talk.'

'I could try. If it was me I might not want to speak to anyone connected with the place.'

'See what you can do. I know it should be Brenda but I'm not sure she would be the right person at the moment.'

Mills took a break to light the fire and grab a mug of tea before settling on the sofa to call Nina.

'How are you?' her friend asked. 'It must've been a dreadful shock. Was the fire an accident? Are they investigating? How long will it take? How's Brenda?'

Mills tried to answer her questions one by one. Finally she told Nina what was really worrying her: that Brenda seemed determined to cut her losses and run.

'Are you allowed to do that?' Nina asked. 'Surely the

insurance money is to cover rebuilding isn't it? No, actually that may not be true. When Dad wrote his car off he didn't have to buy another one with the money they gave him. Perhaps she can just take the money and retire.'

'She said she would have to pay off the mortgage. I think the business has some financial problems. This might just solve them.'

Nina went quiet. 'Changing the subject, Mills, is Phil with you?'

'No, he's in Nottingham. I don't expect he'll be back for a while.'

'Is he down there permanently? I thought the university gave him a part-time contract.'

'It's taking up more of his time than he thought.'

'I see.'

What you don't see, Nina, thought Mills, is his female colleague who seems to be taking up much of his time.

'What about the dog? Has Phil taken him?'

'No, Harris is still here with me. He's fine. My neighbour is walking him during the day. He's perfectly happy.'

Mills promised to keep in touch with her friend as they ended the call. It had occurred to her that Brenda might not have been informed that Tim's body had been identified. She didn't want to talk to anyone else, least of all her boss, so she sent an email, hoping she would bother to look at her messages. Then she settled down on the sofa.

She was woken by the phone ringing. It was dark and she felt her way across the room by the dim glow of the fire that was almost out.

'Hello? Is that Mills?' Her boss sounded anxious.

'Yes. Hello Brenda.'

'It doesn't sound like you.'

'I've just woken up.'

'You've been asleep, have you? I seem to have been on the telephone all afternoon. The police came round to tell me that they've identified the body.'

'I know. Didn't you see my email?'

'You know already? Well it was what we feared but it doesn't make it any easier. Chloe's mother called me – she wants to come round today. I said I was out.'

She waited for a response but Mills had nothing to say to her.

'You'll be pleased to know I've been in touch with the regulators.' Brenda continued. 'They suspended our accreditation straight away.'

'That's hardly surprising.'

'I told them we hadn't been able to get into the building so we didn't know what could be salvaged.'

'What did they say to that?'

'That the police will probably want to set up some group to establish the evidence they had stored in there. The regulator says she may be invited to that. They'll want to know we've followed the code of practice regarding our business continuity plan. She said we must have one. Anyway, I'm sure you can handle that side for me.'

'What?'

It was typical of Brenda to expect her to take responsibility. She had no interest in the boring stuff and relied on Mills too much to make sure they were compliant. She was sure that was why the financial side had suffered recently. Granted, her boss had been treated for cancer and during that time Mills had held the fort but that was over now and, since she started her full time lecturing post, Mills was spending very little time at Yardley Forensics. Her instinct was to tell Brenda to deal with the regulators herself but she knew that would be disastrous if Brenda became belligerent as she tended to do when unsure of herself.

'I have to go into uni tomorrow morning but perhaps we could sit down in the afternoon and see what samples were being processed.'

'Good! We can't meet in the lab so you'd better come to my house at three o' clock.'

'Fine. So what do you have in the way of records at home?'

'Nothing really.'

Exasperated, Mills just wanted to finish the call.

'I'll be at yours by three tomorrow, bye!'

She put the phone down guiltily and went into the kitchen to give Harris his tea.

It was a relief to drive into the car park behind the faculty building next morning. Everything was as normal as it could be; students were rushing up the corridor to their nine o' clock lectures and Nige was in the office bashing his keyboard noisily. He looked up when she sat at her desk and told her he had something for her.

'Nina sent this in for you.'

It was a round tin. She went over and opened it.

'They're chocolate brownies,' he said, peering inside. 'She said I wasn't to have any.'

'Would you like one?'

His hand moved swiftly. 'Thanks, they're very good.'

Mills spent the morning catching up with correspondence and finishing off a forensics lecture she was due to give just before lunch. Fortunately there was nothing that would need her attention in the afternoon.

'Right I'm off straight after I've finished with the first-years,' she announced.

'See you tomorrow?' Nige asked without looking up.

'Not sure. I thought I'd keep it clear until I see what this afternoon brings. To be honest I think we're going to find ourselves in trouble. If we can't account for the samples in the lab it will affect a lot of cases. It's a mess.'

'There must be back-ups of the records though?'

'I hope so, I really do.'

She carried the cake tin out to the car so she could make a quick get-away and went to lecture room three. She could hear the students waiting for her as she walked down the corridor. It was the fourth week of term. They'd got over freshers' week with the novelty of being away from home and, following a couple of talks from the Head about getting down to work, they'd begun to settle. Her lecture was designed as an initial introduction to laboratory procedures and analysis. Her notes were based on what was done at Yardley Forensics, an accredited laboratory carrying out a range of analytical techniques, mainly to support the police. One thing was clear, she thought as she gathered up her notes at the end, the Yardley lab was no longer accredited for anything.

Brenda opened the door as Mills was walking up the path.

'Glyn's here,' she announced in a low voice. 'I thought it best to ask him. He has a good handle on the work across the whole lab.'

Let's hope so, thought Mills. She and Glyn had never hit it off. He seemed threatened in his role as lab manager when she was taken on as a consultant and it was even worse when Alex arrived to develop their digital forensics capabilities. Glyn disliked him and it got difficult when Alex moved in with her. Things should have improved when he left but, although she and Glyn were polite to one another, they were never friends.

She followed Brenda into the sitting room. Glyn was relaxing in a large leather armchair. He looked up and gave a wan smile. There was an uncomfortable silence that Mills felt compelled to fill.

'I guess Brenda has updated you on the news?'

'You mean about Tim?' He was studying the floor. 'Yes, I heard.' Then he looked directly at her. 'Do *you* know why he was there so late?'

'No, she doesn't, Glyn. I told you.' Brenda looked embarrassed. She was standing by the door. 'Sit down Mills. I'll put the kettle on.'

She went out, leaving Mills with Glyn still looking at her in a hostile way.

'But you do give him work to do out of hours. I know that for a fact.'

Mills stepped over to the sofa and sat down.

'I have done, yes. He has sometimes worked at the weekend for me but only during the day and generally I'll be there as well.'

'So he definitely wasn't working for you on Monday night?'

'No.'

'In that case I can't imagine what he was up to. We don't allow lone working out of office hours.'

'Donna said she saw him leave on Monday evening.'

'He must have come back later then.'

'Chloe dropped him off in her car.'

'Chloe?'

'His fiancée.'

'Ah, yes, I've met her. She's popped into the lab once or twice when she's brought Tim into work – when the weather's been too bad for him to use his bike.'

'Glyn, I'm really worried about how we sort out all this mess.'

She felt bad about changing the subject but she wanted to know whether he thought anything was salvageable.

'What d'you mean exactly?'

'I mean do we have any way of retrieving records and samples or is everything going to be lost?'

He looked surprised, as if he hadn't thought about it. Perhaps he hadn't. Anyway it was too late, there was a rattling of crockery coming down the hall and Brenda appeared with a large tea tray. She had made sandwiches, bless her, and Mills realised she was hungry.

'Tuck in. I know you've probably missed your lunch, pet.'

Glyn protested that he had already eaten but proceeded to polish off more than his fair share. No more was said about the fire until Brenda checked her watch, announcing that Donna was due to arrive.

'We can start as soon as she's here,' she said. 'I thought we should have a quick meeting of senior staff to discuss what we should do.'

No-one argued. In Mills' view there wasn't much they could say.

'The site is being investigated and there'll be an inquest.

Until we know what happened I don't see that we can contribute much,' said Glyn, leaning forward to put his cup on the tray. 'I've told Margaret and Debs to stay away until they hear from me.'

He was referring to their two part-time lab technicians. A car was parking behind the others in the drive and Brenda jumped up to peer through the net curtains.

'It's Donna,' she said. 'I'll make some more tea. Can you let her in?'

Mills sighed as Brenda shot out of the room with the tray. She waited for the bell before going to open the door.

'Hello Donna, how are you?' Mills gave her a hug and led her into the sitting room.

Glyn was already standing in preparation to greet her.

'Glyn, how nice to see you.' Donna looked pale.

'And you,' he replied.

'Brenda's just making tea,' Mills explained.

Donna sat down next to Mills.

As soon as Brenda appeared she was in charge. She began the meeting by offering her sympathies for the loss of their colleague. Then she went on to explain the situation as she understood it, concluding that nothing could really be done at present.

'Do you know when we'll be given access to the lab?' Donna asked.

Brenda shrugged. 'They haven't told us anything.'

Anxious that they shouldn't appear negative, Mills explained that the investigation team were working with the police to establish the cause of the fire. 'I'm sure it won't be much longer,' she added. 'As soon as we have permission we'll have to do a thorough review of what we can salvage, what is beyond saving and what is missing. We'll definitely need your help with that.' Mills hoped that sounded suitably efficient. 'I think we should catch up in a few days when it's clearer how long this is going to take. Meanwhile, a list of police cases and the impact on them would be very helpful. We'll have to contact our customers to let them know the situation.'

'Yes, that's in hand,' confirmed Brenda.

Mills looked at Glyn. His eyebrows moved almost imperceptibly. She too doubted Brenda had anything "in hand".

When they'd finished their tea Brenda picked up the tray and Donna followed her into the kitchen. Glyn leaned forward in his chair, rubbing his forehead.

'*Has* she contacted anyone?'

'I doubt it. I don't suppose she knows who to contact unless she keeps a list of jobs here.'

'The majority of the work was from North Yorkshire Police as usual. There was something from Cleveland Police as well but I don't recall anything from outside the force.'

'That will make life easier. I can contact the police forces to see if I can put a list of jobs together. But we need to get to the bottom of where the records are stored.'

Brenda returned with Donna and they stood in the doorway.

Mills took a breath. 'Brenda, where are the lab records backed up? Where can we find the data, if the computers have been destroyed?'

Glyn chipped in. 'There's an external hard drive for the instruments. That's copied every week.'

'In the lab?' asked Mills.

'Yes… oh dear, yes, I see what you mean.'

'I suppose my computer may be damaged too?'

'Yes, Brenda.' Mills couldn't keep the frustration from her voice. 'So there has to be an external back up.'

Brenda was looking into the distance. 'I suppose there will be – but where?'

'Don't worry, it'll be in the protocols, I'll look tonight.' Mills didn't trust herself to discuss it any longer. It was obvious that her boss didn't have a clue what to do and Glyn wasn't going to be much help. She had better get up to speed to produce what the police would need on her own.

'Thank you Mills, I don't think I can cope with this business.'

Donna said if there was nothing else she would be going and made for the front door.

'I'll be back in a minute,' Mills called as she followed the girl onto the drive.

'Donna, wait!'

She stopped by her car.

'I just wanted to ask if you've spoken to Chloe. Brenda said her mother wanted to see her but she's been avoiding her. She's not handling things very well as you probably realise.'

'It has hit us all hard, hasn't it? I mean you don't expect to lose a friend that way. I keep going over how the fire started and why Tim was there. None of it makes any sense. Chloe is in bits over it.'

'You've seen her?'

Her expression changed. She looked as if she might cry. 'Yes. I went to see her. Her mum was there and she was nice but Chloe was like really angry. I thought she'd be upset but she just started as soon as I went in.'

'What d'you mean?'

Donna sighed. 'At first she asked me about the analyses Tim did for you. She was sure you'd asked him to work on something. I told her that if you said he wasn't, then he wasn't. She seemed to accept that but then she turned on me, saying that we were very close me and Tim; that he was always talking about me.'

Her eyes were wet and her mouth twisted as she spoke. Mills put an arm round the girl's shaking shoulders.

'She said… she said that she'd suspected he was seeing someone and it made sense now why he was in the lab – to meet me.'

'But you weren't there.'

'I know. Anyway her mum came in and said it was best if I left. Chloe was shouting and screaming at me.'

'What did her mother think?'

'Only that Chloe was very upset and wasn't really thinking straight.'

She climbed into her car and Mills watched her reverse carefully out of the drive before going back inside. When asked if Donna was all right she simply said that her visit to Chloe had been quite emotional.

'Her mother keeps ringing. I suppose I'll have to talk to her soon.'

'Do you know what she wants?'

'It could be about insurance,' suggested Glyn. 'After all, Tim did die at work, so to speak.'

Brenda sat down heavily on the sofa. 'I can't cope with all this,' she exclaimed.

'It'll be OK in the end. A lot of paperwork though.'

Glyn smiled encouragingly at his boss.

'No I mean it. After all, if we're not going to start again we don't need to go through it all, do we?'

Glyn looked surprised but didn't respond.

Mills felt compelled to say something. 'Brenda, there are ongoing cases that relied on our, I mean your, lab to do the forensic work that will prove whether the defendant is rightly or wrongly accused of a crime. Some of the crimes are very serious and they're depending on us. I don't think we can walk away from that.'

'But if the evidence is destroyed?'

'We don't know until we see inside, do we? I suggest we go along to the lab tomorrow and talk to the fire investigation people to find out when they'll be finished.'

Chapter 3

The investigation team was inside the building when Mills arrived at the lab. She waited by the taped off entrance until a man came down the stairs accompanied by a cocker spaniel.

'This is Snoops,' he explained. 'She's our fire investigation dog.'

Mills restrained herself from making a fuss of the spaniel in case it was inappropriate when the dog was working.

'I like her little boots.'

'They protect her feet from glass and other debris.'

'So is she a detection dog?' asked Mills.

'She's trained to pick up most accelerants including petrol, paraffin, diesel, methylated spirits, acetone, and barbecue lighter fluid. Aren't you Snoops?'

The dog wagged its tail.

'Did she find any of those?'

He looked round as a second man came down the stairs.

'Are you a journalist?' he asked her with a frown.

'Sorry, I should have said. My name is Mills Sanderson. I work … I mean I worked here.'

He nodded as if he recognised her name.

'I've got ID,' she offered.

'It's OK. I think we've sent evidence to you in the past. I'm Ralf and this is Seb. I won't shake hands,' he added showing her his plastic gloves.

'So can you tell me anything about how it started?' she asked.

The two men looked at each other and Seb answered. 'We're pretty sure accelerant was used just inside here and up the stairs. Do you know if the door was secured on Sunday night?'

'No but if Tim was working inside he might not have locked it. His girlfriend was collecting him so he may have left it open for her.'

'Snoops located the accelerant,' said the other man. 'We've taken samples so they'll be sent off straight away.'

He showed her the bag he was carrying. It was ironic, Mills thought, that they might have sent the samples to Yardley Forensics if it wasn't for…

'It's a right mess up there!' offered Seb, climbing out of his protective coverall and flinging it in the back of the van. 'I don't envy you sorting that lot out.'

'Is it safe to walk about up there?' she asked.

Ralf nodded. 'Yes, those metal stairs seem to be indestructible but no-one's to go in yet. A police forensic team will be all over it now we know the fire was started deliberately. Someone from the local station is coming back to secure it before we go.'

'Your insurance company will arrange to have the structure checked out. Presumably you've contacted them?' asked Seb.

'Yes, I'm sure the boss has,' Mills replied but she wasn't confident.

There was still no sign of Brenda when the police officer arrived to guard the building until the forensic team arrived. Mills said goodbye to the fire investigators and Snoops before heading down to see Brenda. She needed to know whether the insurance company was coming to sort it all out.

Brenda's car was in the drive but there was no answer when Mills knocked. She tried the bell several times but wasn't convinced it was working. Finally she called the landline from her mobile and listened to it ringing inside. It rang and rang. Finally, through the frosted glass, she could see a dark figure moving slowly down the stairs. She cut off the call and banged loudly on the door again.

'Brenda, it's me!'

The figure turned and made for the door, opening it a little way.

'Mills?'

She was in her dressing gown, squinting at her through the crack.

'Let me in please Brenda.'

The door was opened a little wider and Mills squeezed through. They stood staring at each other in the hall.

'I thought we were meeting at the lab,' Mills said.

'What time is it, pet?'

'Lunch time.'

They went into the kitchen where Brenda snatched a whisky bottle off the table and shoved it in the bin.

'Want a cup of tea?'

'If you're making one.'

It was obvious her boss wasn't coping and now Mills was about to make it worse by informing her that the fire was started deliberately, a case of arson. She had hardly absorbed the information herself and in the car she'd been imagining all sorts of scenarios including the thought that Tim had killed himself. She decided to wait until she had persuaded Brenda to get washed and dressed. Meanwhile they drank the strong tea together with little conversation.

'Did you go to the lab this morning?' Brenda asked her eventually.

'I did. I thought you were coming too. I saw the fire investigation team and their dog. It was a cocker spaniel with little protective boots on. I wanted to take a picture but I thought it might seem rather flippant. Anyway, why don't you pop upstairs and have a shower while I fix us something to eat – I'm starving.'

When she was alone, Mills peered into the fridge to see what she could make. There was a piece of hard cheese and two eggs. Deciding that cheese on toast would be easier than preparing eggs, she turned on the grill and waited for it to heat up. The toast got a bit burnt but the cheese cooked nicely and when Brenda appeared she sniffed appreciatively.

'Is that cheese?' she asked.

'Cheese on toast.'

'Lovely.'

The food seemed to lift the mood and Mills felt able to talk business.

'What is your insurance company doing?' she asked.

'I rang them yesterday but they asked me lots of questions and I got a bit muddled. They need some number or other and I didn't know it.'

'It'll be on the certificate. Do you have that?'

'Well it'll be in the lab won't it?' she snapped. She was clearly getting stressed.

'If you give me the name of the company I'll see if I can talk to them about it.'

Mills asked herself why she was offering to do it. 'They'll be able to sort out a lot of the issues once they have seen the lab. There will be structural examinations before we can be sure it's safe to go in. I am thinking we might need a specialist company to help.'

Brenda was frowning. 'Why? We know our own lab best.'

'But there are gas cylinders and acids and solvents to make safe. We don't know how the fire has affected the electrics, do we? And the cleaning is going to be a nightmare. We won't be able to manage without outside help.'

'But if we aren't going to carry on…'

'You can't leave it in that state. It will have to be made safe so someone can do something with the building. I assume the mortgage company will want that at least!'

Brenda shook her head slowly and covered her face with her hands.

'To be honest, Mills, I just want it to go away. I want the whole bloody thing to disappear.'

'I'm afraid it's not going to. I guess you'll hear soon enough. The fire investigators have found accelerant on the stairs. It looks like it was deliberate.'

Mills was surprised how calmly Brenda reacted to the news.

'I don't suppose they'll find who did it.' She sat back in her chair. 'It won't affect the insurance though, will it?' she added.

'I don't know. I'll call the insurance company when I get home, if you give me their name.'

Brenda disappeared and came back with a scrap of paper with a phone number scribbled in pencil.

'I hope you have better luck than I did, pet.'

'I'll make sure I do. I'll call you later to tell you how I got on.'

It was a relief to be leaving. Brenda used to be quite efficient but she had her blind spots when it came to 'officialdom' as she called it. She was quite old fashioned sometimes. Mills suspected that she had never really got her mojo back after her cancer treatment.

Mills was just putting the phone down when Nina rang. It had been a long call to the insurers but finally there was a successful outcome. She would meet an assessor at the lab on the following afternoon for an initial view of the scale of the claim. It would be fine they said. She hoped so. Her friend asked how things were going and she told her that the fire investigators had found accelerant so it was arson.

'Murder then,' Nina said.

Mills hadn't really thought about it. She'd assumed it was just unfortunate that Tim happened to be working in the lab at the time. 'Surely it would be manslaughter?'

'Have they had the post mortem yet?'

'I guess so but I don't know the results. There's no reason why I would.'

'Are you in touch with his family?'

'No, not directly, that's Brenda's job. She'll have the contact details… maybe.'

'Perhaps you should contact them if she hasn't – if only to find out when the funeral is taking place.'

She told Nina how she'd been on the phone for hours to the insurance company because Brenda was cracking up under the strain.

'She's leaving me to look after everything. I wouldn't mind but I don't know where to start with tracking all the police cases that they were working on. Brenda says they'll set up a group to look at it.'

'A Gold Group?'

'She didn't say. What's that?'

'It's what we do if there is a special investigation to carry out. It's quite high level.'

'Serious then.'

'Well I guess if there are ongoing cases waiting for forensic evidence there needs to be serious consideration of the outcomes. It sounds as if you need to take responsibility if Brenda's not coping. She's not been well these last few years has she?'

'No, she hasn't.'

Nina promised to let Mills know if she heard anything about a Gold Group being set up and in turn made her promise to keep in touch.

Mills had just got back from walking Harris and was giving him his tea when the phone rang again. She hesitated when she saw it was Phil but she needed to know if he was coming at the weekend and lifted the receiver reluctantly.

'Phil.'

'Hi, it's me. How are things?'

'You don't want to know.'

But he did and it all spilled out. Everything from the fire on Sunday night, Tim, Brenda wanting to finish with the lab, the paperwork and how it was all landing on her shoulders. He made sympathetic noises and said he was really sorry to hear about Tim.

'You must be shattered, Mills.'

'I think I am but I can't afford to be, can I? You know Brenda.'

He did. Brenda was a colleague of his when she'd first met Phil and they'd become an item all those years ago. He was the osteoarchaeologist and Brenda was the expert in textiles when they were both working for the police. A lot had happened since he went abroad to work but strangely it had been an ex-girlfriend of his that had owned the lab before Brenda took it over.

'Anyway, Phil, what are you doing this weekend?'

It was her roundabout way of asking if he was coming up from Nottingham to see her.

'There's a big firework display down here. Apparently it's really something. You ought to come down.'

It was typical of Phil.

'And what about Harris?'

'Ah.'

'Reeth has a bonfire on the fifth.'

'Shame, I'm giving a seminar.'

'How's work then?'

'Amazing. Maria is just brilliant and she's great to work with. She's got these bones from an area by the coast in Norway where the diet was pretty much only fish and we're going to get isotope ratios on them. We could send samples up for your elemental analysis, that's if you can still get them done?'

Quite, thought Mills. She would have asked Tim but now she realised even her research plans would be affected. Phil rambled on about the Scandinavian bones and what a wonderful researcher Maria was. When he'd said she was a professor Mills assumed she was quite old but judging by her photograph on the university website she was probably in her late thirties. Not that Mills was interested.

'I'd better go, Phil. I've got to call Brenda and Nina might be trying to ring.'

She put the receiver down slowly. It was great that he sounded so buoyant, so excited by his work considering what he'd been like only a few months earlier. When he was hospitalised with post-traumatic stress disorder she thought he would still be recovering, at least until the New Year. She'd enjoyed looking after him, assumed they would spend Christmas together in the cottage, but too many years had passed since they were together properly. She would have to accept it.

She scratched the dog's neck. 'So what's going to happen to you, Harris?'

He cocked his head on one side and then the other.

'You'll just have to stay with me until Phil settles down somewhere suitable for you. I don't think a flat on a university campus will suit, will it? I think you'd rather be here, eh?'

She gave him a hug and he wagged his tail cautiously.

It was time to tell Brenda about her chat with the insurers. Her boss took an age to answer the phone and when she did she sounded weary.

'Oh Mills, I've had such an afternoon. Chloe and her mum appeared on my doorstep.'

'How is Chloe?'

'She didn't say a lot but her mother made up for it. She wants to know exactly what happened at the lab. Well I told her, we won't know until the police have finished their investigation.'

'Have they seen the results of Tim's post mortem?'

'I didn't ask. Do you think it's been done?'

'I would think so.'

'Can you find out?'

'Not really. But have you spoken to Tim's parents?'

'No. Should I have done?'

'They are his next of kin.'

'Chloe, or rather her mother, seems to be taking that role.'

'I don't think Chloe gets on very well with Tim's parents. I can't remember exactly what the problem was. Money I think. Do you know if they're local?'

Brenda was livening up. 'Now I should have the address somewhere because I always send Tim a Christmas card and he was still living at home last year.'

Mills heard the receiver drop onto a hard surface then silence for several minutes before Brenda returned.

'Here it is, pet. Have you got a pen?'

'You're giving me the address because…?'

'I thought you wanted to see them.'

Mills sighed. 'OK, go ahead.'

She then asked Brenda how her meeting with Chloe had ended.

'It was a bit strange actually. She still wants to know why Tim was working late at night. I said we were all wondering that. Was I sure he wasn't moonlighting for you, she asked. I told her definitely not so then she got very emotional and asked me outright if he was having a fling with a member of my staff. I have to ask, do you think he might have been meeting someone?'

'When you say someone, do you mean Donna?'

'So there was something going on.'

'No, Brenda. It's just that Donna told me Chloe had accused her to her face. The poor girl was so upset. I can't believe Tim was anything but devoted to Chloe. He was so excited about the baby and the wedding.'

Mills turned the subject to insurance, informing her of the assessor's visit the following afternoon.

'You'll be there, Brenda, won't you?'

'I'll do my best, pet.'

As she put the receiver down it occurred to Mills that the phone number she had for Tim must be at his parents' house. It wasn't too late to give them a call. But it wasn't an easy conversation. Tim's mother had never met Mills and she seemed uncertain whether they would be available for her to come in the next few days. Also, if she had just called to express her condolences then that was sufficient, there was no need for a visit. But Mills had a question before the woman rang off and she did it as politely as she could.

'I wondered if you'd received the results of the post mortem?'

'Yes we have.'

Mills could hear a man's voice asking who was on the phone. A pause then he was speaking to Mills.

'Who is this?'

She began to explain but he cut her short. 'Look, my wife is very upset, I'm sorry.' Then the phone went dead.

Her face felt hot. How stupid, she told herself. How stupid and rude and crass.

Chapter 4

The insurance assessor was already there when Mills arrived at the lab. She was standing beside her car wrapped up in an expensive looking camel coat against the biting cold easterly wind. Mills apologised, although she wasn't technically late.

'No, no, I'm early,' the woman protested. 'I haven't visited Harrogate before so I left in good time. I'm Jessica, by the way.'

She offered a business card as they shook hands.

'Well this is it,' said Mills, waving at the blackened building. 'I'm afraid we can't go in until it's been declared safe.'

'Well that's where we come in. I can arrange for a site survey as soon as possible. Once we have entry we can assess the damage and work out what repairs and refurbishments are required. And we'll make sure it's secure – I'm guessing that's pretty important in this case? Don't worry, you'll be back doing your important work as soon as possible.'

Mills refrained from repeating Brenda's wishes to be shot of the property.

'I don't even know the details of the insurance cover,' admitted Mills. 'The owner isn't too well or she'd be here.'

'No problem, we've got everything under control. I can copy you in on everything we send to Dr Yardley, once we have her authorisation.' She turned towards her car.

'Meanwhile I've got a pile of paperwork I can give you to pass on to her, if you don't mind.'

She explained the purpose of the various documents while Mills stood shivering.

'…and that's the last one. Sorry there's so much reading.'

'That's all right. Look, I've got a few questions but it's getting quite chilly out her. Do you fancy a coffee?'

Jessica's face lit up. 'I'd love one. And I need to find a loo, it was a long journey.'

It was a brisk walk to the nearest decent café which seemed to meet Jessica's approval. They ordered flat whites with Danish pastries and found an empty table in the corner. Jessica disappeared to the "Ladies".

'Have you worked as an assessor for long?' Mills asked when she returned.

'Actually I'm a loss adjuster. I work independently for the company on complex claims. It's my job to get reports together from building surveyors, the fire brigade or the police.'

'I don't suppose the police are normally involved in insurance cases though?'

'You'd be surprised at the dodgy cases I've had to investigate. I even get to check company accounts to see if they're in financial difficulties in cases where I suspect fraud.'

'Really?' Mills sipped her coffee to avoid any further comment.

Jessica asked her to describe the sort of forensics that went through the lab. It would all go into the report and the sooner she understood the scope of the work the better.

Finally she stood up, pulling on her coat.

'I must dash, it's going to take a while to set everything in motion and the sooner we get the building surveyor into the lab the better.'

As they walked back to their cars, Jessica apologised for raising a difficult subject.

'I understand there was a colleague in the building at the time.'

'Yes, unfortunately he died in the fire.'

'I will need to get the report from the police investigation but I wondered if you knew the circumstances?'

'All I know is that he was in there working when the building caught fire.'

'Was it usual for him to work so late?'

'We didn't know he was there until his fiancée turned up to collect him.'

Back at Jessica's car, Mills noticed the back seat was covered with hi-vis work wear and a hard hat. Not used today but next time, perhaps? After Jessica had left, she sat in her Mini deciding whether to take the paperwork directly to Brenda, who probably wouldn't read it. She chose to go through it herself before giving her boss a summary. There was a lot to absorb following the loss adjustor's visit, including the fact that she could investigate the company finances if she felt there was cause. That definitely worried Mills.

Friday afternoon was always quiet in the department. It suited Mills to have the office to herself. She whisked through her inbox and dealt with a couple of forms before clearing her desk to settle down with the papers that Jessica had given her, noting anything she thought Brenda should be aware of. An hour later she rang her boss to report on her meeting with the loss adjuster.

'Is that the person who sent me a message asking for my permission to copy you in on messages?'

'Yes, that's right. She thought it might be helpful.'

'Well I suppose it might.'

Mills agreed. 'She's given me some paperwork already. I've gone through it so I'm emailing you the gist of what it says. It's mainly for our information: what's going to happen – the formalities. But there are some forms to complete. Shall I bring them down over the weekend?'

Brenda didn't respond immediately. 'I was thinking of going to Whitby.'

'Whitby?'

'Yes. Well I thought a break would be good.'

'Do you have people over there?'

'Yes.'

'Friends?'

'Yes. Look can't we do this next week? There's no rush is there?'

Mills was losing patience. 'No, there's no rush,' she replied sarcastically.

Brenda didn't seem to notice the irritation in her voice when she wished her a good weekend. She cursed as she put the phone down and sent the email to Brenda. Not that she'd read it, Mills thought.

She was packing up to go home when Nina rang her mobile.

'I wanted to let you know,' her friend began, 'there will be a Gold Group set up to look at the police cases being processed by Yardley Forensics. Apparently there are some very sensitive samples going through. The reason I'm involved is because I've been appointed to Tim's family. I'm sure you'll find out soon enough.'

'You're going to be their Family Liaison Officer?'

'Yes. I'm on my way to see his parents now. Anyway, how's it going?'

Mills brought her up to date with her meeting with Jessica and moaned about Brenda's lack of interest.

'It sounds as if she isn't coping very well with it. Do you think she feels responsible for Tim's death?'

Mills was shocked. 'What d'you mean?'

'Just that if he hadn't been working in the lab… you know.'

'But it wasn't her fault. It wasn't anyone's fault.'

'Well someone must have asked him to work late, mustn't they? Unless he was doing something for himself. What *was* he doing?'

'We may never know but certainly not until we get access to the lab. Jessica says she'll get a surveyor in as soon as possible.'

'Maybe Tim's family will help,' suggested Nina. 'Anyway, I'd better get going or I'll be late, which won't be a good start to my FLO role.'

As the conversation ended, there was a missed call, followed by a text from Jessica, telling Mills that the surveyor would be on site on Saturday. There was no need for her to be present as the police would be in attendance. If the building was safe to enter, police forensics would be in immediately to make a thorough examination of the premises because of the presence of accelerant.

It seemed as if Brenda was right – she could do nothing

over the weekend. It was frustrating. As Mills drove she went over what she could achieve until they were allowed on the premises. If there was an external back-up for the computers she could be accessing the information but no-one seemed to know if it even existed. She had the lab protocols on her laptop so she could at least go through them to see if it was mentioned.

Nina always felt nervous the first time she encountered the relatives of a victim of a crime. Even if it wasn't as serious as a death, she only felt comfortable acting as their liaison officer after the first meeting with the family was out of the way. She knew how she would feel about any intrusion at such a sensitive time and always trod very carefully. At least on this occasion she would only be seeing Tim's parents, not the poor young woman who was busy planning her wedding until a few days ago. That was going to be much more difficult.

She parked outside a neat semi-detached house in a cul-de-sac lined with trees. There was a newish Audi in the drive and the front garden was neatly lined with evergreen shrubs, all perfectly trimmed. There was not a single dead leaf lying on the square of lawn. Nina locked the car, took a deep breath and headed for the front door.

A man in his fifties or sixties opened the door. He was smartly dressed as if he'd just arrived from work. She introduced herself and he told her to call him Piers. As he showed her into a room that overlooked the front garden, she could see someone was moving about in the kitchen at the end of the hall. He offered her tea and she accepted, taking the opportunity to glance around while he was absent. The room was tastefully decorated and the furniture was old fashioned but not dated. In fact she was admiring the way the cushions complemented the colour of the sofas when a woman appeared carrying a tray and hesitated. Nina jumped up and introduced herself again.

It sometimes happened, more often than she liked. People were surprised by her appearance, her ethnic background. She'd even been asked where she came from on occasions. When she was younger she enjoyed answering "Leeds" for a second time when they asked "but where are you really from?" Nowadays she would patiently explain where her family originated when asked again by an older member of the public. Her colleague, Hazel, said she was too polite and if it was her she'd tell them to mind their own business.

'Do sit down.' Tim's father was offering her a biscuit.

They looked homemade and she said so.

'That's Ann, always baking.'

'I like to keep busy,' she said, pouring tea and offering Nina a cup. 'Oh I forgot to ask – did you want milk?'

'That's fine and the biscuit is delicious.' So far, so good, she thought.

Gaining confidence she launched into her usual speech about what the role of a family liaison officer was. In their case it would mainly be to keep them informed about the investigation.

'Will you be talking to poor Chloe?' Ann asked.

'Yes. I understand she's expecting Tim's baby very soon?'

'Next month.' She sighed as she put her cup down. 'And they were getting married next year.'

'I'm so sorry.'

'She's devastated. We all are but for her, so young and

with the bairn…' she was scrabbling in her pocket to pull out a tissue. 'I'm sorry.'

As she went out, Piers shook his head. 'I don't know how we'll get over this. It seems so senseless.' He put his cup down carefully. 'Have they found out what happened, why he was there, what he was doing?'

Nina wasn't able to help him. She said that it would be a great help if he could tell her anything that might explain why he was at the lab that evening.

'We've both been racking our brains to think if he said anything that evening.'

'He left the lab at the usual time on Monday. Did he cycle home?'

'Yes. His mum had tea on the table at six sharp as per normal and he went out just before seven.'

'Did he say where he was going?'

'No. He spends most evenings over at Chloe's so we just assumed.'

Ann had come back in.

'Didn't we, love? We thought he was over at Chloe's.'

She nodded. 'Yes. Sometimes he stays over so we didn't know anything was wrong until Becky got in touch.'

Nina was making notes. 'Becky?'

'Chloe's mother,' Piers explained. 'She rang us early in the morning. She was at the hospital with Chloe. She said they'd found a body in the fire and Chloe thought it was him. We were rather confused.'

'We couldn't understand what he was doing there,' Ann said.

'Anyway,' he continued, 'when we contacted the police they finally came back to confirm it. By that time Chloe had told us.'

'Her mother identified him. She was in pieces.' Ann held a tissue to her face.

Nina apologised for asking them to re-live it all but asked whether Chloe had been able to cast any light on what had happened

Piers answered. 'She's as puzzled as we are. Tim told her he was working on something. He sometimes went in at weekends to do extra work, so she didn't think anything of it. But no-one is admitting to asking him to work that night. It's a mystery. We had hoped you would be able to shed some light.'

'I hope to, in time,' said Nina. 'Meanwhile, have you been asked for any computer or mobile belonging to Tim?'

Piers nodded. 'He has a phone but it's always with him. He doesn't have a computer, just a tablet but Chloe has it.'

'If you've checked his room, are there any papers or anything that might tell us what he was doing that night?' Nina asked.

'Not that I could see,' he replied. 'But I didn't know what I was looking for. You are welcome to go up.'

'Thank you.'

Piers led the way upstairs and opened the second door on the landing. It was a very neat room. Nothing was out of place. Nina wondered aloud if Ann had tidied it up but her husband assured her that Tim always left it that way.

'I hope my boys grow up to be so tidy,' she commented.

'You have children?'

Why did he sound so surprised.

'Yes twin boys. They're six and my daughter is nine.'

He watched her move round the room to the desk by the window overlooking the back garden. She could see trees, flower beds and a vegetable plot with fruit cages. It was easy to imagine they'd lived there a long time and that Tim had grown up in the house.

'I'll just have a quick look through the drawers.'

It wasn't a question but if he'd objected she would have stopped. She was used to sifting quickly through people's paperwork. As usual it was mostly personal stuff like insurance quotes, bills, invoices. Interesting stuff like bank statements were held digitally. She went back downstairs empty-handed.

As she was leaving, Ann, who seemed more composed now, thanked her for coming.

'We thought he had such a bright future at that place,' she said. 'When he started there he was just out of college but they gave him responsibility from day one. It was the making of him. Then he met Chloe.' She sighed. 'You will go and talk to Chloe, won't you? She has some theories about what was going on at the lab.'

Chapter 5

Donna and Glyn were seated at the far end of the coffee shop when Mills arrived. It had been Donna's idea. She thought it would help them recall the work in progress at the lab if all three of them sat down together to brainstorm. She'd called Mills in the evening, having already spoken to Glyn. He'd suggested meeting in Northallerton as it was sort of between them all. Mills had finally agreed to join them for coffee on Saturday morning. She hadn't relished seeing them again so soon under such dreadful circumstances so she was relieved that Donna seemed determined to keep it business-like.

'I've made a spreadsheet,' she said, pulling a laptop out of her bag and powering it up.

After a few minutes she turned it round so they could see the screen. 'This first column is for the customer, the next is the job and the third is where the sample is located. This last column is to record what progress had been made.' She turned it back round, adding, 'I've already put three jobs in – the ones I started on Monday.'

Glyn peered at the screen. 'What bloods have you got listed? There was one for drugs and another for alcohol, both from the police.'

She typed them in.

'What about the set of urine samples from that company that does the random drug and alcohol tests?' Mills asked.

Donna started typing. 'How many were there? I can't

remember.'

'There were probably twenty. It's pretty much always twenty. And what about clothing? I saw some large packages arriving the Friday before last.'

'Would that be Brenda's cold case?' Glyn asked. 'She was looking at knife cuts in the fabric.'

'It could have been that old arran sweater,' said Donna. 'It's from a murder investigation. I hadn't started working on it.'

She typed for several minutes. 'I left the DNA because I didn't know who they were from.'

She and Glyn went through them together. Although DNA fingerprinting was Donna's area of expertise, Glyn as lab manager was responsible for registering the work and reporting results. Mills helped out when she was there, often liaising with the customers herself. It seemed there were DNA samples from a rape, a fatal stabbing and any fluids found on the sweater.

'I'm sure we're missing a load of stuff,' Donna said.

'We'll find out when we go in.' Glyn leaned back in his chair and drank his coffee.

Mills laughed. 'You think so? I'm worried that everything will have been destroyed.'

Glyn ignored her and looked at his watch. 'If we're done I'd better go. I said I'd be back for lunch.'

Mills shrugged, Donna shut the lid of her laptop.

When he'd gone, Mills fetched them both another coffee.

'Donna, I'm glad we've got the chance to talk. Have you seen or heard from Chloe again?'

'No way. Not after what she said.'

'I expect she was just upset. She'll realise her mistake

soon.'

'Do you really think so? I was thinking you could speak to her. She might listen to you.'

In reality Mills was wary of meeting Chloe. The girl had initially thought she was the reason Tim was in the building at that time of night. In the past he'd jumped at the chance to work weekends for Mills, now she no longer had research funds to pay him, would the girl believe her?'

She let Donna give her Chloe's phone number.

'She lives with her mum, Becky. She's really nice,' Donna said.

'Is there a dad?'

'I don't think so. No, definitely not because Tim told me she was going to get her uncle to give her away. Apparently they're really close.'

'And when is the baby due?'

'Some time around Christmas.'

Donna asked when they would be able to start clearing up the lab. Mills explained that when the surveyor declared it safe the police forensics would go in.

'Hopefully they'll be finished by early next week. I'll contact you as soon as there's news.'

'And let me know how Chloe is when you see her,' Donna called as Mills left.

Nina didn't trust Nige to dress the boys properly for the party that afternoon, so before she left the house she carefully selected clean clothes for Tomos and Owen, leaving them in neat piles on their bunk beds.

'And don't forget to comb their hair! I've left the address on the kitchen table with the presents.'

'Can I just drop them off?' Nige asked.

'Yes, you'll have to because you're taking Rosie to the pet shop for hamster food while they're there.'

Nige was asking her something as she left but she didn't have time to stop. She'd arranged to visit Tim's fiancée at noon and it was already half past eleven. She mustn't be late for the first meeting. She was anticipating it would be a useful visit as Tim's mother had indicated Chloe had something interesting to tell her. Her role as family liaison officer was not confined to keeping relatives of the victim up to date with progress. It provided the opportunity to be informed by the family with intelligence relevant to the case.

The address was in a very nice part of Harrogate. She was driving up a wide road with large detached properties on either side. It was difficult to read the house names but the satnav told her she'd arrived at her destination so she pulled into the side of the road and parked. After walking up and down and across the road she finally spotted the name she was looking for beside a wrought iron gate. She couldn't see the house until she reached the top of a narrow flight of stone steps. It was an attractive old brick building set in a sheltered garden. There must have been another entrance further along the road because she found herself on a wide drive in front of the house.

A middle-aged woman, smartly dressed, welcomed her inside.

'I'm Becky,' she said when Nina had identified herself. 'Chloe – it's the police!' she called.

There were quick footsteps and a very pregnant girl came down the stairs.

'Hello Chloe, I'm Nina. I'm your family liaison officer. I know it must be a very difficult time for you and your family but I'm here to help keep you informed of what is happening.'

Nina followed them into a huge sitting room with enormous windows and doors leading into the garden. She could see an ornamental pond the size of a small lake.

'So what is the news?' Chloe asked, curling up on a large leather sofa.

Nina explained that the lab hadn't been opened for a thorough forensic search yet but the accelerant found by the fire investigators had been identified as petrol.

'That wasn't already in the lab?' the girl asked.

'Definitely not.'

'So that's what killed him.' Her voice was calm. She sat with her hands resting on her bump. 'They said it was the smoke that killed him. I don't suppose *you* know why he was there?'

'No,' Nina admitted. 'I was hoping you might have some information that could help.'

She waited while the girl seemed to be considering whether to answer. She uncurled her legs and sat upright, easing herself into the back of the sofa. When she'd made herself comfortable she looked across at Nina.

'I'll tell you what I know, which isn't much. Tim would do extra bits and pieces in the lab at weekends sometimes. It was for Dr Sanderson who works there on and off. It wasn't regular but when it came he would be pretty busy. It suited us because of the wedding.' She bit her lip. 'Anyway, he said he'd got a lot on and he'd be working some evenings as well.' She shrugged. 'I didn't mind, did I?'

'So it was like overtime?' said Nina.

'Yes, except it turns out it wasn't work for her – or so she says.'

'I was thinking it could be a communication gap,' her mother said to Nina. 'It would be nice to clear that up. She might be feeling rather… you know… upset about it. She may be feeling guilty about what happened.'

'We can certainly clarify it,' agreed Nina, making a note which read "ask Mills".

'If she's telling the truth, there is another explanation…'

Becky held up a hand to interrupt her daughter. 'I don't think that's something you want to raise now. Let's wait until…'

'No, Mum. She said she wanted to know what I thought.'

Becky sank back in her chair tight-lipped.

'What is it?' Nina asked.

'I think he might have been using work as an excuse to see someone.'

'Someone?'

'Another woman. It would explain him going out in the evenings.'

'Becky darling, I can't believe that of Tim. He was working so hard to save up for the baby and the wedding.'

Becky turned to Nina.

'He was a lovely young man. He was totally focussed on doing his very best for Chloe and the baby.'

Nina was puzzled. 'Would he really meet someone at the laboratory?' she asked. It seemed an odd place for a romantic rendezvous.

'He would if it was someone from the lab.'

For a second Nina thought she was suggesting that Tim and Mills…

'Donna Nicholson,' Chloe said triumphantly. 'I think he was seeing her that night.'

Mills was planning a quiet night in so she bought a microwaveable Indian meal in town along with a bottle of Shiraz. It was the weekend before bonfire night and the family at the end of her row of cottages usually let off fireworks quite early in the evening as they had young children. If the people in the Manor House were down from Scotland then there could even be a party with fireworks at midnight. Mills didn't mind, in fact she'd enjoyed the free displays, but this year she was concerned for Harris.

She decided to walk the dog early to ensure they were safely back inside by the time it got dark. He was keen to get up the track, pulling her along until she felt it was safe to let him off. He raced away seeming to enjoy the strong easterly wind that buffeted them to one side. As she passed the Manor she peered down the drive. There were no cars and the gate was firmly shut. Hopefully that meant there would be no late night explosions. The wind was stronger at the top of the track and after a quarter of an hour of being blown along, Mills decided to turn back and face the wind head-on. Harris followed and soon she was putting him back on the lead at the top of the lane.

Muriel was at her window when Mills was opening the gate. Her neighbour came out and called across to her. Harris jumped up at the low wall between them.

'Mills, I just wanted to tell you that Trish is having some fireworks for the kids tonight.'

'I thought they might.'

'Will young Harris be all right with them?' Muriel asked, absently patting the dog's head.

'I don't know. We'll see.'

Inside, Mills decided to eat early so she was ready to distract the dog if necessary. By the time it was dark she'd finished her meal, drawn the curtains, turned the television up loud and was sitting with Harris next to her. She must have fallen asleep because she was woken by the dog jumping across her and off the sofa. He was barking loudly by the back door. She could hear intermittent bangs as her neighbour's firework display began. She tried offering Harris treats but he refused to leave his post, barking every time there was an explosion.

Fortunately the display didn't last long. After ten minutes it was all over. Harris then strolled back to the sofa and climbed on. He seemed pleased that he'd chased the noise away. They dozed the rest of the evening and Mills let Harris out at ten o'clock. It was a beautiful starry night but the wind was still fierce and very cold. She locked up and left him on his bed, shut in the kitchen. Upstairs she went into the front bedroom to look across at the Manor. The place was in darkness, it would be a peaceful night after all.

So Mills was surprised to be woken by the sound of barking. She swore as she put the lamp on. It was nearly one o'clock. She listened for the bangs but there weren't any. Curious, she got up and called to Harris to be quiet. Then, concerned that he needed to go out, she went downstairs, where he greeted her by jumping up and barking. She unlocked the back door and let him out, grabbing a jacket from the hall before venturing into the garden. There was a strong smell of smoke, which she assumed was drifting from the remains of the bonfire at the end cottage. Harris sniffed the ground then ran back inside to the sitting room window where he began barking again. The house smelt of smoke inside now. Mills went to pull Harris away.

'Quiet, you'll wake Muriel.'

It looked quite smoky outside the window. She ran upstairs to look across at the Manor and could see flames. So, they were having a bonfire after all. How inconsiderate was that? She put Harris back in the kitchen, crawled up to bed and tried to get back to sleep. She was dreaming that she was attempting to rescue Tim from the lab when she was disturbed by Harris again. Clearly the fireworks earlier had upset him more than she realised. This time she found her slippers and was pulling on a sweater as she passed the open door of the spare room. There was shouting outside and headlights flashing past. She ran downstairs and out into the lane as a fire engine went past and turned into the Manor.

Muriel was in the road in her dressing gown. Her husband appeared from the house pulling on a jacket.

'There's a fire at the Manor,' he said. 'It's quite a blaze at the back of the garage. I was worried there might be fuel stored in there,' he added as he set off after the fire engine.

'He called the fire brigade,' Muriel explained. 'Something woke me and I couldn't get back to sleep. I could smell smoke so I sent him up the road to check.'

Mills wondered if she should offer to go up to the

house but they agreed that they would leave it to the professionals. The wind was wild and Muriel was shivering.

'Come inside and have a warm drink,' she told her neighbour.

They sat in the sitting room with Harris, waiting to find out what had happened. It was Muriel's view that a spark from a bonfire could have caught the heather behind the Manor.

'Could it have been the bonfire at the end cottage?' Mills asked. 'I thought the smoke came from there when Harris woke me the first time.'

'He's usually so quiet. You wouldn't know he was here normally.'

'That's right – except if he hears a quad bike. He doesn't like them and kicks up a fuss.'

'I've noticed that when I've been walking him. There's a young man that rides through here sometimes that sets him off.'

An hour went by before they saw Muriel's husband passing the window, much to Mills' relief. She was feeling very sleepy and wondered how much longer she could survive Muriel's chatter. She ran to open the door.

'Ah, there you are,' he said to his wife as she followed Mills outside. 'They've got it under control but it's taken a fair area off the moor. The house isn't occupied but they reckon if we hadn't called them it could have caused no end of damage.'

'Well I hope they appreciate it when they hear how you saved their property. Perhaps there should be a reward,' Muriel said with a giggle.

'I told them the family at the end had fireworks. They

said it could've been a spark from their bonfire or a firework that went the wrong way. They've seen that happen before.'

When she woke the next morning Mills was surprised to find she was still dressed. Curious to see what damage the fire had caused, she put on her boots and jacket, woke Harris and they went together up the lane. The smell of smoke still hung in the air but whether that was from the cottage chimneys or the heather she wasn't sure. There was no sign of the fire engine but the gate had been left open. She walked past, waiting until she was some distance up the track before turning back to look. The fire had blackened the ground in a large area at the rear of the property, right up to the stone wall surrounding the Manor's garden. There were scorch marks on the wall of the outhouse that served as a garage.

Mills was puzzled by the suggestion that a spark from the family bonfire had caused the fire. It must have been smouldering for hours before it took hold. On the other hand there was a strong wind that night and there hadn't been any significant rain for weeks, they'd all been commenting how dry it had been. At least there was no suggestion of arson this time. If only the lab fire could be put down to an unfortunate firework incident, kids messing about. Or maybe it had been – just kids playing with fire that got out of hand. If not it left the question: who wanted to burn down Yardley Forensics?

'I know it is Sunday,' she told Harris after breakfast, 'but today I've got work to do.'

Donna had sent her the list of jobs they could remember were being processed by the lab. The least

Mills could do was start writing a formal report about the situation. This Gold Group that the police were setting up would need it and the insurance company, no doubt. She included facts about what the insurance investigation might entail and added dates and times of meetings and phone calls. Hopefully Brenda would read it at some stage.

It didn't take long but she strung it out until lunchtime by fiddling with the formatting. Finally, when there was nothing else she could include, she fixed a sandwich, sharing it with Harris. After a mug of tea, and then another, she couldn't put it off any longer – she rang Chloe.

Mills formulated her sentence while Chloe's mother went to find her daughter.

'I am *so* sorry about what happened to Tim.'

It didn't sound right but what else could she have said?

'Yes.' The girl's voice was emotionless.

'I know Brenda has spoken to you but I thought I should ring, you know to say how sorry we all are.' She was just making it worse.

'Is there some news? Mum's been ringing Brenda but she's not answering.'

'I'm afraid she's away this weekend. That's why I…'

'So why *are* you calling me?'

'I just thought it might help if we could meet to chat, you know. It might help us both understand what happened.'

'I think I know.'

Presumably she was referring to Donna.

Mills took a breath. 'Donna has told me what you said to her and I'm sure you are wrong. She's so upset by your accusation, There's no basis to it I can reassure you, Chloe.'

'Really?'

'Tim was devoted to you, you know that. He never stopped talking about you and the baby and the wedding.' Could she risk mentioning the work for her? 'That's why he did the overtime for me before.'

She sounded quieter now. 'Are you saying he *was* working for you then?'

'No, Chloe. I'm sorry but he definitely wasn't. I wouldn't have let him work late in the week. You know he only ever worked for me at weekends.'

'So what *was* he doing there?' She raised her voice but it was not in anger, more out of frustration.

'We don't know yet but I intend to find out. Hopefully tomorrow they will let us into the lab and we can begin to piece together what he was working on. Trust me Chloe, we will find out.'

Chapter 6

Jessica rang to tell Mills that the surveyor had found a weakness in the floor at the front of the building but he had arranged for supports to be put in. The biggest concern had been the stairs but as they were metal there was very little damage.

'So I can go in now?' Mills asked.

'The forensics team left this morning. I'm on my way there to check the building has been secured adequately. I could meet you to hand over the keys if you like.'

Mills felt her anxiety returning as she approached Harrogate. She wanted to get inside the lab to start sorting it out but she knew it was going to be an emotional time. A young man had lost his life in that building – a memory that could not be cleaned away. She wondered whether, in fact, any of them could face working there again even if Brenda changed her mind about continuing.

The parking area in front of the lab was empty. A temporary replacement door had been fitted on the entrance, with a heavy-looking padlock attached. The windows had been boarded up and the blackened walls remained the only evidence of the blaze she'd witnessed. Glass had been cleared away but here and there shards glistened on the tarmac. It was fifteen minutes before a car arrived and Jessica emerged carrying two hard hats.

'I guessed you would need this,' she said, handing one over.

She checked Mills was wearing sturdy boots before giving her a health and safety talk. Then she unlocked the padlock and swung the door open. Jessica peered inside before switching on a powerful torch and led the way upstairs, warning Mills to take care where she was walking and to avoid touching the blackened walls. The first impression was the overpowering smoky smell and the darkness.

'They said there was some temporary lighting up here,' Jessica called, waving the beam of light around the landing.

In front of them at the top of the stairs was the outer office where Mills had her desk, outside Brenda's inner sanctum. Jessica was clicking switches down at floor level. The charred door was open and Mills could just discern the outlines of a desk, a chair, and a filing cabinet. Her hopes were raised that the metal cabinet still contained paper records. Suddenly a light was flashing and after a moment a bright fluorescent bulb hanging from a beam burst into life above them.

'Thank goodness for that!' said Jessica. 'Now we can see properly.'

She went down the corridor towards the laboratory area. Mills followed her to the next pool of light outside the two main labs. The damage in this part of the building seemed less severe to Mills and she said so to Jessica, who agreed.

'That's because it's at the back and further away from the stairs and landing,' she said. 'The front of the building got the worst of it when the solvent store downstairs caught fire. But the smoke would have been just as bad, particularly if the fume cupboards were drawing air into this area.' She pointed at the door on the right – what they always thought of as "Tim's lab".

'Is that what they think?' Mills asked.

'The report from the fire brigade says the fume cupboards were operating.'

Mills looked round at the equipment, blackened by smoke but otherwise relatively undamaged.

'Tim must have turned them on,' Mills said.

'He normally worked in here?' Jessica sounded puzzled.

'Yes.'

'But his body was found in there,' she said, pointing across the corridor to where Donna worked.

Mills had an image of Tim running to the front of the building to escape the fire and getting caught in the blaze but Jessica's view was quite different.

'The fire was much worse in here,' she said, moving through the doorway into Donna's lab. 'They think he was in here when the fire was started. He might have been unaware of it at first because the fume cupboard would have drawn smoke into the back lab. Unfortunately the petrol spread into the store room below and once the fire reached a certain temperature the solvents went up. He probably didn't have time to get out before he was overcome by the smoke from below.'

They were standing in the middle of a blackened jumble of mangled furniture. The metal benches were intact the rest was a shambles. Mills stared at the equipment heaped on the floor.

'That's roughly where your colleague was found,' Jessica said, touching her arm. 'They say he would have lost consciousness very rapidly – that he didn't appear to have been struggling to get out.'

Everywhere was blackened. Looking closer, Mills could identify only a few of the pieces of equipment, contorted as they were by the heat. Broken glassware crunched under their feet as they moved around aimlessly.

'How do we even start to sort all this out?' Mills asked.

'I'll arrange for a professional company that specialises in disaster recovery to come in and clear it before it's refurbished. I'm thinking that there is little or nothing in the way of equipment that is salvageable?'

Mills was so close to tears she didn't trust herself to answer but shook her head.

'I'm sorry,' Jessica said, putting her hand on Mills' shoulder. 'I'm forgetting that you're not used to all this.' She waved her arm round the room. 'I've seen fire damage so many times and I know it will soon be back to normal but it doesn't change the loss of your colleague. Perhaps we should go downstairs now?'

Mills was relieved to leave the laboratory behind but she did want to look in the store room. It had taken the brunt of the fire so she was keen to see whether any of their valuable forensic samples had survived. The paint had been stripped from the metal cabinets and the heat had distorted the locks on the doors. There was no way she was going to get inside them today.

Thinking that the back of the building had not been so badly affected by the fire she asked Jessica if they could go back upstairs to look at the filing cabinets in her office.

'The key is in my desk,' Mills explained, asking Jessica to bring the torch over.

It was strange to open the blackened desk to find the contents of the drawer relatively unaffected. She fitted the key into the lock of the first cabinet and opened it carefully. The contents appeared undamaged.

'Do you keep all your records in here?' Jessica asked.

'Only completed work documents. Any paperwork for current analysis would be in the lab.'

'Oh dear.'

'Yes and results from any measurements relating to ongoing work would be on the computers in the lab. I think we can assume they are now defunct.'

'What about back-ups?'

'That's what I've got to find out. Our paperwork says we store the results on an external server but that's not something I'm familiar with. I've asked Donna and Glyn but they don't know and Brenda… well she's Brenda.'

'Will you update her on our visit today, Mills? She needs to keep on top of this – she can't expect you to handle it all by yourself.'

Back outside she shut the padlock on the door, giving Mills a spare key. They walked together back to the car where Jessica replaced her yellow jacket with a thick knitted sweater. As Mills handed her the hard hat she thanked her for showing her round.

'Look, can I ask a favour?' Jessica was smiling anxiously. 'I've been trying to contact your boss but she never answers her landline or mobile. I get the feeling she's avoiding me.'

'I think she was away this weekend.'

'I thought I might just go on the off-chance that she's in – I've got some more papers for her to sign – but it might be easier if you're with me. Do you have time?'

'Yes, it's not far.'

Mills set off slowly, keeping an eye on the mirror,

checking that Jessica's car was still following her. If Brenda was at home she would not only make sure her boss met the loss adjuster but that she began to take an interest in the progress they were making.

Mills parked in the drive, waiting for Jessica, who had left her car in the road. At first there was no response but when Mills shouted through the letterbox the curtains moved and there was the sound of footsteps in the hall. Finally the door opened a few inches.

'Brenda, it's me.' Mills could smell the whisky on Brenda's breath as she leaned forward. 'Please let us in.'

The door opened wider and Mills turned with a nod.

'This is Jessica, the loss adjuster from the insurance company,' she explained, closing the door when they were both inside. 'She needs your signature.'

Brenda made a harrumphing noise and led them into the sitting room. Mills went over to pull the curtains back. Brenda had already taken the armchair so she sat beside Jessica on the sofa.

'It's just a few formalities Dr Yardley.'

Brenda didn't respond.

Mills glared at her. 'We went into the lab today, to look round. It's quite a mess but it's all achievable.' She smiled encouragingly at Brenda, who remained morose as Jessica passed the papers to her.

'I need your signature here and here, where the markers are,' she explained gently. 'It's all to do with permitting us to approve the clearance company. As soon as you sign we can go ahead and sort out a contract.'

'I don't have a pen.'

Jessica searched in her bag. 'Here use this.' She watched patiently as Brenda appeared to read through the document then signed without comment.

'The clearance team will try to retrieve anything that can be salvaged,' she said, 'but that will require you to be available to provide information. After all, you guys are the only ones who know what equipment you have and whether it is beyond repair.'

'You can deal with that.' Brenda was looking at Mills.

She and Jessica exchanged glances.

'Wouldn't you at least like to be involved, even on the periphery?' Jessica asked.

'Not even there, young lady. Not even the periphery.' She folded her arms stubbornly.

Jessica picked up the papers, placing them carefully in her large leather briefcase.

'I'd better be going,' she said to Mills. 'I'll let you know as soon as the contract has been placed. They will need you to help them once they start work.'

Mills went to the door with her, apologising for her boss's behaviour.

Jessica smiled. 'It has obviously been a huge shock to her, particularly the loss of an employee. Also she is probably worrying about any repercussions regarding a work-related death. We won't know whether the Health and Safety Executive will want to investigate until the outcome of the inquest.'

'That's next week. I thought I should go,' Mills replied without enthusiasm.

'I might see you there.'

Mills went back inside. Brenda hadn't moved from her chair.

'Glyn and Donna gave me all the jobs in progress they could recall,' Mills told her. 'I made a list and put it in the report I sent you. Did you get it?'

'I haven't checked my emails today.'

'I thought the police would need it.'

'Perhaps you could send it to them, pet.'

Mills was unwilling to spend any more time with Brenda; she left soon afterwards but not before pleading with her to stay in touch with Chloe.

'I can't face her,' her boss had said. 'Not after what happened to poor Tim. I can never forgive myself.'

With that she went into the kitchen and Mills heard the chink of a glass as she let herself out.

Mills arrived in the lecture room only two minutes late. She'd almost forgotten she had a one hour lecture with the second-year archaeology students that afternoon. Her head was aching, probably because she'd missed lunch. The students were still drifting in carrying bottles of water and sport drinks. They chatted among themselves until she shut the door and started by warning them that the topic, "Analytical Techniques in Archaeology" would form part of the exams after Christmas and she would set a short module test so they could check their knowledge. That seemed to get their attention and she clicked on the first slide.

She left the room as soon as she'd finished lecturing, making for the cafeteria to pick up whatever was left at that time in the afternoon. The kitchen staff were sitting together eating their lunch but the woman who worked on the till scraped back her chair, still chewing. The sandwich shelf was empty except for two cheese and pickle baguettes. Mills was tempted to walk away but picked one up plus a chocolate bar.

'That's three-fifty, love. Not much choice now.'

Mills agreed, stuffed the selection in her bag and carried them back to the office.

Nige was there. 'Tea?' he asked.

There was a tiny kitchen down the corridor where they could make tea and instant coffee. He reappeared with two mugs.

'Did you have any milk?' Mills asked.

'Not really, but there was some in the fridge.'

'Nige!'

Everyone brought their own milk and Mills got very annoyed if it was "borrowed" by others.

'I'll bring some in tomorrow and tell everyone to help themselves.'

It was difficult to be cross with Nige when he was smiling.

'How's it going with the lab and everything?' he asked as Mills worked her way through the dry baguette.

She told him about the visit she'd made that morning.

'So, everything is damaged? Even the computers?'

'Yep.' Mills took another bite of the baguette then threw the rest in the bin.

'Wow. That's a real pain. Do you have cloud storage?'

'If you mean data stored somewhere else, I have absolutely no idea Nige. Can we change the subject please, my head is bursting.'

Nige offered Mills paracetamols and stayed quiet for a minute or two.

Then he asked, 'Did you catch a firework display at the weekend?'

'Not exactly, what about you?'

'Nina says there's a display at the Durham Constabulary

Headquarters tonight. I just can't keep her away from work,' he said with a grin.

'I usually go to the one at Reeth.'

'It was good when we brought the kids over that time a couple of years ago.'

'Yes, it was fun.' That was when she was still with Alex.

As if reading her thoughts Nige said, 'That guy you were with then…'

'Alex?'

'Yes. Where is he working now?'

'Not sure. Why?'

'I was just wondering. I imagine he's doing pretty well for himself, digital forensics seems to be the big thing now, doesn't it? Cybercrime or whatever you call it.'

'Probably.' She would go home when she finished her tea and have a lie down.

'Didn't he work at your lab for a while? He'll know where your data is.'

'That was ages ago.'

'Worth a try though.'

'Maybe.' But she didn't mean it.

The pile of wood on the green at Reeth seemed to have grown since the morning. Mills had never missed the fireworks since she moved to Mossy Bank all those years ago. The pubs would be full and hundreds of locals would gather for what was always a splendid display. But this year Mills wasn't sure she could face it. It was the memory of the fire, of course, and nothing to do with the fact she would be on her own. By the time Mills reached home she'd decided to miss the fireworks and have a quiet night in – until Muriel caught her as she was locking the car.

'Mills, dear, I'm glad I caught you.'

'Is everything all right? It's not Harris?'

'No, he's his usual self. We had a lovely walk this afternoon. No, I was wondering if you're going to the fireworks tonight.'

Mills was about to reply in the negative but her neighbour went on to explain that her husband had taken the car. 'He had to go to see his mum in hospital so I thought I might cadge a lift with you.'

'Oh I don't think I should leave Harris – not tonight.' It was the perfect excuse.

'Don't worry, Mills. I've checked and there are no fireworks going off in Mossy Bank tonight. I've asked everyone.'

Mills looked at her watch. There was time to take Harris up the road, a quick shower and something to eat. Perhaps by then she might feel better.

She sighed. 'I don't see why not.'

'If we leave by seven there will be time for a drink and there's a barbecue. I said I'd meet a couple of friends in "The Buck".'

'Sounds like a plan,' she replied and let herself into the cottage.

Mills dosed herself up with headache pills before she left the house. Harris looked disappointed as she pulled her jacket on.

'Don't pull that face,' she told him. 'You really wouldn't like it in Reeth tonight I can assure you.'

Despite that, she could hear him whining as she shut the front door.

In Reeth, they went straight to the pub where Muriel insisted on buying Mills a drink. She sipped half a pint of Black Sheep while her neighbour chatted with her friends. The bar was packed with people dressed up in bulky winter clothes and the heat was making Mills feel worse. She was relieved when they eventually moved outside to watch the bonfire being lit. Muriel moved forward with the crowd but Mills hung back, suddenly aware that she wanted to be anywhere but on the green surrounded by hundreds of people who were actually enjoying the sight.

Fortunately, in the darkness no-one could see the tears that suddenly formed as she relived the night of the fire. Firemen wandered round the green, ensuring the blaze didn't spread too far but all she could see were the hoses, the flames as they licked round the ground floor window. Jessica had been correct – the store room had been the centre of the fire, that's why Tim had been overcome by the fumes. What she couldn't understand was why he wasn't in his own workspace. Why would he need to access Donna's lab, unless he was moonlighting and earning extra cash for someone else – someone who wanted a different sort of forensic analysis.

She desperately wanted to get home to think about it but the fireworks had started and she'd arranged to meet Muriel once they were over. Showers of coloured explosions followed each other but to Mills they were just an irritation. She tried to concentrate but it was impossible. Looking round at the enthralled crowd she searched for Muriel in a sea of unfamiliar faces. Then she thought she recognised a man who was standing a few rows in front of her.

The bangs and flashes seemed to go on forever. Mills

was distracted by the fire that continued to blaze. Firemen from the local volunteer force kept pushing stray branches back into the ashes as it gradually subsided. Eventually Mills couldn't take it any longer and walked back to the car to wait for Muriel. It was another half hour before she arrived, excited by the spectacle and grateful to Mills for bringing her.

'I saw someone just now. I thought it was David Price at first but he was much younger,' said Mills when they were in the car.

'It was probably Justin. He does take after his dad.'

'So he is working on the farm now?'

'Yes, since he's come back from university. Haven't you seen him up and down on his quad bike?'

'I thought it might be him – I saw the bike when I was walking Harris.'

'That dog makes such a terrible fuss with quad bikes. I wondered if he'd been hit by one in his past life.'

'Maybe. But it is the *only* time he barks.'

'Except the other night, Mills, I could hear him then.'

Inside the cottage Mills scratched the dog's ears and asked him, 'What *did* set you off barking in the middle of the night?'

Chapter 7

'And finally, how's the Yardley arson investigation going?'

DI Mitch Turner was looking across at DS Hazel Fuller but she nudged Nina who was sitting beside her. Nina glared at her colleague who grinned back.

'Hazel, the arson attack at the forensic lab – what's happening?' her DI demanded.

Hazel was supposed to be liaising with DI Stewart from Harrogate but Nina was much more familiar with the fire investigation results. Her family liaison role automatically meant she had to keep on top of all the intel. Besides, Hazel was suffering from a hangover this morning after she'd celebrated Guy Fawkes Night a little too heavily.

'Nina's got the latest info,' Hazel replied, taking another swig from her bottle of water.

Mitch sighed audibly. 'Let's hear it then.'

Nina, consulting her notes intermittently, gave the room a summary of what the fire investigation team had found.

'So it was definitely arson?' someone asked.

'Their tests show that petrol was poured on the floor at the entrance, spreading to the storeroom as well. The front door and the storeroom are kept locked out of hours but we don't know whether the deceased left them open while he was working upstairs.'

There was a brief discussion about possible motives for the arson attack but Mitch told them to wait for the forensic report, as that would hopefully identify a suspect, particularly if it was kids messing about round bonfire night. Meanwhile he said it was worth checking with Harrogate for any history of vandalism in the area.

Back in the office Hazel begged Ruby, their researcher, to get her a strong black coffee. Nina tut-tutted loudly but her colleague ignored her.

'He did it again didn't he?' Nina said crossly.

'Who? What?' Hazel was leaning on her desk with a hand on her forehead. 'Have you got any paracetamols?'

Hazel found a packet in her bag and handed it to her. 'Mitch – his dismissive way of treating me, can't you see it?'

'You're too sensitive, Nina. You need to grow a thicker skin.'

'Do you agree with him that it was an act of vandalism?'

'It sounds the most likely explanation. What are the options otherwise?'

Nina opened her notebook. 'Revenge, crime concealment, profit, or extremism.'

Hazel was laughing. 'What have you got there?'

'It's a list of motives for arson. I think extremism is unlikely but the others are worth investigating, don't you think? A young man died in that fire, Hazel.'

Ruby came in clutching two mugs and handed them out.

'Say them again,' demanded Hazel with a grin. 'Listen Ruby, Nina's got a list of motives for arson.'

Nina repeated them, this time she included vandalism.

'What d'you think Ruby?'

Nina saw the researcher's discomfort, knowing she was embarrassed when Hazel teased her.

'Did you chase the forensic report?' Nina asked before

Ruby could respond.

'It's in your inbox,' she replied.

Nina called up the document, scanning it quickly.

'Anything interesting?' Hazel asked.

'No traceable prints and no sign of a container for the petrol or any source of ignition.'

'Sounds like a professional job,' Ruby commented.

'So probably not vandals,' said Nina.

Hazel laughed. 'So either professional extremists or anti-forensic lab protestors.'

Nina ignored her. 'Revenge could mean the fire was started by a professional criminal. It could be someone who was convicted on evidence from the lab and wants to punish it for putting them away.'

Hazel groaned. 'You do realise that could be one of hundreds, maybe thousands of suspects. How long has the lab been open?'

'It has operated as Yardley Forensics for many years. You're right, that would be a nightmare scenario.'

'Hopeless unless some forensic evidence, like DNA, is found at the scene,' agreed Ruby.

'But revenge could also mean someone who works there or worked there in the past with a grudge couldn't it?' asked Nina. 'Anyone with forensic experience would know how to avoid leaving evidence behind.'

'That would be a much smaller number of suspects,' Hazel said more cheerfully. 'Perhaps I should talk to the current employees – and Ruby, get a list of past members of staff, particularly anyone who left under a cloud.'

They worked in silence for a while then Ruby looked over at Nina. 'How do we know for sure that the guy working in the building wasn't the target of the attack?'

'None of the staff knew he was working late,' Nina replied.

'But wouldn't his car have been parked there?'

'He normally rode a bike to work but that evening his girlfriend gave him a lift back there. She went to pick him up but by then the place was ablaze.'

'That's so sad,' Ruby said. 'She's expecting his baby soon isn't she?'

Hazel jumped up and walked to the door. 'I need some fresh air.'

Nina and Ruby looked across at each other and grinned. That meant Hazel was going outside for a cigarette. Nina used the opportunity to ask for some help.

'Ruby, I've got the first meeting of the Gold Group on Friday and I need to be properly prepared. I've a copy of the fire investigation and now I've got the forensics. It might be useful to get hold of a copy of the post mortem report, I know Hazel has a copy but I don't. Someone will need to know what ongoing forensic work the lab was undertaking for us. Is that something you can pull together for me?'

'I don't see why not.'

'You're a star, Ruby.'

That evening Nina called Mills to let her know about the Gold Group meeting. She had to reassure her that she had nothing to worry about but her friend was panicking.

'But they'll want to know what's happened to all the evidence bags, won't they. I've tried to make a list of your jobs but we may have overlooked something. I'm doing my best, Nina, but Brenda is so useless at the moment.'

'Calm down, Mills. The group should be able to help

with all that. Have you been to the lab yet?'

Mills described her visit and the state of the interior.

'But you might be able to salvage something?'

'The paperwork is still in the filing cabinet in my office. I couldn't open the sample cupboards but something might be useable.'

'Well that's the sort of information that will be useful. I'm getting Ruby to make an inventory of forensic samples sent to you where we haven't received results yet. Nige said you were going to contact Alex about external back-up of your records.'

'He said what?'

'Sorry, did I misunderstand?'

Mills repeated the conversation she'd had with Nige, which did not include any offer to make contact with Alex. 'I don't even know if he's still working with the Home Office.'

'Don't you have his mobile number?'

'Somewhere.'

'I don't see why it's a problem – he'll most probably be in another relationship, like you are.'

Mills didn't answer and Nina sensed that things with Phil were not going smoothly. She knew when to back off. If it became important Mills would *have* to ask for help from Alex, however much she might wish to avoid it.

'Are you going to Tim's inquest?' she asked Mills.

'Are *you*?'

'Yes, I guess I'll accompany his fiancée and her mother.'

'I thought I might go,' said Mills. 'I don't suppose Brenda will bother and it'll look bad if no-one from the lab makes an appearance.'

'Hasn't she been asked to attend as a witness?'

'Not that I know of but she's not very communicative at the moment.'

'Perhaps it isn't necessary since no-one was there when the fire started.'

'It won't be accidental death, will it, Nina?'

'No not accidental. Someone started the fire and even if they didn't know he was in there, they were responsible for his death. In fact it seemed to us to be quite a professional job.'

'Why do you say that?'

'The area was swept for any discarded containers for the fuel or sources of ignition such as matches, but there was nothing.'

'Are you involved in the investigation, Nina?'

'It's Hazel's case but as FLO I am, yes.'

Mills went quiet.

'You must be busy if Brenda isn't taking charge,' said Nina, changing the subject.

'Tell me about it. I'll be spending this week liaising with the clearance company that the insurers brought in as well as trying to see what can be salvaged.'

'Well, keep in touch with Ruby. She's compiling the work list for me so I can look equally efficient when I attend the Gold Group this Friday.'

Nige was signalling that tea was ready and she said goodbye to her friend.

'How's she doing?' her husband asked.

'I was going to ask you that. You see her more often than I do.'

'Yes but I'm a man so that doesn't count, does it?'

'Probably not,' she said with a smile.

It was the best part of the day for Nina: sitting round the table with her husband, daughter and two boys discussing what the children had been doing at school. By the time everyone was in bed and settled, the washing-up done, packed lunches sorted, and PE kits in bags, it was nearly time for bed.

'D'you think it gets any easier?' Nina asked as they watched the news together.

'Don't ask me,' Nige replied, 'I've not been through this before.'

Mills had a restless night then overslept, so she was hurrying out of the cottage when Muriel caught her. She appeared to be sweeping her front step but Mills knew she was waiting for a chat.

'Everything all right, dear?' her neighbour asked.

'Yes, fine but I'm a bit late I'm afraid.'

'And Harris?'

'Yes. Are you OK to take him out today?'

'Yes. I enjoy it. He's good company.'

Mills hoped she could go now without appearing rude.

'Mills, I wondered… you know about these things. That fire…'

'You mean the one at the Manor?'

'Yes. I rang the Banfords but they weren't interested once I'd told them there was no damage.'

Daniel and Penny Banford owned the Manor House but only used it as a holiday home, appearing in the summer and sometimes at Christmas. Mills had had dealings with them in the past and didn't get on well with the couple.

'What's the problem, Muriel?' Mills was unlocking her car.

'I just wondered whether they should be worried. You hear about arson attacks, don't you?'

'I'm sure it wasn't anything like that.' She was opening the car door.

'Only my brother-in-law – he's a retained firefighter – he said it was probably a spark from the bonfire across the road but I checked and they didn't have one. You know I'm supposed to keep an eye on the Manor for the Banfords so I feel a responsibility.'

'Don't worry,' Mills said. 'I'm sure everything is fine.' She slammed the car door and started the engine, waving as she drove away. She was supposed to see the clearance company team at the lab in an hour and didn't want to be late for their first meeting.

To her relief the car park was empty so she had a few minutes to gather her thoughts before their van arrived. Once they were in the building it was non-stop activity. She kept copious notes but Bill, the manager, said he would make sure everything was recorded for her.

By mid-afternoon she had finished providing them with the information they required about what was in the building, what she might want to retain, and what could be dispensed with. They agreed to keep the cupboards and filing cabinets locked and to retain all the computers in case they were recoverable. She handed over her key and left them to it, promising to return the following day. She drove home feeling that all was not lost even though the inside of the building looked like a war zone at present. The clearance team had been very understanding and she felt she'd left the lab in safe hands.

It was still light when she got back which meant she could take Harris onto the tops without having to wear a head torch. There was a cold wind but it was dry and Mills relaxed as they marched up the stony track. But they didn't stay up there long, Harris clearly wanted his tea and turned round at the top signifying he'd had sufficient exercise, thank you. Mills strolled down towards the Manor House surveying the blackened area where the fire had consumed the dried out heather. Remembering what Nina had said earlier about the fire at the lab being a professional job with no sign of a fuel can and matches, she decided to have a look around.

The smell of smoke still lingered as she walked across the charred soil. She saw that the Manor had been lucky to escape any damage as the fire had stopped at the back wall. The charred area was large and it took a few minutes to walk round examining the ground. Mills could see nothing lying around. She walked back towards the lane along the perimeter wall of the garden and peered over out of curiosity. On the lawn lay a green plastic container exactly like the one she'd seen her father use to store fuel for the petrol mower. Maybe that was its purpose but Mills thought it might be worth investigating. Muriel would know who cut the grass and would be able to tell her if the can was discarded by the gardener or not.

Now it was her turn to bother Muriel. Her neighbour came to the door wiping her hands on her apron. Politely refusing the invitation to go in, Mills asked her who looked after the lawn at the Manor. The answer was simple. Her husband mowed it for them.

'It's only a small patch of grass. He keeps it under control,' Muriel replied. 'Why are you asking?'

'There's a petrol can on the lawn. I wondered if it was left by him.'

'No, love, he uses the electric mower. You aren't thinking it's something to do with the fire?'

'Maybe.'

'I could ask my brother-in-law, he helped put it out. He said it took several hours of beating at it with the wind being so strong.'

'OK.' Mills nearly left it at that. Even if it had been started deliberately, it would be impossible to know who was responsible unless there were fingerprints on the can. 'I might contact my friend in the police as well, Muriel. So tell your brother-in-law not to touch the petrol can,' she ordered. 'They may want to examine it for evidence.'

Muriel looked excited. 'Well you know all about that, love. I'll leave it to you but let me know what happens – and if they want to get in the garden, tell them to call me.'

Mills took Harris inside and rang Nina at the police headquarters in Northallerton.

Ruby answered the phone. 'Sorry, she's just popped out. I don't suppose she'll be long.'

Mills had met the young researcher several times and they got on well. 'Just ask her to call when it's convenient.'

'While you're on, Nina said you can help me. I'm doing a list of jobs we sent to you before the… you know…'

'The fire?'

'Yes.'

'I can send you my list but I'm not sure if it's complete.'

'That would be great.'

Mills could hear someone calling in the background and assumed it was Nina.

'Hazel wants you,' Ruby said before the phone went quiet.

Then, 'Mills can I have a word?'

'Certainly Hazel, how can I help you?'

On occasions Hazel had been quite officious with Mills and she didn't consider her a friend.

'I need to interview you as part of my investigation into the death of your colleague.'

'Oh yes?'

'I'll be talking to everyone that works at Yardley Forensics. Tomorrow, eleven-thirty at Northallerton police station.'

Mills wasn't sure if it was a question or a command but she knew not to get on the wrong side of DS Hazel Fuller and agreed she would be there. The conversation was over.

She sent the list of jobs to Ruby then gave Harris his tea. She was in the middle of preparing her own meal when the phone rang. Assuming it was Nina she ran to pick up.

'Hi Mills, how's it going?'

'Phil?'

'Yes. I thought I'd give you warning I'm coming up this weekend.'

'That's nice.'

'Yes, I'm borrowing a car so I can bring my stuff back down, now I've got more space.'

'More space?'

'Didn't I tell you? Maria lives in this amazing big house that's split into really big flats. One of them has become empty and she suggested I move in. It means I don't have to clutter your place up now.'

Mills didn't say that she liked having his clutter around. 'That's good then.'

'Yes. I'll come up on Saturday but I don't need to go back until Sunday. I thought I'd catch up with a few people while I'm up. You can tell me what's happening with the lab then.'

'OK.'

And that was it. There was little else to talk about. He enquired how work was going. She asked the same without much interest until finally, when they ran out of things to say, she put the phone down. He hadn't even asked about Harris. Back in the kitchen the saucepan had boiled over and the pasta was soggy. Thanks Phil, she thought, you managed to ruin this as well.

As soon as she'd eaten her spoiled meal she tried ringing Nina at home.

'Are you busy cooking tea?' she asked her friend.

'No, we've eaten and Nige is washing up. How are you?'

Mills explained she needed her advice about finding the petrol can at the Manor.

'If you send me the details I can pass it on to the local team,' she said. 'So you're thinking the fire was started deliberately? Do you have any idea who might want to do such a thing?'

'No, no idea. Sorry.'

'So changing the subject, Mills, I heard you're to be interrogated by Hazel tomorrow.'

'Should I be worried?'

Nina laughed. 'Of course not. I think she's at a bit of a loss of what else to do at present.'

'I've sent Ruby the list she asked for.'

'Good. That's for me to take to the Gold Group on Friday.'

'Who else will be there?'

'I don't know exactly but they'll be the key people involved in the situation or affected by it. It will be headed up by a fairly senior police officer; it will probably include senior ranks from the fire service, the forensic service, maybe even your friend Jessica if she can provide useful information. The main purpose is to make sure we haven't lost any vital evidence from any of our current investigations.'

'Of course,' said Mills, hoping she didn't sound as concerned as she felt.

Chapter 8

Mills had tried not to rush through her lecture first thing in the morning but was anxious not to be late for her interview with Hazel Fuller. She hurried into the police station to find Glyn sitting waiting.

He looked at his watch. 'Donna has been in there twenty-three minutes. What time is she seeing you?'

'Eleven-thirty.'

Glyn laughed. 'You'll be lucky. I'm supposed to be seeing her at eleven but Donna met Margaret when she came out and Debs, who was before her, said the woman detective arrived late.'

'She's seeing everyone then?'

'Seems like it. Is Brenda coming?'

Mills shrugged. She told Glyn about the progress the clearance company was making and how she'd sent the list of jobs to the police in preparation for the meeting on Friday. She admitted that she wasn't sure how helpful the information would be.

'It's all that Alex White's fault,' Glyn said suddenly. 'He should have had the data storage system sorted out before he left. He was the IT specialist.'

Mills ignored his outburst. It was difficult to disagree but simply because he had most knowledge on the computing side didn't mean Brenda had instructed him to sort out the back-up of the lab data. But it was something she really did need to find out.

'I'm getting in touch with him,' she declared.

Fortunately she could hear voices in the corridor; Donna was arriving accompanied by a uniformed officer. He invited Glyn to follow him. Donna sank down on the bench and looked at her with a sad expression.

'How did it go?' Mills asked.

'I don't know. She asked a load of questions and wrote lots of things down.'

'What sort of questions?'

'You know, about Tim and what he was doing. I told her I didn't know. He didn't tell me anything about working late.'

'Don't you think that was odd considering what good mates you were?'

'Exactly. That's what's been worrying me. He always told me about the private work you gave him because he was so chuffed to get the extra cash.'

'Perhaps he wasn't being paid this time. Maybe it was something he was doing for himself?'

She looked puzzled. 'How come?'

Mills had been wondering why Tim's body was found in Donna's lab. The explanation that he was trying to escape the fire didn't work because if he was in his own lab the fume cupboards pulling in the smoke would have alerted him and he could have gone along the corridor and down the back stairs to the fire exit. The front of the building took the worst of the fire so he would be mad to try and escape through there. That meant he was already in Donna's lab but using it to do what? Her work involved fingerprints, examination of clothing for evidence, and DNA profiling.

Without explaining why, Mills asked, 'Did Tim know how to carry out a DNA test?'

Donna thought before replying. 'He would know how to use the equipment because he was there when it was delivered. He sat in on the training and we've got the lab protocol which describes all the steps.'

When Mills explained that Tim was found in her lab she frowned. 'You think he was doing DNA profiling?'

'Possibly. I wondered if you could confirm it – if we were able to salvage any of the equipment.'

'The information would be on the computer if it had been run since my last analysis.'

Finally there was something that Mills could do towards establishing why Tim was there that night.

They sat side by side in thought. Then Donna said, 'The only reason I can think why Tim would run a DNA test would be if he wanted to check something about his family tree. Or even Chloe's now that they're having a baby.'

Then she asked if Mills had spoken to Chloe. She reassured Donna that she'd put Tim's fiancée straight about her relationship with him, that it was purely a working one.

At twelve-fifteen Glyn reappeared and left with Donna to find some lunch. Another ten minutes went by before Hazel came down the corridor. She greeted Mills like an old friend, asking her to follow her to the interview room. There were two packs of sandwiches on the table plus two paper cups from the local coffee chain.

Hazel picked up a pack of sandwiches, turned it over, put it back down and took the other one. 'I thought we could eat and talk at the same time,' she said. 'Hope you like tuna.'

Mills was hungry. She didn't like tuna but started

opening the packet.

'They're lattes,' Hazel added as she took one of the cups. 'So, Mills, last but not least.'

She was still wondering if Brenda had been on the list.

'I understand from your colleagues that you gave Tim private work on occasions which he carried out at weekends. Did your boss know about this?' She looked up and smiled.

'Yes she didn't mind. I paid him to analyse samples associated with my research.'

'Is that what he was doing the night of the fire?'

'No, I knew nothing about what he was doing that night.'

Hazel was reading her notes so Mills took a tentative bite of her sandwich.

'I'm trying to understand why Tim Fletcher was there, if he wasn't working for you.'

Mills replied that it was a mystery to everyone. Hazel asked if she could suggest any possible reason and Mills explained her theory that he was using equipment in Donna's lab.

'But why would he be doing DNA profiling at night?' asked Hazel. Mills couldn't answer her.

She then asked whether Tim might have set fire to the building himself. Could there be another member of staff who felt aggrieved and attempted to destroy the place without realising Tim was in there. Finally, when Mills had nearly got through the tuna sandwich and was gulping the tepid coffee to take away the taste, she was asked whether it was possible that Brenda was responsible.

'Why would she do that?' demanded Mills, hoping she

sounded suitably affronted.

Hazel smiled. 'People do sometimes – for the insurance money. It's not unheard of.'

Mills didn't reply. She finished the coffee and waited to be allowed to go while Hazel studied her notebook, flipping pages backwards and forwards. Mills assumed she was reviewing what her colleagues had told her. Minutes passed. Eventually Hazel asked her questions about the state of the lab, when it would be clear, what would happen to it. Mills said they would be back in there as soon as possible, hoping she sounded convincing.

Finally Hazel's questions petered out and she escorted Mills to the front entrance. There was no handshake or thank you, she just told her she'd be in touch if she had any more questions, turned her back and walked off. Mills had planned to contact Nina in the police headquarters down the road to suggest they meet for lunch but it was late and she was full of tuna sandwich anyway. It was time she was at the lab to help with sorting out what could be retrieved.

This time she'd come prepared. She'd looked out a pair of overalls she used for working in mucky places when on archaeology field trips and picked up a hard hat from the department. She was surprised to see several cars parked outside the lab in addition to the company van. A skip had been delivered and it was already half full of blackened wood and indefinable objects. She pulled on her protective gear and went upstairs. Extra lighting had been installed and inside was a hive of activity. She found Bill in the storeroom, standing in front of one of the blackened cabinets where they kept the forensic samples.

He turned to greet her. 'Good timing. They've got into the cupboard but I told them not to touch anything.'

He opened the doors to show her then went off, leaving Mills to examine the contents of the cupboard. Clearly the samples had been exposed to very high temperatures and this immediately concerned her since any chemical analysis, for drugs or alcohol for example, would be compromised. Some of the plastic bags were partially melted and she could see plastic pots that had been distorted by the heat. She pushed the doors closed and went to fetch the supply of large polythene bags she'd brought with her.

For the rest of the afternoon she was packing samples into bags and carefully labelling them. After an hour she rang Donna to ask if she could come in to help by completing chain of custody forms for each package. She arrived half an hour later and together they had cleared one cupboard by the end of the day.

'What are you going to do with them?' Donna asked as she helped carry boxes full of samples outside.

'That's easy, I've arranged to take them straight to the Harrogate evidence store now.'

'But don't we need to go through them?'

'No, they go directly back to the customer. We'll sort the other cupboards tomorrow and I'll deal with the documents in the filing cabinet if there's time.'

Donna helped Mills load the boxes into her car but didn't seem keen to leave when they were finished.

'I wanted to ask you something, Mills. About what's going to happen to us now? I didn't know if I should be looking for another job now that... you know...'

Mills reassured her that she would be paid at the end of

the month as usual and Brenda would get in touch about arrangements during the interim. Silently she wondered if Brenda would be able to pay her staff in the short-term, knowing her financial problems and blaming her boss yet again for not taking responsibility for the company.

It was early evening by the time Mills got home and she was relieved to see that Muriel had been in to put the lights on as arranged. She'd left a note explaining that she'd given Harris a quick run and fed him. Also the fire service had been back to the Manor with a policeman to look at the petrol can which they'd taken away. They think it is significant, the note said.

The Gold Group was to be held at police headquarters first thing in the morning so Nina was up earlier than usual to ensure she was fully prepared – even allowing five minutes to scrape frost from her car windscreen before setting off. She wore her best black suit under her winter coat with a neatly ironed white shirt. Her notes were in her bag and she was in such good time she was able to pick up a latte from the coffee shop. Hazel joked that she looked like she was going to a funeral or appearing in court but Ruby said she looked really nice, adding that she liked the way she'd put her hair up. At exactly ten to nine Nina went upstairs to the meeting room.

The table was arranged with cards at each place giving the names and titles of the attendees. As she'd anticipated, they were representatives from all the key "stakeholders". The room was empty except for one woman who, like herself, had arrived with her coffee. When she introduced herself, Dr Ruth Barnes explained she was nominally "Forensics" from the Regional Scientific Support Unit based in Wakefield. As they chatted about heavy traffic on the M1, other members of the group arrived and at nine the meeting began.

Nina made copious notes, although there was little information that was new to her. The fire service manager reported on the incident, the detection of accelerant, how the fire had spread and the discovery of one fatality. A scientist from the fire investigation team issued copies of the report showing that petrol had been used to start the fire. They had a coffee break before Nina was able to report on the situation regarding the forensic samples that were in the lab that night. She was pleased to be able to pass on the message she'd received from Mills confirming they were being packaged and sent to Harrogate.

Nina listened intently as Dr Barnes then explained the samples would be collected from the forensic store for transfer to Wakefield where their very experienced laboratory would work to retrieve as much information as possible.

Nina expected that would be the extent of her contribution once Dr Barnes had given her view of what should happen regarding the data that was available on those samples already processed. However, as the only representative of the investigation team, Nina was unexpectedly grilled by the chairman about when they expected to arrest the arsonist. She had to admit they had little to go on.

The meeting finished with a list of actions designed to ensure that no valuable forensic evidence was lost as a result of the fire. Most of them fell on Nina and Dr

Barnes so after everyone disappeared they exchanged mobile numbers. Ruth asked her to keep in contact so they could manage progress on the forensic material that urgently needed analysing. Nina left her at the top of the stairs and went back to the office where she bumped into Hazel, who was on her way out.

'I'm going to see that Brenda Yardley woman. She's definitely avoiding me but I've pinned her down to a time so I can't be late,' she explained, pulling on her coat and dashing off.

Ruby grinned. 'She's been like this all morning. She was typing up the notes of the interviews she held yesterday and muttering grimly under her breath.'

'Oh dear, well I think I might be doing the same.'

'How did it go?'

'It was fine but I've got a list of things to do now, most of which rely on Mills keeping me up to date with progress on the lab. They asked about the arsonist, I don't suppose we've got any further?'

'Nope, that's why Hazel is seeing the owner of the lab. She's still got her in her sights. I did a check on the finances at Yardley Laboratories and they're not good I'm afraid. She's running on a big overdraft at present, and has been for several months.'

Nina didn't respond. In ordinary circumstances she would be agreeing with the researcher that arson could often be carried out for the insurance payout so it didn't look good for Brenda. But Mills was a key part of the team at Yardley's and she didn't want to even consider that the lab had been torched to pay off debts – not yet.

Hazel liked her interviews to take place in formal

surroundings and would have much preferred to invite Dr Yardley to Northallerton. However, the stupid old bat said she was indisposed, wasn't sure she could manage to come all the way into town, even though Hazel had offered to meet her in Harrogate police station. So she was parking in the weed-covered drive of an old house that had seen better days. The curtains moved as she climbed out of the car but it still took several minutes before someone answered the door.

The woman was wrapped in a woolly black shawl over a thick sweater and corduroy trousers. The house was cold and Hazel pulled her coat round her as she took the chair offered to her in the old fashioned room.

'I spoke to all your staff yesterday.' She reeled off the names of her five team members.

The woman looked surprised. 'Oh, right then.'

'So now I'd like to ask you the same questions.'

The old woman nodded. 'Fire away.'

Hazel got the same answers she'd received from the others; there was nothing new to be learned.

'What about any staff that might hold a grudge against you or your company?'

Dr Yardley screwed her face up. 'They all seem happy to me but you've spoken to them, pet. What do *you* think?'

'What about anyone no longer in the company? Do you have a list of ex-employees?'

'Well there's only: Alex White – Dr White the digital forensics whizz-kid. He's my only "ex-employee" as you call him.'

'So why did he leave?'

'He was surplus to requirements.' She folded her arms.

'You were over-staffed?'

She nodded.

'So you didn't have any problems with him? He didn't leave under a cloud? You don't think he left bearing a grudge then?'

'Well he wasn't happy but it was just the way it fell. Last in first out they say, don't they?'

'So you couldn't afford him, Dr Yardley.'

She didn't answer.

'Money a bit tight, isn't it?' suggested Hazel. 'We've looked at your financial situation and it's not good, is it?'

Her face was a picture. 'You've looked at my accounts?'

Hazel didn't reply but waited to see what happened next. She watched her sink further into the sofa.

'I'll admit it's been a rough time recently but I've been ill and had to take my eye off the ball. But things are picking up – or they were.'

Hazel closed her notebook. 'The insurance will come in handy then,' she said without looking up.

'Yes.' There was a pause. 'I know what you're getting at young lady but you're wrong.'

Hazel got up to leave. That was when the woman asked whether they were going to interview this Dr Alex White. 'Mills will be able to help you,' she said. 'They used to be together. They split up when he left. I think it was a bit, you know, acrimonious.'

Chapter 9

Phil eventually turned up much later than expected, when it was beginning to get dark. Mills had been shopping earlier and had spent the rest of the day tidying the house and preparing dinner. She'd even given Harris a brush.

And now the dog was making a big fuss of him.

'I think he's put on weight,' he remarked.

'Well so have you,' she said. He was looking much healthier than before he went away.

'Too many takeaways, I'm afraid.'

When he went outside to fetch his things Mills followed, interested to see what he was driving. It was a Jaguar, just two years old.

'Who lent you the flashy car?' she asked casually when they were back inside.

'Oh, it's Maria's. She didn't need it this weekend.' He disappeared upstairs with his rucksack.

'Harris hasn't had his walk yet,' she called. She'd been waiting in, expecting him to arrive early. 'Do you want to come before it gets totally dark?'

They went up the track as usual with Harris on the lead as it was dusk. A frost was already settling on the grass, an icy wind cut across their path. A pair of headlights appeared up on the fell to their left.

'Who's that?' Phil asked.

'It's probably Justin Price from the farm up the dale. He comes over this way sometimes.'

'Why?'

'I don't know but hold onto the lead if he comes down the track, Harris really doesn't like quad bikes.'

They stopped as the sound of the engine came close with Harris barking furiously. They stood aside as the bike thundered past, Harris straining to follow.

'It's not as if he had a dog with him,' Phil remarked as they started back down towards the cottage.

Mills explained about the moor fire as they passed the Manor but he listened without comment. He was more interested in what progress had been made with the lab fire investigation and Mills told him everything she knew while she poured them wine and cooked their meal. She'd made a lamb tagine especially because it had been a favourite of his in the past. Perhaps it was that dish or maybe the wine but their conversation became more relaxed, more like the old days, as they had dinner. By the time they were washing up it was almost like old times.

Over coffee in the sitting-room with Harris stretched out in front of the fire they had their first proper conversation for a long time. Phil began by apologising in a roundabout way for the last few months. His post-traumatic stress disorder had knocked him sideways, he didn't realise how bad he'd been until he went to Nottingham and things began to improve. Not that he didn't appreciate everything that she'd done for him while he was in hospital and afterwards but somehow that period of his life would always be associated with living back in the Dales.

'I'm just glad you're over it,' Mills said forcing a smile.

He went on to enthuse about his new life in academia. He was enjoying the freedom of working when he wanted, how he wanted. He liked adapting to his new surroundings and described in detail his environment, dwelling on the move to join Maria. When he suggested Mills came down to visit she agreed enthusiastically, but thinking about Harris who was snoring gently.

'You'll like Maria, she's such a… I don't know… such a free spirit!'

'Have you decided about him?' she asked, pointing at the lurcher.

'Sorry but the lease says no pets.' He looked at her guiltily. 'Is that going to be all right?'

'I suppose.'

Her original plan to help him recover from PTSD using a dog had come to nothing. It seemed she was now the proud owner of a beautiful lurcher. Phil continued to describe his work at the university – it sounded fascinating and was so close to what *she* had wanted to do that she was actually a bit jealous.

He eventually asked how her research was going. There was nothing to tell. Her time was being totally consumed by Yardley Forensics.

'But surely Brenda…'

'She's doing nothing. Gone into meltdown and delegating all responsibility.'

Phil whistled. He said he recognised the problem. Working with her he'd seen it happen a few times. When things got tough she'd walk away and put it in the 'too difficult' pile. His advice was to do the same but that wasn't possible for Mills. She had Glyn and Donna to consider as well as Margaret and Debs. However, it was nice to have someone sympathising with her over the situation. Phil understood and that meant something.

'So what are your plans for tomorrow?' Mills asked as

she was heading for bed.

She had gambled on the fact that he knew no-one in the area and planned a pub lunch before he disappeared back down to Nottingham. But she was wrong. There was a guy he'd met in the clinic at Catterick when he was being treated for PTSD. He'd kept in touch and planned to meet him in the morning. She could hardly argue with that.

'What about a quick lunch in Reeth?' she suggested.

'Maybe, depends when I get away. I'd hoped to drop in on Nige and Nina when I leave here tomorrow.'

'OK,' she replied as she shut her bedroom door.

Mills was up early in the morning as usual. Harris didn't let her lie in for long at the weekends. The rain was a light drizzle, the wind was sharp but she took him right to the top of the track and followed the contour towards Muker just below the mist. She turned back after half an hour, calling Harris away from where he was investigating a dead rabbit. She wanted to get back in time to dry her hair and change before she made breakfast. She had bacon and sausage to cook before Phil left for Catterick.

He was already up and dressed when they arrived back at the cottage.

'You've got time for breakfast?' she asked.

He looked at the clock.

'Yes, I said I'd be there by ten.'

She pushed her hair behind her ears and turned on the hob. Soon the kitchen was filled with blue smoke as the sausages split and the bacon burned. She cut up tomatoes and threw them into the pan but abandoned the idea of cooking eggs. As she was shovelling the undercooked sausages and overdone bacon onto the plates that she had meant to warm, the smoke alarm went off. The toast was burnt. She flung open the back door and Harris ran outside as Phil came running in.

'Can I help?'

She handed him a plate and threw the toast in the bin.

They ate in the kitchen with the door open while the atmosphere gradually cleared. She made tea and some edible toast. When Phil said it was the best breakfast he'd had for ages she pretended to believe him. Soon it was time for him to leave. He said he'd be back when he could so Mills said it would be nice if they could give Harris a walk before he went back to Nottingham – as he wasn't taking the dog with him. He was already opening the front door and didn't answer.

She was washing the greasy frying pan when the landline rang. Very few people called her at home at the weekend except her father, and only when it was important, so she dried her hands on her jeans as she ran to answer it.

'Dr Sanderson? It's Bill, you said it was all right to call you at home.'

'Bill?'

'We're clearing the lab in Harrogate?'

He apologised for calling her on a Sunday but they were cracking on and he thought she should know that someone had tried to break in overnight. They hadn't succeeded, just damaged the boarding on the ground floor windows.

'Probably kids looking for things to sell for drug money. I thought I'd let you know in case there's anything important on the computers.'

'There are confidential documents in the filing cabinet in the office.'

'What would you like us to do?'

Mills tried to think straight. In the absence of anything occurring to her she offered to go down and collect everything herself.

'Does that mean you'll be here before we finish today? We were planning to knock off at three.'

She said she would be there if they could provide her with some cardboard boxes.

She was already in her old clothes so she simply wrote a note for Phil explaining where she was going, asking him to give his dog a quick walk before he left and if he wanted to stop in Harrogate on his way down to Nottingham she would be at the lab until three. Leaving the key under the mat as they used to when he lived there, she told Harris to be good and left. It was Phil's fault she wasn't there to say goodbye to him when he returned.

On the way down to Harrogate Mills tried to decide what to do with the computers and documents from the lab. It would be convenient to have everything at the cottage if she was going to have to go through the paperwork but she didn't know if the computers were accessible and if they weren't she'd have to call on an expert. It would definitely be a better option to take everything to Brenda, who had plenty of space in her big house which was also handy to Harrogate and Yardley Forensics.

It was still drizzling when she arrived at the lab but the door was wide open and someone was carrying unidentifiable articles out to the large skip. On Friday the skip had been brimming over so this empty one was a replacement. She could see that the boarding on the ground floor windows had been damaged. On close examination it looked as if someone had tried to lever it off but the board was so big they had only broken the corner.

The stairs had been cleared of soot; paint was missing at the bottom becoming less patchy as she climbed to the top. She discovered that the filing cabinet had been washed clean. She found the key in her sooty desk drawer and unlocked it. Pulling out the top drawer she could see that the papers were not seriously damaged. The other drawers held records for completed analyses so any information relevant to the case would have been transmitted to the customer already, they would have their own copies. But the top drawer held the data for more recent jobs, some of which had not been finished and signed off. Where the work had just begun the correspondence was in the filing cabinet but any preliminary results would be in the respective laboratories and notes in the analysts' notebooks – it was those that Mills was most concerned about.

She found Bill in Tim's lab disconnecting the laptop that stored all the data from the mass spectrometer. The soot had been removed and Mills felt hopeful that it might be undamaged.

'I tried turning it on but nothing,' he said. 'It might need charging of course. Perhaps try with a new power supply.'

The laptop from Donna's lab looked in a worse state. He asked if there were any others and she showed him the computers that she and Brenda used. He fetched boxes and while she loaded the contents of the filing cabinet, he disconnected the computers, gave them a quick dust down and had them ready for transferring to her car.

'Is there anything else left in there that you need to keep?' he asked as he helped her carry the boxes outside.

She went round the entire building on her own, examining bits of equipment but finding nothing else worth saving. She walked into town through fine drizzle to get a sandwich, hurrying back in case Phil had turned up but apparently no-one had come looking for her. She sent him a message but when, at three, he still hadn't responded she said goodbye to Bill and thanked him for contacting her, before setting off to Brenda's.

Her boss was watching television when she drew up outside the house. Mills could tell by the flickering light in the front room. When she rang the bell the hall was suddenly illuminated and Brenda opened the door, fully dressed and looking quite alert. Mills explained what she had in her car.

'I didn't know what else to do with the stuff,' she explained.

Brenda had her slippers on so she said she wouldn't come outside in the rain. Mills carried everything straight into the dining room, placing the boxes on the large table in the middle of the room. Her boss seemed happy with the arrangement.

'I bought a couple of cakes in town,' she told Brenda, who had a sweet tooth.

She made a pot of tea and they sat in front of the fire in the sitting room. For once Brenda appeared not to have been drinking.

'You'll laugh at us, pet. I went to church this morning, the first time for many years. When I was a kid I went every week regular as clockwork but it petered out in my teens. It was a nice service today.'

Mills didn't know what to say then she remembered to ask her about the inquest.

'Will you be attending on Tuesday?'

'Tuesday?'

'Tim's inquest, Brenda. I think you should be there.'

'You do?'

'Yes. Depending on the outcome there could be an investigation by the Health and Safety Executive.'

Mills wished she hadn't said that. Brenda was looking anxiously at her.

'I've been sent a letter, pet. Apparently I have to go. Will you be there?'

'Yes I will. I could pick you up and take you.'

Brenda nodded. Despite that wobble she appeared to be in a better state than previously, perhaps her visit to church had calmed her.

'Good. Now, do you have a power cable that'll fit any of the computers?'

They found one that plugged into their own computers and tried to power them up. Both were serviceable, which meant that the administrative records for the business had been saved. Mills was pleased to be able to copy a list of all their current jobs and customers onto a memory stick.

'I'll send the list to Ruby when I get home,' she said triumphantly.

In the absence of the correct connector for the laboratory laptops Mills reluctantly agreed to take them with her. Nige would know where to find a suitable power cable.

Nina was ironing the children's school uniform when she received a text from Chloe's mother to say that her daughter had gone into labour over the weekend and had delivered a baby boy, four weeks premature. Mother and baby were fine but little Tim would have to stay in hospital for a few days.

'Oh.'

'What's up?' asked Nige.

Nina swallowed the lump in her throat. 'It's just my liaison family; she's had a little boy and called him after his dad.'

'The one that died in the lab fire?'

'Yes.'

She pressed another couple of shirts before asking, 'Did Phil know what Mills has been going through when you saw him?'

'He didn't say.'

'Honestly?'

'He was far too busy telling me about his research.'

'It's good he's getting back to his old self but I was surprised he wasn't spending time with Mills today.'

'She had to go out.'

'Really?' She finished the last shirt and switched the iron off. 'I might call her.'

Nige looked up. He was watching the television but went to take hold of the remote control.

'It's OK Nige, I'll go upstairs.'

Mills sounded tired when she picked up but denied it was a bad time. She explained what she'd been doing down in Harrogate.

'Phil told Nige you were busy,' Nina said. 'It was nice he came by. I was out shopping but they had a good catch-up. It sounds as though he's enjoying getting back into research.'

'Hmm.'

Nina gave her the news that Chloe had delivered a baby boy and called him Tim.

'Poor Chloe,' said Mills. 'Do you think she'll be at the inquest?'

'Her mother seems to think she will.'

'Brenda's been called to attend.'

'It will be hard for her.'

'It's hard for all of us.'

Mills put the phone down and sat back by the fire. Harris was stretched out on the rug but the cottage seemed very quiet now. Phil had emptied the spare room of all his things, leaving only a scribbled note thanking her for letting him stay, repeating his invitation to visit Nottingham and confirming that Harris had been out.

Her evening was disturbed by Muriel's signature knock on the door.

'Sorry to disturb,' she said as she came through to the warmth of the sitting room.

Harris was up, wagging his tail excitedly.

'No I haven't come to take you,' she said, patting him. 'I saw my brother-in-law today and he said the fire at the Manor was definitely set deliberately.'

Mills invited her to sit down, offering her a glass of wine. It was a good excuse for a drink.

'So do they have a suspect?'

'I don't think so but it's a police investigation

apparently. I told him to keep me posted but I know you have friends in the police force.'

'I can ask.'

'It's so odd though, isn't it? There's never anyone around or if there is you'd see them, especially if they're a stranger.'

'But presumably it happened in the middle of the night.'

'Yes and we didn't hear a thing did we?'

'No.'

'But Harris did, didn't you boy? It was him that woke me up,' said Muriel.

'That's true. Perhaps *he* knows who did it,' Mills said jokingly.

She tickled the dog behind his ears.

'If only he could talk,' said Muriel.

Her neighbour stayed for the rest of the evening. Normally Mills would be hoping she would go but tonight she felt in need of normal company and was happy to listen to the village gossip. Muriel had a job cleaning a few local holiday cottages on a Saturday morning and she always had stories about what the occupants had been up to. She and her husband also kept their gardens tended in the summer but not at this time of year.

When Muriel finally made her way back next door Mills felt ready for bed. But once she turned the light out she could not get to sleep. She tried to forget the blackened lab, the laptops downstairs, and Chloe's baby with no father. She tried not to think about Phil back at Nottingham with his fun housemate Maria. She concentrated instead on something that wasn't her problem – the fire at the Manor. She went through the hours that led up to the blaze, trying to recollect when exactly she'd woken up. She'd first thought it was a bonfire night celebration at the Manor but recalled it had been after midnight which is why she'd been surprised and irritated. Harris had woken her so she'd assumed he'd heard fireworks being let off at the Manor. But the fire wasn't a bonfire and there were no fireworks. So if he wasn't barking at the fireworks was it possible he'd heard a quad bike?

Chapter 10

Mills was in the office early on Monday morning but it was typical of Nige to arrive late when she needed to see him. He finally appeared at ten o'clock balancing a reusable coffee cup in one hand and a pile of books under the other arm. The books fell noisily onto his desk.

'Nige,' Mills began as he pulled off his anorak, 'can I borrow your laptop charger?'

She'd tried her own but it didn't have the right sort of connection. Nige's laptop, on the other hand, was the same make as the lab ones so she was sure it would fit – and it did. She explained why she needed to charge them as she waited for the first one to show signs of life. Just as she was giving up hope the screen lit up with the company logo and she let out a whoop of joy.

Nige came across to see as she tried the password. She only knew the one for the mass spectrometer because she'd accessed data from it for her research. The password was successful so she knew this was Tim's work laptop.

'This had a better chance of surviving the fire than the other one. It was mainly smoke damage in Tim's lab.'

'So you'll be able to retrieve the data from his instrument. Will that tell you what he was working on?'

'Maybe.'

She was opening the files and scanning the dates. There had been no analyses since the Friday before the fire, which meant he hadn't been using it the night he died.

She frowned. Still at least they hadn't lost any data. She disconnected the power supply, plugged it into the second laptop and waited.

'Nothing?' asked Nige after a few minutes.

'No, I think it's dead.'

She left it charging but after an hour the screen was still blank. Nige had gone off to a lecture but when he returned he asked if she'd had any luck.

'You still may be able to save the hard drive,' he said. 'IT will help you.'

They went down to see the experts together because Nige reckoned he knew some of them quite well. An acquaintance of his offered to have a quick look and told Mills to come back after lunch.

'Don't worry, Mills,' Nige said as they walked back upstairs. 'If all else fails wait until you see Alex and get him to retrieve the data.' Then he added, 'You have contacted him about the back-up haven't you?'

Mills said she was on to it. She waited for Nige to go to the cafeteria before she felt comfortable about ringing Alex's mobile number, hoping there would be no answer so she had an excuse to send a text.

There was a pause after he picked up. 'Mills?'

'Yes, it's me. How are you?'

'I'm... er... fine. And you?'

'Yes, well no, not really.'

She decided to tell him about the fire straight out. She told him what had happened to Tim and how Brenda wasn't coping well so she was dealing with it all herself. She described the state of the lab and how all the forensic work had been curtailed.

'What a mess,' he said when she'd finished. 'If there's

anything…'

'That's why I rang Alex. We've lost track of how the computers are backed-up. Brenda can't remember and I don't think I ever knew. The manual says it's done daily but where does it go?'

He sighed. 'We are talking about something I did two years ago.'

'So you did set it up?'

'Yes, I believe I did but I'd have to have a think about what I would have used. Are any of the computers functional?'

'Yes mine and Brenda's and the one from Tim's lab.'

'In that case it will be easy to see where it goes.' She waited for him to suggest what to do. 'Mills, are you still there?'

'Yes.'

'I suppose it would be best to come up.'

'Are you sure?' That's what she'd been afraid of. 'Can't you send me the instructions?'

'No, I'll come up on Friday. Have *you* got the computers?'

'No, they're at Brenda's house.'

It was half true; she could take the others back to Brenda so she wouldn't have to meet Alex. She gave him the address and he said he would aim to be there by early afternoon.

'I'll let her know.'

Alex began asking her how she was getting on, wanting to know what she was doing, and was she still in Swaledale. She told him she had a lecture and had to go.

After lunch she went to the IT department to find the laptop waiting for her.

'Sorry, the hard drive is too far gone. I can't get anything back for you.'

Mills thanked him and carried it away despondently. She wondered if Alex might be able to do better since he was a specialist in retrieving digital data. She would leave a note with the laptop in case he could help.

Nina arranged to meet Chloe and her mother at the Harrogate Justice Centre on the morning of the inquest. She had ensured that the Coroner's Liaison Officer had met with them to explain the process and she'd handed them the various reports that were made available by the Coroner the previous week. Nina was sure it would be very straightforward because there was no jury and the body had already been released to Tim's parents. They had not wanted to see all the reports or talk to her but she was pleased to see them coming through the entrance lobby. She gave them a little wave and they nodded as they passed her. She was still waiting when Mills arrived with Brenda in tow. They were both smartly dressed in black suits, Mills in trousers and Brenda in a long skirt that billowed as she walked. Their faces were abnormally pale, perhaps accentuated by their funeral attire.

She greeted them in an appropriately sombre manner, taking the opportunity to ask Mills if they had discovered yet why Tim was in the building the night of the fire. It was the only question mark over what had happened that night and she was concerned that they would be asked. Mills shook her head but explained that there might be some information if they could get access to the data from the lab where he was working.

'Alex White is coming to help sort out the digital

records,' Mills said, her face colouring.

Nina raised an eyebrow but didn't comment. She'd seen Chloe arrive with her mother and excused herself to greet them. When she asked how the baby was doing, Becky said her daughter had come straight from the hospital and the good news was that he would be coming home in a couple of days. They stood awkwardly for a few minutes until it was time to go into the courtroom. There were perhaps thirty people attending the inquest, mainly from police, fire and forensic services who would be reporting the details of what had happened the night of the fire. She ushered Chloe and Becky to join Tim's parents and sat beside them.

Inquest proceedings were distressing by their nature. Nina had attended many but they were always difficult to sit through. This one was no different. It began in a matter of fact way with the coroner explaining the reason for the inquest: to establish who the person was, where they died, when they died, and how they came by their death. Then a series of witnesses were called. First the fire service representative described the nature of the fire, the timings and how it had spread. He gave the precise time when Tim's body was removed from the building and declared dead at the scene. His fiancée sat rigid beside Nina.

Next the fire investigation report which showed that petrol had been used to start the fire. A woman from the forensics team went through how they had established with a fair amount of confidence that the door hadn't been forced that night so the deceased had probably left it unlocked, making it easy for the arsonist to spread accelerant inside. There were two questions the coroner finally wanted to establish: who had started the fire and why someone was working in the building that night. Clearly the police had got no further forward in identifying the perpetrator. Now Brenda swished past Nina on her way to be questioned.

She was a strange woman, thought Nina. She didn't know her except what she heard from Mills. She'd always thought she must be very confident, an expert in forensics herself running a successful business employing several people. But as this figure in black looked anxiously at the coroner when he told her to speak up, Nina didn't recognise the image she'd had in her head. When he asked if Tim Fletcher was in the habit of working late she replied that no-one was given overtime but he did sometimes work at the weekend for Dr Sanderson on special projects. Was there any hazard in working alone? Brenda seemed confused but on further questioning explained that Dr Sanderson would be present if there was. Eventually it was established that no-one knew why he was there that night but, yes Tim Fletcher did have a key to the building and would have let himself in. Tim's parents were whispering to each other.

The coroner's conclusions were no surprise to Nina. The evidence of arson confirmed the verdict of unlawful killing by person or persons unknown. As they filed out Nina watched Mills supporting her boss, who seemed overcome by the proceedings. Tim's parents left hurriedly as if avoiding Chloe, who was in tears. Her mother told her to sit down for a minute as she wanted to speak to Nina.

'My daughter has a lot to cope with now and I don't want her to be distracted from the baby but I have to fight her corner. Is there no blame attached to that woman?'

Nina waited for her to continue.

'I mean the owner of the place where he worked. Surely it was her fault?'

'What do you mean?' asked Nina, although she was pretty sure she knew what she was saying.

'Whatever the reason why he was there, the fire was in her building and she is responsible for his death.'

Nina tried to explain sympathetically that the coroner blamed it on whoever set fire to the place but Becky argued that the building should have been better protected against such an eventuality. Chloe was back beside her mother keen to return to the hospital. She thanked Nina for helping them through the inquest before she went. Left in the entrance hall with Chloe's mother, Nina suggested a coffee to discuss her concerns.

Brenda said she needed a drink, setting off for the nearest pub with Mills holding her arm. After a double whisky she seemed to recover sufficiently for Mills to try to persuade her to eat some lunch. She agreed to a bowl of carrot soup and Mills ordered two, with a portion of chips. She brought Brenda up to date on progress at the lab until their food arrived. Her boss didn't appear interested but kept going back to things that were said that morning.

'Did you hear them ask why Tim was in there?' she asked. 'They made out I had him working overtime, as if I could afford to do that!'

'Is it that bad?' Mills asked casually.

'Pretty bad, pet, I was looking at losing another

member of staff but not that way.'

Mills looked at her, thinking it was a joke in bad taste but Brenda wasn't smiling. Her eyes were glistening as she stood up to order another drink.

'Alex White is coming up on Friday to sort out the back-up,' Mills informed her when she returned with another whisky.

She had to remind her who Alex was.

'Oh him,' she said without enthusiasm. 'Is he still around?'

'No, he works for the Home Office now, in London. He said he could come up on Friday to sort things out.'

Brenda nodded, took another sip of her drink and smiled. 'He'll be glad to see you,' she said mischievously.

'I doubt it and anyway I won't be there – I've got an appraisal,' she lied. The appraisal was next week but Brenda wasn't to know.

Her boss was objecting to Alex coming to her house when Mills was distracted by a text message. It was Nina asking if she was still in town.

'Sorry, I'd better reply to this,' she said.

Her friend wanted to meet up for a quick chat. Mills said she'd be back at the Court House in half an hour. That suited Nina fine, she'd replied.

Brenda drained her glass. 'You know the police may treat him as a suspect. When that sergeant asked me about ex-employees with a grudge I had to tell her about him.'

'Seriously? You think he came back here to burn down the lab to get back at you for firing him?'

'I'm just saying. Do you think I should let her know he'll be up here? I really don't know if I should let him come to my house.'

Mills had had enough. 'I'm sorry Brenda but he's coming to you, where the computers are, on Friday and that's the end to it.'

'What about the computers from the lab? You've taken those away.'

'They're in my car. I'm dropping them off now when I take you home.'

As soon as they finished eating she paid for their meals and ushered Brenda to the door. Mills wanted to get away before she said something she regretted later. She was back at the Court House in precisely thirty-five minutes leaving a disgruntled boss back at home with all the computers.

'Mills, you look rather harassed,' Nina said as they hugged.

'It's just Brenda. I could shake her sometimes.'

They found a wooden bench and sat side by side.

'She seemed a little out of it this morning,' Nina observed.

'Out of it? She certainly is! She just doesn't appreciate the gravity of the situation.'

'Would you say she's under pressure? I only ask because Hazel has told Ruby to get details on the financial side of the business. I think the insurance company has been talking to her.'

Mills remembered Jessica saying she sometimes asked for such information if she suspected a building had been set on fire for the insurance money. She muttered that Brenda was always a bit unpredictable.

'So did you expect a verdict of unlawful killing?' Mills asked to change the subject.

'I think so in the circumstances. He might've adjourned the inquest in case we find out who started the fire but that could drag on for months. I believe they felt the family had been through enough and the chances of prosecuting anyone now are pretty slim. What about you? Are you happy with the verdict?'

'Happy?'

'Sorry, that's not the right word.'

'It seemed appropriate.'

'Exactly, that's what I meant. I think Tim's family understood that but Becky, Chloe's mother, is looking for compensation. I thought you should know.'

Mills had no idea how to respond. 'Thanks for telling me. I guess the insurance will deal with that.'

'Well hopefully she has employees' liability insurance. I believe it's a legal requirement and has to cover at least five million pounds.'

'Wow, you've been doing your homework.'

'I had half an hour to kill while I waited for you.'

'In that case I guess we'll be covered.' Mills hoped her optimism was justifiable.

Nina leaned towards her. 'I only say this because Becky may be appointing a solicitor. Tell Brenda to be aware that she may find herself being sued. It's just that it may be the only way that compensation can be paid by the insurance company since the fire was not due to the company's negligence – on the contrary, everything was in place: the fire alarm, the fire escape and all the procedures in case of fire. And we still don't know what Tim was doing there.'

Mills shook her head. 'But the good news is that Alex is coming up to look at the laptop from Donna's lab. If Tim was using the DNA equipment we'll know.'

'Is he?' Nina seemed uncertain how to react.

'Yes, he knows how the data is backed up.'

'That will be interesting. Where's he going to stay?'

'Not with me, if that's what you mean. He's going to Brenda's just for the day to check things out. I won't be there,' she added hastily.

Nina grinned. 'Worried about seeing him again?'

'More what I might say to him,' Mills admitted.

Nina looked at her watch and jumped up. 'I'd better go and report back to the office. They'll want to know the outcome of the inquest. Keep me posted, won't you, about how it goes with Alex.'

Mills walked slowly back to her car trying to rationalise Brenda's outlandish accusation. Was her boss deliberately pointing the finger at Alex as a disgruntled employee capable of arson, just because she'd made him redundant? Or was she simply trying to divert attention from herself?

Chapter 11

Ruby had worked through until lunchtime without a break. She'd taken the list that Mills had sent her and produced a spreadsheet of all the jobs in the first column then populated the rest with information about the crime. She left a space for progress, to be completed when Mills was able to access any data that was stored remotely. She sent Nina a copy to pass on to the members of the Gold Group and, in particular, the forensic science regulator.

When Nina appeared they sat at their desks eating while they went through the list together. First was an item of clothing from a cold case, a stabbing. It was a wool jacket that had been sent because of Dr Yardley's expertise in textiles. They wanted to confirm the type of knife that had been used from the way it had damaged the fabric. It was to corroborate the pathologist's report.

Next there was a soil sample taken from the playground where a girl had been murdered plus samples of soil from the shoes of the defendant. These analyses were required urgently and Nina told Ruby to add a note for the samples to be sent on to Wakefield immediately.

'This next one is interesting,' said Ruby. 'It's a sample of heroin for analysis. They've asked to check the purity.'

'Let's hope the sample is still viable,' said Nina.

'There are three men on remand for the crime and one of them has previously been found guilty of trying to interfere with evidence. I thought I should mention it in case it was relevant.'

'Are you thinking that the fire could be an attempt to destroy evidence?'

Ruby nodded as she chewed on her sandwich.

Then there were two sets of unrelated blood samples. One was a batch from a local firm for routine drug screening, which wasn't of interest to the police forensic service. The second was also for a private customer but was relevant because it was a duplicate sample of blood from a man suspected of driving while under the influence of alcohol.

'Apparently there was something wrong with the breathalyser and the tests didn't agree,' explained Ruby. 'Anyway, the blood sample the police had analysed found him over the limit but the man's solicitor has advised him to get his own duplicate sample analysed. I suppose he's hoping that the margin of error might bring it below the legal limit.'

'That sample may not have survived very well at a high temperature,' Nina commented.

A padded jacket had been submitted for a full examination to search for anything relevant such as hairs, fibres and bodily fluids. It was from the victim of an attempted rape.

Finally there were several DNA samples that had been submitted for a range of crimes, including a blood sample found on the clothing of a suspected murderer. He had been on remand for some time and it was another urgent requirement. Ruby made a note for the sample to be progressed to the Wakefield labs as soon as possible.

'What are these cigarette ends on the list?'

'They're from the scene of that fatal stabbing. The cigarettes were recovered from where Jennifer Carr was murdered outside her house. It's as if the killer had been waiting for her. DNA from those cigarette ends is the only link we have to the crime. It's really sad; she had a ten-year old daughter.'

Nearly the same age as Rosie, Nina thought. 'They'd better be fast-tracked. And this last one?'

It was a sample of clothing that might have evidence of DNA from a sexual attack.

Ruby screwed up her sandwich wrapper and aimed it at the bin. She leaned back in her chair and shrugged.

'Any of the offenders associated with that list of crimes would have reason to destroy the evidence. The drink driving charge might not warrant it but the murders and sexual offences could.'

Nina had to agree but pointed out it was not a line of enquiry that would be popular with the bosses.

'How about I do a little bit of background,' suggested Ruby. 'Where the suspects are, or rather were, the night of the fire.'

'I'm sure Hazel won't think it's a good use of your time.'

'All right.'

Nina thought the researcher had given in far too easily but decided her work wouldn't suffer if she did a bit of digging on the quiet anyway.

'I'll get in touch with Wakefield,' Nina offered. 'I'd like a chance to speak to Dr Barnes anyway.'

When she did finally get through to Ruth Barnes it wasn't until late afternoon.

'We've been through the list of ongoing jobs and I think we should send all the samples on to you as soon as possible,' she said.

'That's fine. We can handle pretty much everything.'

'I can send you a list giving all the details right now.'

'Excellent.'

'You know that the samples might have had their integrity compromised by the fire.'

'Yes, I understood that would be the case. I'll make sure we have a full discussion before any work is started.'

Nina took a deep breath. 'I wondered if you'd experienced anything like this before. You know, a forensic lab being destroyed?'

'I haven't, no.'

'But there have been problems such as falsifying data or tampering with evidence.'

'Yes, that's true.'

'Do you think it's conceivable that someone might set fire to a lab to destroy evidence?'

'What are you saying? Do you think this has happened with Yardley Forensics?'

Nina sighed. 'We don't know. It's just one possibility I suppose.'

'In my experience criminals are capable of anything if they think they can avoid detection.'

Mills had spent the day working at home preparing for her staff appraisal the following week. Nige had warned her that the reviewers would want to know what research she'd been doing and, more importantly, what she planned to do. It was going to be difficult to convince them that she'd achieved a great deal in the past year. She'd hoped to have started her planned investigation into the composition of bones from different parts of the country but that had been put to one side when Phil was going through his illness. The fire at the lab had completely taken over her time and she couldn't remember what she'd told the Archaeology Department she would have achieved in the past year. She also had to satisfy the Forensics Department, which paid half her salary. Perhaps she should do an investigation into what happens when a forensics lab burns down, she mused.

'Fancy a walk, Harris?'

The lurcher leapt up, running to where his lead was hanging in the hall. He ran up and down until Mills had her boots and jacket on.

A cold wind was blowing as they took the usual route up to the tops. It was cloudy and she guessed it would get dark early that evening. A nice long walk now and Harris wouldn't want to go out later, she thought. So she kept going when they reached the end of the track, turning left along the hill in the direction of David's farm. She let Harris off on the moor where he ran about looking for rabbits but when she reached the first gate she put him back on the lead – he wasn't used to sheep yet. This field was empty but as the track went slightly uphill they reached another wall with a narrow gate stile. Here they would join the farm track that would take them up to the top of the fell where she would follow the narrow footpath back along and down to Mossy Bank.

A quad bike was coming down the track towards the farm and Harris went mad as usual, barking and pulling on his lead. Mills waved, assuming it was David Price. He stopped almost beside her and cut the engine. The dog calmed down immediately.

Mills then realised it wasn't David. 'Justin?'

Of course it was David's son. She hadn't spoken to him

since he was a young boy but Muriel had confirmed he was back on the farm. She explained that she'd mistaken him for his father and he laughed awkwardly. She asked if he was working for his dad now, a really stupid thing to say. Justin said he was and started the engine, setting Harris off again as he disappeared towards the farm.

On her way back home Mills tried to analyse rationally why she thought Justin might have something to do with the fire at the Manor. It was the quad bike that had started it, or rather Harris and his reaction to it. The dog had woken Mills the night of the fire by barking furiously. No-one was breaking into her cottage and there were no fireworks being let off. In her experience the only other thing that would cause Harris to bark was a quad bike. So is that what he heard and, if so, was it Justin?

'Well, Harris, if that is what you heard and Justin did set fire to the moorland by the Manor in the middle of the night – why on earth did he do it?'

Next morning Mills had a tutorial group with the first-years. She hadn't prepared for it so it wasn't surprising that the students weren't very motivated. She cut it short, asking them to prepare presentations for the following week, and headed to the cafeteria. She wanted to leave but she'd told Brenda she had her appraisal so she thought it best to stay in the office in case her boss tried to contact her on the landline. She was sure Alex would have questions that Brenda wouldn't be able to understand, never mind find the answer to. So long as she could avoid having to meet him face to face.

Ruby had sent an email asking if she could annotate the list of forensic samples she'd compiled with who was responsible for the work. They were keen to find out which samples Tim Fletcher had been analysing. It only took Mills a few minutes: Donna covered drug and alcohol testing, DNA and clothing examination; Tim analysed the soils. Ruby had already put Brenda's name against "knife penetration in outer garment". The researcher had added that all the samples were being sent to the Regional Scientific Support Unit for analysis. They wouldn't find the forensic evidence in a pristine state, thought Mills, but she decided that was their problem not hers.

She opened her laptop and stared dejectedly at her "Personal Review and Development Plan". She'd completed the "Teaching" section because it was quite straightforward but she had to come up with some exciting prospective work under "Research" before the end of the day. She left that section, moving on to the questions that would be discussed at the review on Monday. By the time Nige appeared she'd filled nearly a page with "Challenges faced in the past year" but very little under "Knowledge gained" and "Contributions to the Department." So she asked for his help. Her problem was that she was being reviewed by two senior members of academic staff: one from Forensics and the other from Archaeology. He advised her to complete her plan in two parts, one for each department.

'So now I've got twice as much to do,' she complained.

Nige spent an hour helping her complete the form. He'd been through it so many times himself he couldn't see what her problem was.

'Just put down what you want to do but don't be too ambitious because it will be reviewed this time next year.'

By the time Nige went to lunch Mills had completed every section, although some parts of the form were decidedly skimpy. She was just finishing the "Contributions to the Department" when Brenda rang.

'Mills, you have to come. I don't understand what he's wanting.'

There was a rustling and then Alex spoke. 'Hi Mills. I need to know where you want me to store the information I retrieve.' He lowered his voice. 'To be honest I really need someone who can tell me whether what I get off the laptops looks like what you're expecting. Brenda doesn't know what's working and what's bust.'

More rustling, it was Brenda, sounding overwrought. 'Mills, it's me again. You have to come down. I know you're busy today but you can come tomorrow morning can't you? Alex says he can stay overnight.'

Mills thought through the options rapidly. 'It's fine. I've had the appraisal. I'll come down now.'

At least she would only be there for an hour or so. Although she was familiar with the software that Tim used in his lab, it occurred to her that Donna was actually the best person to tell Alex what her lab software looked like. She rang her and they arranged to meet at Brenda's. Mills set off feeling a little less reticent about meeting Alex.

Donna was already there when Mills arrived. She and Alex were seated at Brenda's dining table poring over the inside of a laptop. He was explaining what he was doing but looked up when Mills joined them.

'Hi there, I'm looking to see if I can get anything from Donna's laptop. While I do this, do you know what's wrong with the other one?'

'Nothing,' said Mills. 'I've had it running. Our office computers seem fine too. But Donna's wouldn't charge.'

'No, I'm hoping we haven't lost everything.'

'If it's all been backed up it won't be a problem, will it?' Mills asked.

Alex was fiddling inside the laptop. 'Depends how often it's been done. I'll have a look at yours to see in a minute.'

Mills powered it up in readiness then went to find Brenda, who was in the kitchen.

'How are you?'

Her boss didn't answer but carried on washing up dishes.

'Can I make some tea?' Mills asked.

Brenda turned round from the sink. 'What, love?'

'Tea. Shall I make tea for us?'

'You can. I'm just washing some mugs.'

Mills found a damp tea towel and began drying the dishes. It looked as though there were several days of washing up there.

She tried again. 'Are you keeping well?'

'Not bad, considering.'

'When did Alex arrive?'

'Lunchtime. He said it might take a while. I said he could stay here.'

'Did he want to?'

'He said he was seeing friends in Leeds tomorrow but not until later.'

'You don't mind him staying after what you were insinuating the other day?'

'What do you mean?'

'You were almost accusing him of starting the fire.'

There was a shout from the next room and Mills ran in.

'He says he can read the hard drive!' said Donna excitedly.

There were wires sticking out of Donna's laptop leading to another that Alex was typing on furiously.

'Have a look at this and tell me if it seems familiar.'

Donna peered over his shoulder and grimaced.

'Wait a second.' He typed again. 'Is that the name of one of your files?'

'Yes, that's the program we run for the DNA profiling software.'

'In that case I think we have it. I'll transfer all of it over to the other laptop if I can.'

They stopped for a mug of tea then Alex asked Mills to show him her computer. She typed in the password and left him to browse the contents. He said he was looking for the back-up setting. It didn't take long.

'There it is: every evening at seven o'clock.'

'And where does it go?'

'Onto a remote server. I'm surprised you haven't been sent a bill since I left. Perhaps we paid for five years up front.'

He spent some time showing Mills exactly where the back-up could be found and gave her details of the service he'd set up. She was surprised that they could sit together having a matter of fact conversation after the way they'd separated. Alex was definitely less arrogant. He'd changed and she wondered if she had too.

'Do you think that you'll be all right with that?' he asked when they'd finished.

'I think so.' She looked at him properly for the first

time since she'd arrived. 'Thank you.'

He grinned. 'It's a pleasure. I'm just sorry it's been such a disaster.'

She assumed he meant the fire. She asked him to show her how to recall the results on the server back to her computer.

Donna had been sitting quietly while Alex helped Mills but when they'd finished she pointed out that anything Tim had done after seven o'clock would not have been saved. Mills told them she'd already checked Tim's laptop and there was nothing recorded that evening. So Donna asked Alex if they could look at what he'd copied from her laptop. Everyone sat in silence as Alex typed and Donna told him where to look for the most recent DNA results. When Alex stopped typing Donna put her hand to her mouth and gasped.

'He was using the DNA profiler,' she said. She gave Alex some more instructions. 'There, stop there. Oh my goodness, he's been using it since September. He's set up a file of his own, I didn't notice.'

'Can you tell what sort of samples he was analysing?' Mills asked.

She took over the keyboard and scanned the files. 'He's only used the parameters for swab samples.'

That made sense to Mills. She'd been worrying that he'd been moonlighting and, if so, blamed herself for giving him private work in the past. She'd had nothing to offer him since the summer and he was desperate to earn extra for the wedding. Had he found another lucrative side-line? It was possible. But she didn't share her thoughts, she felt strangely responsible for his actions.

'Did he know how to use the DNA analyser?' asked

Brenda.

'Didn't you say he went to the training course when the manufacturer installed it?' Mills asked.

'Well he was a bright boy,' said Brenda with a sigh.

Mills suspected that Brenda had the same idea that she had about Tim's motives: he'd been offering DNA testing to the public as a way of making money for his bride's perfect wedding day.

Chapter 12

Donna said she would take the laptop to check when Tim was DNA testing in an attempt to establish what he was looking for. Mills suddenly realised how late it was and picked up her bag to leave.

Alex looked up. 'You're not going already? I thought I could take you and Brenda out for dinner as I'm not leaving tonight.'

Mills froze.

'That's nice of you, Alex,' Brenda said with a forced smile, 'but I don't eat a proper meal in the evening, it's too near bed-time for me.'

He turned to Mills.

'Sorry, I've got to get back for the dog.'

Without missing a beat he said, 'No problem, I'll come up to you. I've got all evening. I'll bring your computer.'

Everyone was looking at her. What could she say – she was cornered. 'Fine,' she replied with a shrug.

'Does the fish and chip van still come round on a Friday?'

'Yes.' She pulled on her jacket and started to follow Donna to the door.

'Then I'll pick them up on the way through,' he called.

It was nearly five o'clock. He might just make it, Mills thought.

All the way home she was cursing herself for not telling him she didn't want him coming to the cottage. It would have been much better to go out for a meal or she could have met him somewhere half-way; although that would still make it like a date and she definitely didn't want him thinking that. And what would they talk about while they ate fish and chips? She couldn't even make an excuse to leave as she would be at home.

The cottage was empty when she arrived so she automatically went next door. Muriel tended to have Harris with her if Mills was late, "to keep him company, poor lamb". The dog was pleased to see her, greeting her by jumping up and nearly knocking her over. Apologising to Muriel for being late yet again, she took Harris by the collar and guided him next door. She hastily tidied the sitting room, turned up the heating before putting plates in the oven to warm and laying the tiny table in the kitchen. Without thinking she put out the tomato sauce – he'd always had it on his chips – then quickly put it back in the fridge. She looked at her watch. The fish and chip van had been parked in Low Row when she came through so Alex would probably catch it there or in Gunnerside.

It wasn't too long before there was a knock on the door. Alex was distracted by Harris while Mills unloaded their supper onto two plates, calling him into the kitchen.

'I got cod,' he said. 'I hope that's all right?'

'Fine.'

'D'you have any ketchup?'

'I'll look.'

She handed him the bottle and he squirted it all over his chips. It had always irritated her. She asked if he wanted a beer but he said no as he was driving. She made tea.

'Has Brenda recovered or is she still being treated?' he asked once they were eating.

'You mean from her cancer?'

'Yes. She doesn't seem very well.'

'The fire has affected her badly. She doesn't want to rebuild the business.'

She thought he'd be pleased to hear that after being made redundant. She was trying to judge his mood in case Brenda's suspicions had any basis. She watched him halt with his fork raised halfway to his mouth.

'No,' he said. 'She can't do that. What about Donna and the others. What about you?'

'I'm working full-time at the university, if you remember,' she said pointedly. She'd taken the post when he left Yardley's. That was why he thought he should stay on instead of Mills being kept as a consultant.

He poured more sauce on his plate, dipping a chip studiously. 'Did I get the impression that Tim was moonlighting? Is that why he was in the building that night?'

'Hopefully Donna will find out a bit more now that she can access the files – and thanks for that, by the way. I'm meeting her tomorrow to see what she's got. At least we'll have something to tell Chloe.'

'Chloe?'

'Tim's fiancée. She's just had his baby. She's pretty angry with us all, as you can imagine. They were getting married next year.'

'Hence the moonlighting.'

'I think so.'

'Well it's an expensive business. I'm lucky, Sasha's parents are loaded so they're paying for most of ours.'

Mills was suddenly conscious of what he was saying. He was beaming at her.

'You're getting married?' she asked, uncertain whether she'd understood correctly.

'Yes, next July.' He was still grinning.

'Congratulations! That's brilliant news.'

'I wanted to tell you face to face.'

What had he expected, that she would be heart-broken or something? She kept up the smile while she thought of something appropriate to say.

'So how did you meet?'

'On the internet,' he replied. 'We chatted for a while and then decided to get together. By then we knew quite a bit about each other. She's a lawyer.'

'Wow.'

'Yes, very clever. She does company law in the city. She works really hard.'

'And how's your work at the Home Office?'

'It's great. It's more research than anything, almost like being back at uni but much better paid. Have you heard of eDiscovery?'

'No.'

'Electronic discovery is about handling data once it's been put into a database. It can be reviewed to take out irrelevant documents and reduce the volume of data that has to be handled.'

'Sounds fascinating.' She was teasing him.

'It's really important with so much forensic data being generated. Just think if at the click of a mouse all the communications between a criminal gang could be collated and indexed against individual members. It's really important.'

While he'd been going on about his work, Mills had been trying to think of a way to find out where he was on the night of the lab fire.

'Do you have any pictures of Sasha?' she asked, knowing he was bound to have loads.

He pulled out his mobile. 'These are the most recent.'

She made out she needed to look closer and when he'd handed her the phone she saw a slim attractive woman with perfect hair and teeth. She casually scrolled back, looking at the dates.

'What's this?' she asked, pointing to a grotesque face painted like a skull.

Alex looked and laughed. 'That's the Dia de Muertos,' he explained. 'We went to Mexico City to see the Day of the Dead celebrations, can you imagine? Sasha organised it all as a surprise, she's great like that although she gets very little time off. I said we should have a holiday and she surprised me by booking ten days in Mexico. We went to Mexico City to see the Halloween celebrations over the weekend then on to Cancun to chill out. Trick or treating seems pretty tame after the Dia de Muertos.'

So he was thousands of miles away on that Monday night.

'Sasha sounds great fun,' said Mills as she cleared away the plates.

'She is, she's so full of life.' He was looking at his phone with a soppy grin on his face.

He was certainly punching above his weight there, thought Mills.

'I've got a bottle of wine,' she said, opening the cupboard. 'It's white I'm afraid and not chilled but I'm having a glass.'

'OK, just a small one.'

She went into the kitchen to find her last bottle of wine,

hidden in the top cupboard, for emergencies only. She poured them both a large glass. She felt herself thinking of Alex as a friend now there was no danger of them picking up their relationship again. It was quite a relief, enhanced by the fact she no longer suspected him of arson.

'So you're enjoying being in London?' she asked as they left the dishes and moved to the sitting room. Harris clambered onto the sofa, resting his head on Alex's knee.

'Yes, the best thing I ever did.' He looked across at Mills. 'What about you – is there someone?'

'Yes. He's working down at Nottingham University at the moment.'

'Oh what does he do?'

'He's an archaeologist too.'

She wasn't going to admit it was Phil, the ex she'd told Alex all about when they were together, the one who left her and went off to Colombia, who she didn't hear from again. It sounded too humiliating. She let Alex witter on about his wonder woman Sasha. She sounded pretty dynamic and Mills couldn't help asking how come they'd met on the internet.

'It's different in London.' Alex said. 'It's so big. The only way to get to know people is online. I guess it's not so different here. Everyone is so dispersed. You should try it – oh, sorry, I forgot, you have someone.'

Did she seem so alone that he had sensed it? Alex was stroking Harris in a gentle mechanical way. The dog clambered further across his knees.

'He's making himself comfortable,' Mills observed as she refilled his glass.

'I'd love to have a dog but Sasha is not so keen.'

'Where will you be living?' Mills asked, thinking that a shared house or even a small flat would not be an ideal environment for a dog.

'We'll rent a flat somewhere on the edge of the tube line,' he said.

'Maybe a cat then?'

He laughed. The conversation was relaxed, time went quickly. They finished the bottle and Alex looked at the clock.

'I should be going.' He stood up, carefully moving Harris out of the way. 'I shouldn't have had the wine.'

There was an awkward silence.

'You can stay if you want to,' Mills said hesitantly.

He obviously sensed her reluctance. 'No, I'll be all right. Brenda's expecting me.'

He kissed her on both cheeks, thanking her for a nice evening and promising to send her a wedding invitation. Mills stood on the doorstep, relieved that the evening was over but pleased it had not been the ordeal she'd anticipated.

Mills left Harris with Muriel on Saturday morning. She was meeting Donna at her parents' house in Birstwith, a small village not far from Harrogate. She parked outside a neat cottage and the door opened as she reached for the bell. Donna introduced Mills to her mother, who brought coffee and biscuits through to a cosy dining room where her daughter had the laptop set up.

'This is what I've got so far,' Donna began, as she sat Mills down beside her. 'He was definitely only doing DNA testing; I've checked the other databases and there is nothing new there. However, he has been doing quite a lot of samples for DNA over time. It started late August and he's been working at least once a week, usually on a Monday evening.'

'So how many tests has he done all together?'

'About fifty. Sometimes he only tests two samples in a week but occasionally up to six. The interesting thing is the way the samples are labelled in the files. You'd expect he would use a numerical system like we normally do but look...' She typed on the keyboard and a list appeared. 'They begin with three letters then a number, which is the date. The second letter is often the same. Sometimes there are two, occasionally three or even four with the same second letter.'

Mills was puzzled but Donna was smiling. 'I think,' she said, 'that these are familial groups, people from the same family so they have the same second initial.' She turned to Mills. 'So why do people ask for a DNA test?'

Mills thought. 'Paternity testing is the most common I suppose – or family tree stuff, if you've got a database to work from.'

'Exactly. Tim wouldn't have access to ancestry databases – unless you include the police database but he hasn't been stupid enough to try to access that. No, I think he's been doing it for family reasons like paternity testing or inheritance claims.'

'But wouldn't he have to advertise? Where would the work come from?'

'I don't know – maybe social media? Chloe might help us. He must have a list of clients somewhere.'

Mills sat absorbing the information while Donna typed on the keyboard again, revealing a page of numbers that meant nothing to her.

'What's this?' she asked.

Donna grinned. 'If you analyse the results of the tests in batches of codes with the same second letter – see, there's a pattern.'

Mills couldn't see it.

'It proves that they're familial groups. Often they are good matches. Less often they're not. They'll be the ones where the members of the family turn out not to be related.'

'Shouldn't there be counselling for that situation?' Mills asked.

'Of course, it's not a good way to find out your dad's not your father or your sister is really your mother.'

'The other question is whether Tim was actually doing the work properly, drawing the correct conclusions.'

Donna sighed. 'He was a good analyst and he did do the training. I don't think he would want to give anyone dodgy results. I just worry that he was under a lot of pressure to get the cash for this wedding of the year that Chloe was planning. Tim told me he was saving for a two week honeymoon in Hawaii.'

'How much does a DNA test cost?' Mills asked.

'You see paternity tests advertised for under a hundred pounds.'

Mills was wondering if Tim's dubious line of business could in any way have been the cause of the fire and, in consequence, his death. She asked Donna to spend some time writing up what she had found in a report.

'Make it as objective and scientific as you can, Donna. It might be important if we find that this business has anything to do with the fire.'

'Do you think that's possible?' Donna sounded

shocked.

'I'm going to let Brenda know and I'll tell Chloe what we've found, it might make her feel more positive towards us. I'll ask her to look into Tim's social media and messaging. Meanwhile I'll inform the police.'

Mills had another reason for wanting to see Brenda again. She was relieved to find that Alex had already left for Leeds but her boss was there, dressed but still looking drained. She listened as Mills explained what Tim had been doing in Donna's lab. Her expression changed from curiosity through indignation to sorrow.

'What a stupid young man,' she said finally, sitting down at the kitchen table.

Mills was going to change the subject but Brenda jumped up again.

'Fancy thinking it was right to offer DNA testing from *my* laboratory,' she said vehemently. 'It could have ruined us if it had got out. We must find the people and let them know he was in no position to offer such a service!'

Mills had to agree. Eventually Brenda calmed down.

'I've got something to tell you – about Alex.'

'I know,' Brenda said. 'He's getting married.'

Mills smiled. 'No, Alex was in Mexico when the lab burned down.'

Her boss looked up at her and nodded slowly. 'That's good.'

Mills saw that she was genuinely pleased.

'You know he invited me to the wedding, pet.'

'And me.'

'I won't be going all that way though.'

'Me neither.'

When Mills rang Chloe, telling her she had news of why Tim had been working in the evenings, she was invited over immediately. Mills asked Brenda to accompany her but she refused, saying she had things to do. Mills didn't believe her but went alone.

Mills knew Chloe lived with her mother but was surprised by the affluence of the area when she drew up outside the house. She was even more surprised by the house itself – large, detached and with a big garden. Because Tim was scraping together funds for the wedding, Mills had assumed Chloe's family had no money. She could hear the bell ringing inside and soon Chloe was leading Mills into a comfortable lounge and offering her tea. She heard the girl speaking to someone in another room before hurrying back to sit on the sofa next to Mills.

'You said you had some news.'

Mills nodded. She explained how they had finally discovered what Tim was working on.

'Did you know anything about it?' she asked Chloe.

The girl didn't answer but there were tears forming. 'No, he didn't tell me. I thought he was meeting someone.' Her voice was a whisper.

Mills felt uncomfortable. 'I know. We think he was saving up for your honeymoon.'

She sniffed. 'We said we wouldn't have one.'

'Donna said he wanted to take you to Hawaii.'

She smiled wanly. 'He used to say he'd take me there one day.'

Her mother came in with a tray. She sat with them for a minute while Chloe shared her news. Mills could tell she was as affected by it as her daughter. Eventually, Mills felt she could ask if Chloe had access to Tim's emails.

'Yes,' she replied. 'They'll be on his tablet. His mother gave it to me in case there's anything on it that needs cancelling – you know, wedding stuff.'

Her mother looked as though she was going to break down. 'It's almost time for little Tim's feed,' she said and disappeared.

'If you have his password…'

'Oh yes, I'm always using his iPad – it's got lots of photos on it. And it's the same as his phone.'

Mills was surprised. 'You don't have his phone?'

'Yes, he left it the night he…' She took a deep breath. 'I found it in my car.'

'When you have time,' Mills continued, 'can you look for any communications with people he was doing the DNA tests for?'

Chloe promised to make a note of the names and contact details of any of Tim's customers if she found them.

Her mother came back in with a tiny bundle. She walked round the room as little squawks emitted from the blanket. Chloe was taking her baby and Mills felt it was time to go.

As her mother showed Mills out, she touched her arm and asked in a low voice if what Tim had been doing was illegal. It was a difficult question that Mills took a while to answer.

'I don't think what he was doing was necessarily illegal, although using the lab without Brenda's permission was not exactly lawful. He certainly was giving her cause to dismiss him, although I think she might have just stopped him doing it if she'd found out.'

On the drive back Mills considered her answer, wondering if she was right. She parked in Bedale to pick up a sandwich and as she sat in the car to eat it she rang Nina. She told her what they now knew about Tim's DNA testing service, adding that she hoped Chloe would find out who his clients were from Tim's iPad.

'Do you think this makes a difference to anything Nina? I mean what he was doing was wrong but I don't think it was against the law, was it?'

'It depends. It's a crime to take DNA from someone without their knowledge so he would have had to get written consent from all the participants.'

'I wonder if he realised that.'

'If you get the names we can check. I'll catch up with Chloe next week to see what evidence she's found. Thanks for letting me know.'

Mills had mixed feelings. She'd been a friend of Tim's and even though he was dead she felt as though she had just betrayed him.

Chapter 13

Sunday was when Mills promised to take Harris on a really long walk. The clouds were grey but thankfully it wasn't raining yet so she told the dog they were going out. He ran round excitedly, trying to pull his lead from its hook in the hall. She was in her boots ready to leave when Chloe rang to tell her that she'd found Tim's list of customers, complete with names and email addresses. Mills asked her to send over the details because she had to contact them to explain the situation.

'Sorry, boy,' she said as she put Harris on his lead. 'It won't be so far after all.'

She was tempted just to pop him up the track but he was now so excited that guilt prevailed and she set off down to the river. Turning east she followed the path, crossing the fields as far as Gunnerside, stopping for Harris to have a drink of water from the river by the bridge. They walked back on the top road in a fine drizzle, where they were passed by several cyclists making their way along the Swale Trail. By the time they were back in Mossy Bank it was lunchtime and raining heavily. The list had arrived from Chloe so she hurriedly fixed herself a sandwich and settled down to go through the names.

Although Donna had calculated maybe thirty analyses had been carried out, Chloe's list contained only ten names. Mills thought perhaps he'd been practicing in the early months before accepting real samples. She sat in front of her computer pondering what to do with the information. Without phone numbers or addresses she could only send them emails and wait to be contacted.

It took her an hour to write and re-write a suitable message. She didn't want to alarm them so she began by saying that she understood they had submitted samples for testing at the laboratory. She didn't know if Tim had used the Yardley Forensics title so she included his name in her introduction. She then apologised, explaining that the test had not been part of their accredited work so they couldn't guarantee the accuracy of the results. She finished by offering to refund the fee or arrange for a new test by an accredited laboratory. Mills had wavered over offering another test but it seemed the only way to ensure no-one made a fuss. Brenda wouldn't cope well if someone sued the lab. She sent the same message to all ten customers on the list.

There was nothing she could do now but wait. She was glancing through her inbox when she found a message from the Forensics Department Administrator. It was a reminder that her "Personal Review and Development Plan" must be submitted by the end of the week. Horrified she realised she'd forgotten to submit it. She quickly found the file, put an electronic signature at the bottom with Friday's date – they'd never know – and sent it off. She sighed. She was unprepared and not looking forward to her appraisal the next day.

The rain had stopped, most of the clouds had cleared and the sun was appearing intermittently. Mills looked down at Harris who stared up at her expectantly.

'Come on then, let's go for a walk.'

Mills had an ulterior motive for taking the higher route

to Muker. It would bring her past the Price's farm. Despite the fact she'd seen little of David and Jean in recent years, at one time she had known them quite well. Perhaps this was an opportunity to renew their acquaintance and have a chat about the family, particularly Justin.

However, once the farmhouse was in sight she couldn't think of a reason to call on them unexpectedly. Unless someone was out in the fields she had no excuse to meet them on her walk. She slowed down as she neared the farm and was about to put Harris on his lead but she could see there were no sheep in the nearest field and let him loose again. As she'd planned he rushed off towards the front of the house and disappeared.

'Harris! Harris!' She ran shouting loudly as if in a panic. He was just sniffing around at the front door. Good boy, she thought. 'Harris! Bad boy! Here!'

Barking came from the barn so she was confident the farm dogs were inside. She kept up the shouting, knowing Harris would ignore her, as he always did. Finally, the front door opened and a woman appeared. Mills immediately recognised Jean, introduced herself and reminded her that she lived in Mossy Bank. Once she realised who Mills was, Jean expressed delight to see her and opened the door wider to reveal a teenage girl standing behind her.

'Do you remember Lucy?' Jean asked.

'Hi Lucy, I think you were a baby last time we met.'

'Is it that long ago?' the girl's mother asked. 'Tell Millie how old you are, Lucy.'

'Thirteen,' she answered shyly.

It was her opportunity to ask about Justin. 'So your

brother must be over twenty.'

'He's twenty-three next month.'

'He's working on the farm now,' Jean added.

She told Mills how David's father had died five years ago and they'd been struggling until Justin came back from college. Now he was doing his share things were a lot easier and they were expanding the flock. The only problem was finding enough room for them. Mills thought they owned most of the grazing between Mossy Bank and the farm but Jean explained that some of it was rented from the Banford estate. Mills hadn't known that the Manor had land associated with it.

'Oh yes, they used to have a lot more but they sold off the land to the east. David did put in an offer for the pasture in our direction but they wouldn't accept it, even though half of it isn't used for grazing at all.'

Mills knew the Banford family lived in Scotland. Lizzie Banford had been living alone in the Manor when Mills first visited her grandmother in Mossy Bank. She was a lovely old lady who'd been a good friend to Gran but her son, Daniel, and his wife Penny were different all together. Their son, Gareth, had been quite a handful as a teenager. She mentioned him to Jean, thinking he must be a similar age to Justin.

'I believe he's the reason his parents decided not to sell to us. He's some sort of ecowarrior – I don't know why they listen to him. Apparently he became a vegan at university and is against farming with animals, full stop.'

Mills remembered him as a Goth dressed in black. He wasn't a bad lad, just a typical teenager, she'd thought. Lucy was out in the yard now, making a fuss of Harris and Mills took the opportunity to put him back on the lead. Jean was asking what "Millie" had been doing since she was a teenager. It was inevitable that they would continue to call her that because at seventeen that's what everyone had called her. Her daughter was listening intently as Mills talked about her forensic work.

'You must come over for a meal,' said Jean. 'David will be pleased to see you after so long – and Justin, of course.'

Mills told her she'd met Justin briefly the other day and sometimes saw him on his quad bike in Mossy Bank.

'He drives past the Manor in case anyone is there,' his mother explained. 'He's determined to get them to change their minds about selling the land.'

Mills walked back home through the fields she now knew were owned by the Banfords. Justin was clearly keen to persuade them to sell and she feared he may have started the fire at the Manor as some form of retribution or to threaten them perhaps? Both seemed rather extreme measures. She remembered David being very ambitious about the future of the farm, so perhaps Justin was the same.

Mills waited until five to eleven before she left the office to attend her appraisal. There had been some confusion about the format of her review because her time was split between departments. She'd expressed a preference for having the appraisers there at the same time, simply because it meant one appraisal not two. She was aware she wasn't properly prepared for the interview and would probably make a mess of it. It wasn't her normal approach to things but life was getting on top of her.

They were seeing her in a small meeting room at the

end of the corridor. When she arrived her appraisers were already seated. She recognised Professor Dunn but not the younger man. He stood up and introduced himself as Professor Pringle, offering his hand. He was dressed very casually in jeans and a sweater, in contrast to Professor Dunn who always sported a bow tie.

'Dr Sanderson, would you prefer I call you...' Professor Pringle was reading her form.

'Just Mills.'

'Mills?' He sounded puzzled. 'Right. As you know Professor Dunn is from the Archaeology Department and I represent Forensics.'

She sat opposite them. Professor Dunn appeared to be taking the lead. He explained that the purpose of the meeting was to highlight her successes and challenges, looking at targets set last year and planning new ones. It was all going to be very informal, he said with a smile. Professor Pringle didn't say a word. His head was down, he was reading her submission. It was hardly his fault, he would have only received it that morning. Mills wished she felt more enthusiastic about her roles. When they asked her to expand on her research she tried to sound excited by the prospect of working on analysis of bones for evidence of diet to identify geographical origins. Neither of them seemed to understand what she was getting at but nodded and made notes.

Now they moved to her targets from last year. What had she achieved? There was the international conference last year, where she'd given a paper. But it was only published in the conference proceedings, no points for that. As a new lecturer she wasn't expected to have a long list of publications but a couple was the target and she'd had none. She felt herself redden. She said she'd had a heavy teaching load so they referred to her paperwork again. Apparently it wasn't overly onerous, in fact the archaeology lecturing duties were quite light and Professor Dunn might look into that.

He was frankly disappointed in her progress while Professor Pringle sat quietly saying very little until suddenly he asked about her proposal to study the effects of disaster recovery in a forensic laboratory. Here was something she could talk about but first she had to admit that she was doing consultancy work for Yardley Forensics. To her surprise he was impressed that she had such a responsible role. They discussed the fire, its effect on the forensic evidence and what would happen next. Dunn looked bored, fiddling with his papers and finally looking at his watch declared they should draw things to a close.

Targets were imposed by Dunn for more teaching and papers in scientific journals. He looked at Pringle who shook his head.

'I'm happy with the proposed research area. I'm a consultant for the Forensic Science Services so I know it will be of significant interest to us. I might even be able to get some funding for it.'

Mills shook their hands, nearly skipping down the corridor to tell Nige. She had to wait for an hour before he emerged from a full morning's practical session but her time wasn't wasted. While she waited she read and re-read the email responses from three of Tim's customers. The messages were similar and yet they were not. They were all customers with questions about their relatives. Mills was sure that at least one had not asked permission before sending the samples in. It was from a woman who had submitted her DNA and a swab from her uncle. The results had confirmed he was her father but could she have them retested before she tells him? The other two emails were from men who had requested paternity tests. Neither had received the results.

Mills needed to talk to these people to explain the law and persuade them to use an accredited testing laboratory, one that was used to dealing with these family cases. She replied to all three of them, asking if she could ring them or meet them for a confidential chat as soon as possible. To her surprise she received a reply from one of them almost immediately giving his mobile number and asking if he could speak to her now. She rang it nervously.

A man with a strong Scottish accent answered the phone, softly asking if it was Dr Sanderson. She told him that they couldn't offer a service now and advised him to use a recognised DNA service.

'I tried one but they wanted all sorts of official paperwork. I just wanted a quick test – just to confirm it.'

'I'm afraid the paperwork is a legal requirement. It was wrong of our technician to offer to do the test without it.'

'Am I going to get into trouble?' he asked anxiously.

'No, it was our error. Now, about getting you a refund.'

'No, I haven't paid anything. He said he'd let me know when he had the results then I could transfer the money and he would email the letter.'

'As a matter of interest how much was he asking for?'

'He said sixty pounds, much cheaper than those places online.'

'And how did you hear about us?'

'I found it in the small ads of the Harrogate Advertiser.'

Nige came into the office, threw his papers on his desk and sat down wearily. Mills quickly ended the conversation, thanking the Scotsman for his understanding.

'How did the appraisal go?' he asked.

'Dunn gave me the third degree but Prof Pringle from Forensics was keen on my research proposal and even hinted he might find me some funding.'

'I said it would be fine. Dunn is always difficult but he can't do anything that will affect your position.'

Mills hoped he was right.

Ruby waited until Hazel went to lunch before telling Nina about the further intel she had dug up on a couple of the samples involved in the Yardley fire. First was the teenage girl found dead in a kid's playground near her home. A lad from the same estate had been charged. Several witnesses had named him as the suspect and he had no alibi – on the contrary, CCTV put him close to the scene at the time of death. He was being held on remand so Ruby reckoned the chance of someone trying to destroy the soil evidence from his shoes was small.

However, the next one was much more interesting. There was no question that the three men charged and detained were found with seven kilograms of heroin in their car but the analysis was to determine the quality of the drug.

'Why is it important to know the quality?' she asked Nina.

Her colleague looked up from the bowl of salad she was eating, swallowing hard. 'The sentence is based on the potential harm distribution of the drug will cause so it's about quality as well as quantity. If you think about it, one kilo of high quality heroin could be equivalent to five kilos of low quality once it's cut and on the streets.'

Ruby went back to the detailed report, pointing out that one of the gang had a record of interfering with witnesses.

'Do you think this could be the one?' she asked.

'Have a look for known associates and check what they were up to when the fire was started,' ordered Nina.

She searched details of the previous case concerning the man who had threatened witnesses. His colleagues were known to the police so it was easy to obtain their current whereabouts. One of them was still living in the area. Ruby made a note of his car registration and requested an ANPR search on the date of the fire.

Ruby had just completed her search, when Hazel returned complaining about the sandwich queue. The researcher closed the file quickly, sending Nina a message. 'A known associate of the heroin case was in Harrogate on the night of the 28th October.'

By the end of the following day Mills had received responses from nine of Tim's customers. To her relief the ones that had received results agreed to accept a refund. The others, like her first caller, were happy to go elsewhere. It puzzled her that there was still someone who hadn't replied. She would wait to see whether they would respond eventually. Meanwhile she rang Brenda to tell her what she'd been doing to rectify Tim's work.

'I've had a visit from that insurance woman,' her boss complained.

'Jessica?'

'Yes. She's been harassing me again.'

Mills asked what she meant.

'She came here armed with bank details: standing orders, direct debits, income and expenditure. She asked to see my cash flow forecasts and commitments. I'm telling you, it was the third degree.'

'Why was she so interested?' asked Mills, knowing the answer.

'Apparently it's her job to understand the finances of the business. It's her job to pay me my insurance!'

Mills sighed. 'She has the right to investigate whether we would benefit from the lab burning down,' she explained.

Brenda ignored her. 'Next time, I told her, she can deal with you. I'm not letting her in.'

Mills remained silent.

Brenda continued, 'By the way, she said the lab is completely cleared out now. I thought we should be talking to the estate agents.'

'Are you really going to sell up? What about Glyn and Donna and the others?'

'They're bright people. They'll soon find something. We'll give them good references.'

'And redundancy payments?'

'There's enough to cover that, I'm sure.'

As Mills put the phone down she planned to contact her colleagues at Yardley Forensics to discuss how they could make Brenda change her mind. She was concerned about their futures, of course, but at the moment she was worried that Jessica suspected Brenda of burning down the lab herself.

Chapter 14

Mills had discovered a mysterious pie in her refrigerator so went next door to thank Muriel. Her neighbour said she shouldn't have bothered but invited her inside. Mills had a reason for wanting to speak to her and gradually led the conversation round to the Price's farm. It wasn't difficult because Muriel always liked to gossip.

'Is it true that David wants to buy some of the Banford estate?' Mills asked.

Muriel nodded. It was apparently common knowledge that the Banfords had put some of their rough pasture up for sale.

'That was over two years ago,' she explained. 'Word is that the price was set too high so it came down a bit in the spring. I was told that the only offer came from David but the Banfords didn't accept it.'

'Was it less than the asking price?'

'I suppose it must've been.'

Mills thanked her again for the pie. 'By the way, Muriel, what sort is it?'

Her neighbour laughed. 'Did I not say? It's one of my chicken pies. I thought you could use it since you're always rushing about.'

Mills went back home and turned on the oven. As she waited for it to heat up she considered what Muriel had said. The land was certainly a source of bad feeling between David and the Banfords. But could it be a reason for Justin to set fire to the moor?

Mills had more important things to worry about. The computer she'd brought back from Brenda's had been standing in the hall since Friday and she was supposed to be sending any forensic data she could retrieve to the relevant customer, namely the police. The cable stretched far enough for her to set it up on the low table in the sitting room, just. She sat on the floor next to Harris and searched for the file Alex had set up for her. She sighed as the long list of result files appeared on the screen. They contained data that she would have to check before sending them off.

Stopping only to rescue and eat a rather burnt and very dry chicken pie from the oven, she spent the evening working. It was after midnight when she went to bed having dealt with the forensics from convicted drug dealers caught in possession of heroin. Tim had analysed it for purity and she had the result which was needed for sentencing.

Ruby was giving Hazel the heroin analysis when Nina arrived next morning.

'The boss will be pleased,' Hazel said. 'This should ensure they get the maximum sentence.'

Nina asked Ruby if she'd mentioned to Hazel that the defendants had motive to set fire to the forensic lab to interfere with the testing. She shook her head. Their colleague was on the phone and Nina didn't pursue it but later on she rang Mills to ask if she'd told Dr Barnes at the Wakefield lab that the heroin had been tested successfully. It would save them repeating the work unnecessarily.

'I'm glad you rang,' Mills said.

She told her friend that she had a list of Tim's customers from Chloe and would send it on to her. She added that she'd spoken to nearly all of them to inform them of the situation.

'There is just one that I'm waiting to hear from.'

Nina made some notes. 'We need to think about whether this has any bearing on the arson case,' she said at last. 'I've been considering potential motives from the forensic cases your lab was working on. We need to include these other people.'

She asked Mills to tell her what the DNA testing was for in each case. 'And you say you've spoken to these people?'

'Yes by email or phone, except one of them.'

'And why did that one want the test?'

'I'd have to look back but it was probably a paternity case.'

'Right, let me know when you've spoken to them won't you?'

Nina passed on Dr Barnes' contact details before she put the phone down then turned to Ruby. 'Mills is in touch with Tim Fletcher's customers. It sounds as though he was doing routine paternity cases, nothing more sinister.'

'By the way,' said Ruby, 'I checked on that associate of the heroin dealers. He's known to the guys down in Harrogate because he lives there. They've had a word with him about the night of the fire and he hasn't got an alibi. Basically he can't remember what he was doing. They asked what you want to do.'

'We've got nothing on him unless you've dug anything out.'

Ruby shook her head. 'Hazel's theory that the owner torched it for the insurance is more plausible. The loss adjuster has been talking to her about the company finances and they don't look good.'

'What else is on your list of forensic jobs besides the heroin testing?'

'There's the cold case and the stabbing. We don't have a suspect for either so I can't do any checks on those. The murder case guy is on remand. That just leaves the drink-drive blood sample. Do you want me to check on him?'

'Give me his details and I'll have a chat with him. I can't believe he would be so worried about a guilty verdict that he burned the lab down.'

'His name is Derek Plant. He's probably the only one on the list who knew where the evidence was being tested though.'

'Right, in that case I'll try to see him later today.'

Nina discovered her drink-driver was an accountant who worked from home in Wetherby. She arranged to drive down to see him in the afternoon and sent a message to Nige warning him she might be home a little later than planned. She had a clear run to the outskirts of the town where she found Mr Plant's large detached house set back from the main road up a wide drive. She parked next to the top of the range BMW, which she assumed he was driving when stopped and breathalysed. She was anticipating an awkward conversation, since he was adamant that he was innocent, as his confirmatory blood test would surely prove.

A young woman opened the door and invited Nina

inside, saying she would call her husband down from his office. Nina waited in the hall, peering into the living room hung with large abstract paintings. It seemed empty except for two enormous leather sofas and a white rug in front of the modern fireplace. Nina concluded there were no children in the house or it couldn't possibly be kept so beautifully pristine. There were footsteps on the stairs and Mrs Plant reappeared, followed by a gaunt man dressed immaculately in navy trousers with a pink sweater over a striped shirt, open at the neck.

'Sorry, my wife didn't ask your name.' He was offering his hand.

'Nina Featherstone,' she answered automatically. 'Detective Sergeant.'

'Well, Detective Sergeant Nina Featherstone, to what do we owe this pleasure?'

He was ushering her into the living room and over to a seat. Nina noticed that his wife had disappeared.

'I wanted to let you know about the progress of your blood alcohol test.' She'd been rehearsing how to approach the conversation on the way down.

'I had assumed that much.' He was seated opposite her on the matching sofa.

'I understand you requested to have your duplicate sample analysed to confirm the police result.'

'I did.' He stretched his legs out straight in front of him and leaned back with his hands behind his head. 'I wasn't confident in the way the original test was carried out and my solicitor recommended a second one.'

'Do you know where that test was sent?'

'Oh yes. It went to Yardley Forensics in Harrogate.' He sat up. 'Have you seen the results?'

Nina shook her head. 'Unfortunately there was a fire at the laboratory at the end of last month.'

He appeared surprised.

'You hadn't heard?' Nina asked.

'No.' There was a pause and he smiled. 'I suppose that means there won't be a second test and the case will be dismissed?'

Nina evaluated his response. Was he too quick to suggest he was off the hook? 'Actually, no, the sample has been salvaged so if the result is not available yet the test can be carried out by our Regional Scientific Support Unit in Wakefield.'

His demeanour changed instantly. 'My solicitor says the sample must go to an independent laboratory. Is this support unit independent?'

Nina admitted it was a facility in the West Yorkshire Police area and offered to enquire if there was an alternative independent laboratory that could do the test.

'You do understand?' he asked. 'When they stopped me the breathalyser was all over the place. They tried several times but it was always a different answer, anything between a hundred milligrams and twice that.'

Nina didn't comment. If the breathalyser was faulty she couldn't make a judgement. The court would rely on the blood test.

'I should talk to my solicitor,' he continued. 'It's, what, six weeks now since the sample was taken. Is the test still going to be reliable?'

Nina couldn't tell him. Whether he tried to destroy the evidence or not, it seemed possible he might walk away without a blemish on his record. Mills would know whether the blood could still be tested but all in all he seemed an unlikely candidate for a midnight raid on a laboratory armed with a can of petrol and a box of matches.

Wednesday afternoon in the department was always quiet. The students were given time off for sports activities, although only a few of them were seriously involved in university teams. Mills was marking when she received a call from Professor Pringle asking if she could spare a few minutes. On the way she popped into the cloakroom and checked her hair in the mirror. She knew there was no reason to be nervous but she was.

'Mills, come in!' He looked pleased to see her. 'And you must call me Simon.'

He was probably forty, maybe forty-five; tall and gangly with curly black hair that needed a cut. He wore jeans with a denim shirt. The collar was turned up in an affected manner.

'I wasn't sure if you'd be… well you are. Please sit down. Coffee? Tea?'

Mills refused politely. He drew up a chair for her and dragged his own from behind the desk.

'I expect you wondered why I asked you to meet me.'

She smiled and nodded.

He put his head on one side. 'I was impressed with your interview the other day,' he said. 'Prof Dunn didn't understand the potential you have. I thought the plans you presented were very "of the moment". Maybe that's why he didn't get it.' He laughed before becoming very serious. 'I think you've really got something with your approach. Disaster recovery, that's what it's all about isn't it?'

Mills was taken aback by his apparent interest. She presumed he was talking about her proposal to research the effect of losing a forensic facility. She repeated her idea of using Yardley as an example. He beamed at her throughout. When she had finished he jumped up, grabbing a leather jacket off the back of his chair.

'Why don't we continue our discussion over coffee?' he suggested.

She followed him past the cafeteria, realising that they were heading towards the bar/café on the periphery of the campus. He offered Mills a drink and she asked for a latte. He ordered himself a large red wine and carried it to a corner table.

'I'll tell you what I was thinking,' he said as he placed the glass down carefully. 'I'll talk to the powers that be at Wakefield and suggest this project on disaster recovery.'

Mills listened, slightly bemused by his enthusiasm.

'They probably don't have many resources for research but with their collaboration the project will carry weight with funding bodies, I'm sure of that.' He picked up his glass. 'So tell me what ideas you have.'

Mills stumbled over her words, knowing she sounded uncertain of where the work would lead. She was interrupted by her coffee arriving and she used it as an excuse to stop for a minute. Her companion was smiling at her in a patronising way that made her feel about twelve years old.

'I am currently dealing with a situation where all the important laboratory's records have been jeopardised,' she continued. 'The forensic samples are possibly damaged and there is no certainty the company will ever work again.' She suddenly felt very emotional. 'A colleague died in the fire and it seems he was working outside hours to run his own forensic business. It's been a disaster.'

She covered her embarrassment by drinking the rest of her coffee.

'I can see it has affected you significantly,' he said. 'I suggest we call it a day for now but continue another time. What about Friday?'

Mills was relieved to know their conversation was over. 'Yes that's fine.'

'Good. How about lunch? I'll give you a call around mid-day?'

Mills nodded and left him at the bar ordering another large glass of merlot.

Mills had gone straight home after her meeting with Simon Pringle. It was Tim's funeral the next day and she wanted to check that Brenda would be attending. But she was disappointed, her boss was adamant she was too unwell to go. When pressed to say what was wrong she couldn't explain but sadly she wouldn't be able to make it. Mills didn't attempt to persuade her, she knew it would be pointless. Brenda was a stubborn old woman and Mills would have to represent the company that owned the lab where Tim died.

She was therefore relieved to spot Nina when she arrived the following morning. The funeral was being held in Wilsill church where Tim and his family worshipped. Although it wasn't a historic building it was set in open fields surrounded by a dry stone wall with open views all round. Nina was walking slowly up the path toward the church door as Mills parked behind the row of cars and ran to catch her up. They stood outside together, holding their coats tight at the necks in the chilly air.

'Brenda's not coming,' Mills told her friend.

'I expect it's a difficult time for her.'

Nina was so tolerant of everyone, thought Mills.

People gathered in the cold waiting for the family to arrive with the coffin. They watched the black cars pull up in front of the church, the crowd parting as Chloe, her mother and Tim's parents climbed out and led the procession inside. Mills and Nina took their places in the back pew where Donna and Glyn were already seated. Finally, when everyone was settled, the coffin was carried in.

The ceremony was simple with traditional hymns and readings from the bible. While Glyn sang loudly, Donna seemed too emotional to join in and Nina, like Mills, followed the service uncertainly. Tim's father made a very short but moving speech about his son not having reached his potential. Tim's sister read a familiar passage from Corinthians about love which was more usually heard at weddings. Mills thought perhaps the young couple had chosen the passage for their forthcoming marriage ceremony. Chloe's shoulders began shaking during the final hymn "Love divine all loves excelling" and Mills wondered whether this was the church where they planned to get married At the end of the service the congregation followed the family outside, to watch the coffin with its covering of white and yellow wreaths being carried to the waiting car on its way to the crematorium in Harrogate. The ashes would be scattered by the family in due course. Meanwhile Tim's father was inviting them back to their house for refreshments.

Glyn said goodbye to Mills – he'd brought Donna and she was asking to be taken home.

'Are you going back to the house?' Mills whispered to Nina.

'I think I should. And so should you.'

'Really?'

'You're representing the lab, Mills. You can't leave yet.'

She drove to Tim's parents' house, following Nina, and they went in together. It was full of people who were chatting noisily, clinking glasses and grabbing sandwiches, pies and cake. Even Chloe had gained her composure, wandering round with a wan smile, while relatives and friends made a fuss of the tiny baby in her arms. Nina found Tim's mother in the kitchen to offer her condolences then led Mills to where Tim's father was pouring drinks. He had removed his jacket and loosened his tie. Mills told him she was representing Yardley Forensics in Brenda's absence and was very sorry; that Tim had been a valued colleague and they all missed him enormously. He nodded but didn't speak to her.

When Chloe had finished talking to an elderly woman in a black silk shirt, they expressed their condolences and Nina made a fuss of baby Timmy. The girl insisted they eat something, sending them off to the table covered in plates of food. Armed with sandwiches and sausage rolls Mills and Nina withdrew to the hall and sat on a wooden pew by the front door where the guests' coats were hanging.

'Have you heard from the remaining DNA test customer?' Nina asked as soon as they were alone.

'No. I've sent another message. They may be away.'

Nina frowned. 'You have the email addresses then?'

'Yes.'

'Perhaps we can trace them for you.'

'Is it important?' Mills had finished her chicken sandwich and was examining a sausage roll. It looked home-made.

'Perhaps. We're looking at the cases you were doing forensic work for to eliminate any suspects but these DNA test people might have cause to destroy the laboratory don't you think?'

Mills hadn't thought for a second that could be the case. 'Seriously?'

'We have to eliminate any possibilities.'

'Are you still investigating the fire then?'

'Maybe.'

Mills knew better than to push her friend too far. 'I can give you their email addresses – and Chloe has Tim's phone if that helps.'

'It may do. Ruby will know what to do with it,' she said with a grin. 'Where is Dr Alex White, "cyber forensic investigator", at a time like this?'

'He's a digital forensics investigator and he's in London with his future wife.'

Nina looked surprised.

'And before you say anything, I'm fine with that.'

There were footsteps on the stairs and Chloe came down. She was a slim figure in her black wool dress but the slight bulge reminded Mills that she had given birth to Tim's son less than a fortnight ago.

'Are you two all right?' she asked. 'I've just given Timmy a feed and put him down for a nap.'

'He's such a good baby,' Nina said.

'Yes, he's a treasure.'

'Just a thought,' Nina continued. 'You don't happen to have Tim's phone handy?'

'Yes, I carry it with me all the time. It's one of the few things I have apart from Timmy of course.'

Nina explained how it might help to find the person who set the fire if she could borrow Tim's phone. Chloe went to fetch her handbag, returning with the phone in her hand.

'I will get it back won't I?' she pleaded.

'Of course you will, Chloe, as soon as possible.' She placed it in her bag with exaggerated care. 'And I suppose we should be going, Mills.'

She stood up, giving Chloe a hug, saying, 'Look after that little treasure of yours and please say goodbye to your mum and Tim's parents – we don't want to disturb them.'

Chloe smiled at Nina. Her face became more serious as she turned to Mills and muttered goodbye.

'What will you do with the phone?' Mills asked as soon as they were outside.

'Ruby might be able to find your missing DNA customer if they've been in contact with Tim by phone. It's another way of tracing them if your email messages don't work.'

'Do you really think one of them could be the arsonist?'

Nina shrugged. 'We don't know until we ask, do we?'

Chapter 15

Nina gave Tim's phone to Ruby, telling her there was no need to bother Hazel with it.

'Just have a quick look to see if there are any messages relating to DNA testing and if you can identify the caller. I've got a Gold Group meeting this morning.'

She picked up her file and hurried to the meeting room, almost colliding with Ruth Barnes as she turned down the corridor.

'We're not late, are we?' she asked, looking at her watch.

'No, we're just in time to grab a coffee.'

Ruth admitted she needed a few minutes to gather her thoughts; there was quite a lot of progress to report.

The Superintendent who chaired the meetings arrived with a woman Nina hadn't seen before. He introduced her as Jessica Hayes, the loss adjuster from the insurance company handling the aftermath of the fire. Since the fire service had presented their final report at the previous meeting the main item on the agenda was "Impact on forensic investigations". That was followed by "Ongoing investigations" and "Financial issues".

Nina listened with admiration as Dr Barnes gave a very clear and detailed account of where the samples were in the process, which ones may have been compromised and those that were undamaged. The analyses were being fast-tracked and she expected everything to be completed by the middle of the following month.

There were questions when she'd finished her report and the Superintendent asked Ruth whether she'd received any results for samples that had already been analysed at Yardley Forensics. She paused then shook her head, explaining that she wouldn't be sent that information – it would go back to the customer.

The chairman then looked across at Nina. 'Have you received anything from them?' he asked.

She coughed before replying. 'The heroin sample Dr Barnes mentioned has been analysed by the laboratory and the results came back to us recently. I believe they are processing some other results that were retrieved from their off-site back-up.'

Ruth made a note then looked up. 'Can you ensure that they let me know what has been tested so we don't repeat needlessly?'

Nina nodded. She would get onto Mills straight away.

The item concluded with a discussion of the cases that could be compromised by damage to the samples. Ruth was concerned about a blood sample since at elevated temperatures the level of alcohol could reduce, bringing it below the legal limit. There was no possibility of obtaining a second sample. Nina added that she'd spoken to the man who had provided the sample and he wanted it tested at an independent laboratory.

The chairman thanked Ruth for her comprehensive report then turned to the next item on the agenda which had the enigmatic title "Ongoing investigations". Perhaps Nina shouldn't have been surprised that, once again, she was expected to report any updates regarding the arson attack. She tried to be brief as she explained that they'd finally established what Tim Fletcher had been doing.

Ruth was quite shocked that Yardley Forensics would allow such goings-on and Nina had to explain that the company knew nothing about it. The Superintendent wanted to know whether there was a possible motive for the arson attack resulting from this DNA testing. Nina confirmed they were currently considering the possibility. It was true, she was, but now Hazel would have to take notice. There was an action on her to bring the results of all the enquiries to the next meeting.

The chairman then explained that he had invited Jessica Hayes to the meeting because she had been looking at the financial records of Yardley Forensics as part of the fire investigation. He asked her to expand for the group. She spoke clearly, looking round at them, emphasising points by tapping gently on the table. Nina heard how Brenda's company was in a poor financial state. The bank was owed money, suppliers' bills were unpaid, and in a short time staff would not receive a salary. The insurance company had obtained copies of bank statements that showed the predicament was due to rising rents and falling turnover.

'You must understand that we become suspicious when a company in dire straits has a sudden reason to make a big insurance claim.'

Nina was forced to confirm that they were already looking into it. According to Jessica Hayes, the insurance company would continue to pursue that particular line of enquiry and was liaising with DS Fuller.

At the end of the meeting Nina picked up her file and made a dash for the door. She had a list of actions that would keep her busy for the rest of the day. She just hoped Mills was around.

Mills was in her office when she received Nina's call. It was a rather serious conversation compared to their normal friendly chats. It sounded as though Nina had been put on the spot at the Gold Group and it was all because Mills had taken her eye off the ball. Feeling guilty she had agreed to work on the data on Saturday before going over to discuss the results with Nina on Sunday. When she told Nige of the arrangement, he sighed dramatically, saying that meant he would have to make the roast dinner for them all.

They were disturbed by Simon Pringle opening the door slowly. Nige gave Mills a quizzical look but she just smiled at him.

'Hi, are you ready to go?' Simon asked.

Mills grabbed her bag. She'd meant to comb her hair before he arrived but it was too late now.

'There's a pub I know that does a really good lunchtime menu,' he said as they walked out to the car park.

She followed him to an old green sports car with a fabric roof. He opened the passenger door and she clambered down into the leather seat. The car had a dank smell. He slammed her door and was soon settling himself in the driver's seat. It was very cramped. He described how the car was his pride and joy. It was an MG he'd been doing up but Mills couldn't hear much of his explanation once he started the engine. They lurched out onto the road with the smell of the exhaust wafting in.

Mills had accepted they were going to be driving a little way to this pub he favoured but it seemed an interminable journey as she began to feel sick. The hedges were racing past as they swung round bends and screeched to a halt at junctions crossing country lanes. In the end she shut her eyes and hoped they would soon be there. When finally the engine was switched off she opened them again.

'Here we are: "The Star at Harome"!'

Mills knew the name, it had a Michelin star. He was opening her door and offering a hand to help her out. She didn't want to take it but couldn't get out gracefully without it. Her legs felt a bit wobbly as she steadied herself and he took her arm to steer her through the entrance. She had to admit it would have been a super place to eat, if she'd felt less queasy. Simon had apparently booked. They were taken to a table and when they were offered drinks he ordered a pint of local ale. Mills asked for tonic water and studied the menu. Simon suggested the three course lunch but she chose a ham sandwich – the simplest thing she could find. Simon selected the "fish of the day" and told Mills he was putting this "working lunch" on expenses.

He asked about her PhD so she described her time at Manchester working on bog bodies. He encouraged her to talk about her role at Yardley Forensics and she found herself pouring out the concerns she had about its future. He was expressing sympathy when they were interrupted by the food arriving. Simon ordered a large glass of wine but Mills had hardly touched her tonic. She nibbled her sandwich slowly while he tucked into his fish, which did look delicious. He confirmed it was cooked to perfection.

'This is almost my local, you know,' he confided.

Mills became impatient to discuss her proposal; it was, after all, why they were meeting. She asked him whether he thought there might be funding for such work. He simply smiled and nodded, loading his fork with food and lifting it to his mouth.

She tried again. 'I suppose they'll need a detailed proposal?'

He nodded. She waited. Finally he put his knife and fork together neatly on the empty plate and sighed before suggesting they look at the desserts. Mills declined, thinking they should be leaving, but he went ahead and ordered one anyway.

'We could have a coffee here,' he said when he'd finished eating a sugary pudding, 'but I thought it would be quieter and more comfortable to go back to mine.'

Mills thought quickly. 'I'm afraid I have to get some calculations done this afternoon. The results of forensic analyses carried out at Yardley's before the fire, the police need them urgently.'

He didn't look pleased. 'So you need to get back to the university?'

Of course she did. She would've needed to if she'd gone back to his place, wouldn't she? What was he thinking?

The drive back was as bad as before. Mills was relieved to climb out of the MG, without the help of Professor Pringle this time. She leaned down into the car to thank him for lunch and suggested they meet up soon after the weekend to discuss the project. 'Meanwhile, I'll start to put something together,' she added.

He nodded, she slammed the door and he drove away.

Back in the office she told Nige that she'd probably just blown the chance of a project with the Regional Scientific Support Unit.

'You did the right thing, Mills,' Nige said. It was unusual for Nige not to make a joke of her situation. 'If you ask my opinion, his behaviour was inappropriate.'

'You think so? I couldn't decide but it made me feel a little uncomfortable.'

Nige and Mills left the office together. He was on duty at home that evening as Nina was working late again; he would see Mills on Sunday when she came over. She told him there was lots of work to do before then and they said goodbye in the car park.

It was usual on a Friday for Mills to pop next door with Muriel's money for looking after Harris. Her neighbour liked cash because it saved her going to the post office, which was daft because she was in Reeth every Friday morning for the market anyway. Mills, on the other hand, had to remember to go to the cash machine during the week so she had the right money.

Muriel was busy baking so Mills went through to her kitchen where she was mixing something.

'I'm making an apple pudding. We're having pork chops so I thought it would go nicely. What are you cooking?'

Mills thought about the empty fridge. 'Fish and chips from the van I expect.'

Muriel gave a disapproving tut. 'You youngsters don't know how to cook!'

Mills laughed. 'I do but I don't have time today or tomorrow. I've got loads of work on.'

'You work too hard, young lady.'

Mills wouldn't ever admit it but she rather liked the way Muriel fussed over her. She still missed her mother often, and wished she was closer to her father.

'Talking of fish and chips, someone said they saw young Alex at the van last week. I said that was most unlikely but then I thought there *was* a strange car outside that night.'

Mills admitted he had visited. 'But it was only about work.'

'That's what I thought,' said Muriel with a grin.

'Yes, he's getting married next year, isn't that exciting?'

Mills couldn't see Muriel's face as she was busy opening a cake tin. When she looked up she was beaming. 'Try one of these.'

Mills selected a chocolate muffin.

'*I've* got some interesting news,' Muriel said. 'The Banfords are down this weekend. They rang me yesterday. They thought they should check the fire damage before there are any more viewings.'

'Viewings?'

She laughed. 'They're not selling the house but I heard they're putting some of the land back on the market.'

Mills said she should go but Muriel was busy packing a plastic box with sausage rolls. She handed them over saying they were surplus to requirements. It was rare for Mills to leave Muriel's empty handed.

Harris deserved a good walk so she took him down to the river until it started raining, when they almost ran back up the hill. The fish and chip van would be passing in an hour so she decided to fill the time by calling her father because he'd left a message for her weeks ago. But it wasn't him that answered.

'Hi Fiona, it's me.'

Her relationship with her father's young wife was

amicable but strained. She usually answered the phone so they were forced to converse but they had very little in common. Mills asked how Flora was getting on at school.

'Oh she loves it and she's made lots of super little chums. Her best friend is Hermione. Her mother owns a boutique that sells these gorgeous children's clothes. She's organising a fashion show and asked Flora to take part, isn't that fun? She suggested I put Flora down with an agency, she says she's got the face they're wanting at the moment.'

Mills let her witter on until the topic was exhausted then asked if Hugh was around. After a moment's wait he came to the phone.

'Hi Millie, how's things?'

'Fine Dad, sorry I didn't get back to you before.'

'No problem. It wasn't anything really but Fi said we should keep in touch.'

'So things are all right with you? Fiona says Flora is enjoying school.'

He laughed. 'She should do the fees they charge. It's all quinoa for lunch and yoga classes.'

'I guess it means childcare is easier.' Mills was referring to his previous issues with Fiona and nannies.

'Oh we still have someone full-time. She fiddles around with a duster and does a bit of ironing. Occasionally she even cooks a meal.' Mills could hear Fiona shouting in the background. He continued, 'Apparently she takes Flora to school and collects her as well, which means Fi can attend the gym and her life drawing classes.' There was more shouting. 'Anyway apparently the reason I rang before was to ask you about Christmas.'

'What about it?'

'Fi wants to know if you will be joining us.'

There was a muffled conversation then Fiona's voice. 'Sorry Mills, what he meant to say was "would you like to come to us for Christmas?". Flora would love to have her... well, to have you with us over the holiday.'

She nearly said it, thought Mills. She nearly called Flora my sister.

'I don't know what I'm doing yet,' she replied, aware she sounded ungrateful. 'I haven't really made any plans.'

'It's just that we will need to know because if we're on our own we'll probably go skiing or to my parents for the holiday. You can bring someone if you want – that would be fun.'

Mills agreed to let her know in a few days. More importantly it was time to drive down to catch the fish and chip van. Normally the queue for supper on a Friday was the place to pick up the gossip but tonight the rain was relentless and everyone remained in their cars until the van appeared. It was only as they were forming a queue that Mills recognised Daniel Banford in front of her. He seemed to recognise her.

'Hi,' he said.

Perhaps he couldn't remember who she was. It was an opportunity not to be missed.

'Hi, Daniel, I'm Mills from down the road at Laurel Cottage.'

There was a hint of recognition.

'I took the archaeology course your son attended. How is Gareth?'

It was his turn to order and pay. Mills noted it was for two cod and chips. So it was only for him and his wife.

Then he turned to her. 'Gareth has just finished his

masters in environmental studies at Newcastle. He's busy looking for a job.'

He collected the order and went off to his Range Rover where she could see someone seated on the passenger side. Mills asked for haddock and small chips. She was waiting while it was cooked when Daniel returned.

'Penny says it would be nice to catch up. Why don't you drop in for drinks tomorrow – early evening, around six?'

Normally Mills would have found an excuse to avoid socialising with Daniel and Penny but she was curious about the fire and, particularly, the sale of their land to David Price.

'That would be lovely,' she replied.

Next morning Mills was up early, showered and dressed before Harris was out of bed. She gave him a quick walk, sharing her toast with him when they returned. She washed the dishes, set up her laptop and printer in the kitchen, the warmest room in the cottage, and with a cup of coffee freshly made she began to trawl through the analytical data from the lab.

She established there were three tests completed before the fire stopped further work, in addition to the heroin result she'd already submitted. They were, in date order, a blood alcohol measurement, a DNA test on two cigarette ends, and a preliminary run on a pair of soil samples. She began by preparing the standard format reports for each of the tests which was quite straightforward because it only required her to enter dates and the names of the analysts involved. She realised this was purely a displacement activity. It was time to tackle the analyses themselves.

She chose the blood alcohol measurement because it was not only the earliest date but it was also the simplest. The results sheet was straightforward and all she had to enter was the simple value of 158 mg per 100 ml, nearly twice the legal limit. Normally the report would be signed by the analyst and she or Glyn would provide the authorising signature. Donna would have to sign the form over the weekend before she saw Nina.

The DNA on the cigarette ends immediately presented Mills with a problem. The analyses had been completed and the profile was identical on both stubs. But Mills didn't know what she could do with it now. They no longer had a connection to the FINDS database so she couldn't submit it for checking if it matched anyone with a conviction. It was then that she decided it would be sensible to make contact with the Regional Scientific Support Unit, as Nina had told her to do, and hand over the results for them to submit.

She rang Donna and arranged to drop in the following day for her signature. While she was on the phone Mills told her about the soil analyses that Tim was half way through.

'Can't help you there I'm afraid, Mills. His mass spec was always a mystery to me. Anyway, I thought *you* knew how it worked.'

'I guess I do but I'm not really authorised to calculate results. I'll have to warn them over in Wakefield.'

It took her all afternoon to untangle Tim's data but finally she had a set of data that seemed to make sense. She hoped the soils had survived the fire so Wakefield could repeat the analyses because without Tim the results would not be certified so they couldn't be used in court.

Chapter 16

It was Daniel's wife who opened the door and invited Mills inside the Manor. It was only a few years since they'd last met but she wouldn't have recognised the gaunt figure. Penny Banford had been tall and tanned with bleached blond hair, always immaculate. Now she had let her hair return to its natural colour, "pepper pot grey" Mills thought they called it, but on her it was a rather unattractive mixture of greys and white.

She followed Penny into their lounge where Daniel was turning off the television. He took her jacket, offering a drink.

'I've been experimenting with cocktails,' he confided with a sheepish grin. 'This is my chance to show off.'

She settled on a vodka martini, which was what Penny said she would have and was ushered to an armchair by the log fire. While Daniel left the room to prepare his concoctions, Penny sat down opposite her, asking if Mills was still working at the university. This led to them discussing Gareth's education.

'Where did he study?' Mills enquired.

'He did his first degree in Edinburgh. We insisted he stayed in Scotland, no fees you see. But for the master's he chose Newcastle to be near his girlfriend, Frances.'

Her husband appeared with three cocktail glasses.

Here was her chance. 'I think Justin Price studied agriculture at Newcastle, didn't he?' she enquired casually.

Daniel frowned as he handed her the martini. 'Yes,

Gareth did say he came across him but he and Price's lad hold very different views so they didn't spend any time together.'

'Gareth's research project was on sustainable farming,' Penny added.

'He's not come down with you this time?' Mills asked, hoping to steer the conversation round to the reason for their visit.

'He's back in Edinburgh, hopefully writing job applications,' said his father. 'He wants to work in sustainability, which is admirable, but he hasn't managed to find a position yet.'

'To be fair he's working at present for "Friends of the Earth" as a volunteer,' said Penny.

Her husband pulled a face. Mills sipped her drink. It was very strong and she was reminded that she'd only eaten an orange for lunch.

She tried a different approach. 'So are you down here for long?'

This time it worked. Daniel, sprawled on the sofa, explained at great length how they had put some land on the market, the problems associated with pasture prices and capital gains tax.

Penny drained her glass. 'We wanted to see the fire damage for ourselves, in case it affected anything.'

Mills described the alarm the fire had created in the village and expressed surprise that no-one knew what had caused it.

Daniel nodded. 'Exactly, I've got a crime number because they found a petrol can in the garden but there's been no further news. I don't think we'll ever know. We're just pleased there was no damage to the house.'

Soon Daniel was fetching refills. Emboldened by the alcohol Mills asked who might buy their pasture. The Banfords exchanged glances before Daniel said he wasn't sure, there were a number of farmers in the dale who might be interested.

'Will it go to auction?' Mills asked.

'I don't think so,' said Penny in her haughty voice. 'We want to know who we will be passing the land over to.'

Daniel changed the subject quite suddenly by asking Mills what she was working on now. That's a good question, she thought, but she told them about the fire at Yardley's and her plan to do a project on disaster recovery. She was conscious that time was getting on and she could probably leave without seeming impolite.

They saw her out, watching her make her way down the drive. Once the door closed she was plunged into darkness, stumbling along the rough track as her torch dimmed and went out. Fortunately she triggered a security light as she reached the end cottage and was able to reach home safely.

Inside Laurel Cottage, she made herself a toasted sandwich to soak up the alcohol, turned on the TV and sank onto the sofa. She only woke when the ten o'clock news came on and Harris was asking to go out.

Surprisingly Sunday turned out to be quite a good day. Mills had expected Nina to be demanding information she couldn't supply but a quick detour to visit Donna had solved two problems. First of all she was able to sign the analysis report for the blood alcohol test and then she said she had logged the DNA from the cigarette ends so they would already have the details on file. That meant the only issue was Tim's case, which showed the soil from the suspect had come from the park where the girl was murdered. Mills had to explain to Nina that she wasn't accredited to calculate the results.

'Don't worry Mills. We'll tell Wakefield to repeat the samples. Do you think they'll have survived the fire?'

'They are soils, Nina. They aren't flammable. I think they'll be fine.'

'In that case all you have to do is let them know which samples are completed and which need to be re-tested.'

'Are you sure?'

Nina smiled. 'Yes, you've done a grand job under the circumstances.'

'That's a relief.'

Mills began to shut down her laptop but it wasn't quite over.

'These DNA samples Tim Fletcher was testing,' Nina began. 'Can you give me any more details?'

'You've got their names and email addresses and Ruby has Tim's phone.'

'I know. She's working on that in case any of the customers contacted Tim by text.'

'I've got the addresses of the ones wanting a refund,' Mills offered.

Nina waited for her to power up her computer again before she could go back through her list of customers.

Minutes later, Mills looked up from the screen. 'Out of the nine replies I've had so far, only five actually received results and all of those accepted a refund so I have their addresses. I'll email them to you.'

There was silence while she sent them to Nina's office.

'Thanks Mills, that's great. We can check them out

quickly and easily tomorrow.'

'You will be sensitive, won't you?' Mills asked. 'They were all familial tests.'

'Understood. But what about the one you haven't heard from?'

Mills shrugged.

Nina bit her lip. 'Can you send them a message asking them to ring you?'

'Sure.'

Her friend looked at her. 'You won't forget to contact Wakefield, will you?'

Mills reassured her. 'I might be visiting anyway.' She told her about Professor Pringle's offer to find funding for her.

'Oh, yes,' said her friend with a laugh. 'Nige told me about your professor friend and his pub lunch.'

Mills reddened. 'I'm sure he didn't mean anything by it.'

'Even so, you should be careful Mills. What would Phil think?'

'I doubt he'd be worried.'

'You don't mean that.'

'It's true, Nina. He hasn't spoken to me for over a week.'

'Have you contacted him?'

'No but…'

Nina raised her eyebrows. 'I rest my case.'

Nige appeared from the kitchen. 'It sounds as if you ladies have finished your work-related conference so can I set the table?'

Mills put her laptop away while Nina called the children to come downstairs. Rosie wanted to show Mills her latest art project and the boys were asking her to play a game that involved throwing balls. She divided her attention between them as best she could until Nige announced dinner was ready. Soon she was squashed between Rosie and Owen at the table enjoying a noisy family meal. It was traditional when Mills visited that they went to the park after lunch and today was no exception. The kids played on the swings and bought sweets on the way home. Back indoors Rosie went off to finish her project while the boys played happily. Nige had made no secret that Wales was playing South Africa in a rugby match that was being televised at five so Mills offered to help Nina with the washing up.

She finally left at eight when the boys had been bathed and Rosie had read a story with her. On the drive home she made the decision to call Phil and ask him to finally decide whether Harris was going with him or staying with her. It seemed the easiest way to find out where she stood. However, her first priority was to contact the customer who hadn't replied to her message about his DNA samples. And then it was far too late to call Phil – she'd do it tomorrow.

DI Mitch Turner called a meeting first thing Monday morning to sort out "this mess", as he called it. He was referring to the fire at Yardley Forensics. His main concern was evidence from the Jennifer Carr murder.

'We need the results from the cigarettes as soon as possible. The press know it's all we've got and they're beginning to ask why we haven't identified a suspect yet.'

He was looking in Nina and Hazel's direction. He wanted to know if the fire itself was still an "open case"? He was looking straight at Nina now, which was unfair because Hazel was responsible for the investigation. She turned to Hazel, who was looking intently at her notes.

'There have been a few new pieces of evidence that have come to light,' said Nina. 'We know that Tim Fletcher was analysing DNA samples unbeknownst to Yardley Forensics. I have the customers' contact details and am checking their backgrounds. Meanwhile we have worked through the forensic cases sent to the laboratory but haven't found any leads yet.'

'What about the heroin dealer?' Mitch asked. 'Didn't he have a contact seen in the area?'

'Yes, but he lives in Northallerton and we've nothing on him.'

'Hazel?' Mitch asked.

She looked up. 'No, nothing except we're checking up on the owner of the lab. The loss adjuster suspects it could be fraud to collect the insurance money.'

There was murmuring in the room.

'Good, follow that up, Hazel.'

They were dismissed and Nina walked back to the office with her colleague.

'Are you serious about Brenda Yardley destroying her own lab?' she asked.

'She'll clear her debts and more. Who'd blame her?' replied Hazel.

'Her staff?'

Hazel shrugged. 'If it was me I'd be tempted,' she replied before picking up a file and walking out.

'Right,' said Nina turning to Ruby. 'Any luck with the DNA customers?'

'As you know, they all contacted Tim Fletcher by email. I found the messages on his phone and linked them with the addresses that Mills sent over. I've done background checks but found nothing on any of the names.'

'So you've confirmed them all?'

'Yes, all but one that is.'

'Oh?'

'There's one that hasn't replied to Mills.' Ruby passed Tim's phone to her. 'Her name is Jordan Henderson.'

'Jordan's a boy's name, Ruby.' Nina corrected her as she read the message. 'He wanted to see him?'

'Yes. And Fletcher calls the number.'

'Did they meet?'

'I don't know.'

'Can we trace the phone?'

'I tried, it's a "pay as you go". It's unobtainable.'

'Really? Can you check whether Mills has had a response yet?'

Ruby picked up the phone and responded with the answer ten minutes later. 'No.'

Hazel came in, slamming the door behind her.

Ruby looked up. 'Would you say Jordan was a boy or a girl?' she asked her.

'Boy,' she responded sharply then sat at her desk and began tapping fiercely on her keyboard.

Ruby pulled a face. 'Well whichever it is, he or she doesn't live in the area, that's for sure. I can't locate a local address for him or her.'

'We need the whereabouts of this guy.' Nina could see Hazel was listening and lowered her voice to a whisper. 'See if you can find this Jordan Henderson by widening the geographical area.'

Mills took Nina's advice and rang Dr Ruth Barnes first

thing in the morning. She passed on details of the samples that had been completed by Donna already and told her that the soils would need further work even though Tim had already done some analysis.

'We might need some advice on the procedure you used,' Ruth told Mills.

She jumped at the opportunity to visit the Wakefield lab. 'I could come down one day this week,' she offered.

Ruth suggested Wednesday when she would be available for a chat before introducing her to the analyst who would be testing the soils. Mills hoped there would be time to talk to Ruth about the proposal she was discussing with Simon Pringle.

Aware she'd been neglecting her academic duties, she was busy marking course work when Nina rang to ask about Tim's customers. She wanted to know if Jordan Henderson had responded.

'No, still nothing from him. He's the only one that hasn't replied.'

Nina said she would tell Ruby.

When Mills had finished her conversation, Nige looked up. 'You might not get a response from Jordan Henderson,' he said.

Mills was taken aback. 'How do you know?'

'Liverpool played Watford away yesterday and he got a red card.'

'What *are* you talking about Nige?' Sometimes his jokes could be really irritating.

'Jordan Henderson, midfielder aged twenty-eight, captain of Liverpool, plays for England.'

'A footballer?'

'Yes and quite a vocal one. He was sent off and will

miss the local derby with Everton.'

It took Mills a moment to absorb the information before she sent a message to let Nina know there was a footballer called Jordan Henderson, and her husband could tell her all about him. A weird coincidence, she added.

Motivated by the prospect of chatting with Ruth Barnes later in the week, Mills started work on a draft research proposal, thinking that it would be good to pre-empt any approaches that Prof Pringle might initiate with Wakefield. She didn't want to be reliant on him or indebted to him in case he turned out to be what Nige had described as a "typical mid-life professor looking for a distraction". She had laughed and said she had no idea what he could possibly mean but she was sort of touched that he seemed to be looking out for her.

Time passed quickly as she found the words came easily. It took some effort to keep the approach scientific but by the end of the day she was happy with what she'd produced. She was stuck when she came to the cost of the project and sought Nige's advice. He told her to decide how long it would take her, charge for her time and add the standard figure for overheads. He agreed to look through a copy of her proposal that evening and come back with any comments first thing in the morning.

She drove home feeling positive for the first time since the fire, until she remembered Nina's instructions for her to ring Phil. She promised to do so that evening, after she'd walked Harris and had something to eat. Except when she'd taken off her jacket and made a fuss of the lurcher she noticed a message on the answer machine. Phil had beaten her to it.

'Hi Mills, it's me. Can you call me when you get this?'

She stuck to her plan so it was nearly eight by the time she rang. She'd rehearsed what she was going to say as she walked gingerly up the track, her head torch bobbing as she followed Harris's dark shadow.

'Phil? It's Mills.'

'You were working late!'

'Not really. I had to take Harris out then I was cooking dinner.'

'Oh.' He'd sounded faintly displeased. 'So how are things, what's the latest on the lab fire?' His tone had quickly become more upbeat. 'Have they got to the bottom of it yet?'

'I don't think they ever will. It was Tim's funeral last week. Brenda wouldn't go. She thinks they suspect her of burning it down herself.'

'Did she?'

'Don't be silly!'

There was a pause.

'So what about your news?' she asked, wishing to change the subject. She wasn't going to tell him about her project plans because he'd probably laugh at them.

'Me? Well, there is something actually. Maria and her friends are planning to go to Spain for New Year. Her family is over there.'

'That's nice.'

'It is, they have a parador near Malaga.'

'Isn't that like a hotel?'

'Yeah. They've got loads of room and her parents can put us all up.'

Us? thought Mills. 'Are you thinking of going?'

'It sounds like fun.'

Mills waited to find out if she was invited. Wanting him to ask her but unsure how she should respond.

'There's plenty of space if you want to join us.'

It was the way he said *us*, as if he was part of a gang and she was the outsider. She didn't feel welcome.

'I have to look after Harris.' She knew it sounded like what it was – an excuse.

He argued that the dog could go into kennels but she was adamant.

'Anyway,' she added, 'I need you to look after him over Christmas because I'm going down to be with my family and they're in an apartment that doesn't allow pets.'

He hadn't said what he would be doing over the Christmas period. He went a bit quiet but agreed he would do his share.

'By the way,' he continued, 'Nina said we should go over for a meal again soon.'

'Did she?' So her friend was meddling again.

'Yes. I could come up next weekend if it works for you.'

'I guess so.'

Mills sat staring at the phone when the call was over. She didn't really know what she wanted but perhaps she did need to get away and spend some time with her father and his new family. She would have liked for Phil to suggest they spend Christmas in the cottage together but could see that a trip to Malaga would be more fun for him.

'Does that make me boring Harris?' she asked the lurcher who was sprawled out in front of the fire. 'I bet you'll love being the centre of attention down in Nottingham over Christmas.'

Chapter 17

'Ruby, Jordan Henderson is a well-known footballer.'

'Yes, Nina. He plays for England.'

'You know?'

'I just found out.'

'Well my husband is the world's expert. Anything you want to know, he can tell you.'

'Do you think it's a coincidence, the name I mean?'

'Possibly. It's clear that our man isn't *the* Jordan Henderson.'

'No. There isn't anyone with that name in the region – except the footballer, who comes from Sunderland. But he wasn't even in the country on the day when our man wanted to meet Fletcher.'

'Really?'

'I checked. He was playing for England in Croatia.'

Nina laughed. 'You know as much about him as Nige.'

'It's my job, Nina. So, my opinion, for what it's worth, is that it could be a pseudonym. Is that the right word?'

'Yes. It's like calling yourself Mickey Mouse or Homer Simpson. I think all we can say is that he is probably a Liverpool fan. The fact he hasn't replied to messages from Mills or from us suggests he has something to hide. Did you say it was a paternity case?'

'Yes, there was one male and one female swab resulting in a match.'

They were interrupted by Hazel storming in. 'Mitch is getting his knickers in a twist, Nina. He wants the DNA from the Jennifer Carr case to be processed as soon as possible. Ruby said you've got the report.'

'Yes, Mills gave it to me yesterday. I've passed it on to Wakefield to enter onto the national database,' Nina responded calmly.

With the wind taken out of her sails Hazel relaxed slightly. 'Thanks. You know what he's like, wanting everything done yesterday.'

'It's understandable,' said Nina. 'Those cigarette ends are the only link we have with Jennifer Carr's killer. If they'd been lost in the fire we'd have nothing.'

'I still think we should be interviewing the husband again,' Hazel said, settling herself at her desk.

Ruby coughed loudly. 'Excuse me! Apart from the fact he doesn't smoke, he was in Dubai at a hotel exhibition at the time with his spa equipment company.'

'A good alibi though isn't it?' Hazel replied. 'I'd say almost too convenient.'

'You're not suggesting a hired killer?' Ruby laughed.

'It's not impossible,' Hazel snapped.

'If it was,' said Nina, 'he may be on the DNA database. We'll have to wait and see.'

As soon as Hazel was out of the office she rang Mills to ask her, when she was in Wakefield, to check with Ruth Barnes that the DNA from the cigarettes had been submitted to FINDS.

'It's really urgent. I've left messages for her,' Nina told her. 'Ring me tomorrow as soon as you know it's been entered on the database.'

'Were they definitely from the killer?' Mills asked.

'It's all we've got so let's hope so.'

Mills had been in the middle of a discussion with Nige over his comments on her research proposal. She was grateful that he'd spent time looking at it for her and thanked him for his suggestions which were definite improvements. She made the corrections quickly, printing out the final version to give to Simon Pringle. She'd decided to hand him a copy just before she visited Dr Barnes, so he didn't have enough time to interfere with her plans. However, she was nervous about approaching him with a *fait accompli*.

He had an office to himself in the corridor that was the Forensic Department domain. The name on his door read: Professor S Pringle, Toxicology. When she knocked gently, he called for her to enter.

'Yes?' He was staring at his computer monitor.

Mills waited for him to finish whatever he was doing. When he did, he jumped up and came round from behind his desk

'Mills, to what do I owe this pleasure?' he asked, smiling as he indicated for her to sit then perched himself on the edge of his desk in front of her.

She explained that she'd completed the proposal for Wakefield and as she was visiting Ruth Barnes tomorrow, she was going to take the opportunity to talk to her about her ideas.

Pringle was frowning as he accepted the document she offered him. He looked at the paper, muttering that it was fine but unfortunately he wouldn't be able to go with her until the following week. There was an awkward silence.

'I'll tell her that you suggested I submit the proposal,' Mills said, standing up ready to make a rapid exit.

'Let me know how it goes,' he called as she reached the

door. 'What about a drink later in the week?'

Mills fled back to the office. She hadn't handled that well, she told Nige. Pringle would probably never speak to her again, she told him. He said not to be so silly and suggested they went to the cafeteria for a sandwich. Mills thanked him but she was going to Harrogate, Brenda had a meeting booked with the insurance company and Mills wanted to be there to limit any damage that her boss might cause.

As it turned out, Jessica didn't stay long. The loss adjuster knew more about the business than Brenda did and the discussion was getting nowhere. Mills kept apologising because she knew so little about how the finances were run. When Brenda told her to talk to the accountant, Jessica replied she already had, that was how she knew the extent of her company's financial difficulties. After that Brenda refused to co-operate any further.

In the end Jessica packed the files away in her bag and picked up her coat. Mills followed her into the hall.

'I'm sorry but I can't sign off on the insurance until I'm satisfied that this isn't a case of fraud.'

Mills looked at the floor.

'Do you understand what I'm saying?'

Mills nodded. 'But surely you can't believe…'

'I'm just doing my job.'

She was no longer friendly Jessica, here to help. Her tone was cool. She pulled on her coat and opened the front door. 'You'll be hearing from us – or the police.'

Mills shut the door after her and went back to talk to her boss. Brenda quickly pushed a tissue up her sleeve. Her eyes were red-rimmed. Mills put an arm round her shoulder.

'You'll tell me if you've done anything silly, won't you, Brenda?' she asked.

'So you think I've done something?'

'You're being so obstructive with the insurance company and the police. It makes people suspicious.'

She sat upright. 'I can assure you, miss, that I have done nothing wrong, except to let the business go downhill.'

'You were ill, that wasn't your fault.'

'Don't soft-soap me, Mills. I took my eye off the ball afterwards. I could see it coming but didn't know how to stop it.'

'You should've said.'

'You were never around. The university is where you work now. I couldn't expect it.'

Mills felt she'd let Brenda down and said so. Then she suggested a cup of tea before they both burst into tears. Later Mills persuaded her to get legal advice. She suggested contacting a local law firm but Brenda said she had a cousin who was a solicitor and she would call him.

'I'll ask Nina if there's anything we can do to prove you didn't cause the fire,' Mills offered, unable to bring herself to mention the word "arson".

It seemed bizarre to be discussing alibis but what if, by chance, Brenda had been seen by someone that night.

'Don't be daft,' she said. 'I was in bed when I got the call from the fire brigade.'

Mills pictured Brenda standing in her winter coat, her pyjama legs poking out below.

'Do they think,' she went on, 'that I drove down there with a can of petrol then rushed back here and leapt into bed?'

The entire premise seemed so absurd to Mills she had to smile.

But Brenda remained grave. 'It would be funny if it wasn't so bloody tragic.'

Before she left, Mills promised to ask Nina for advice and urged Brenda to talk to her solicitor cousin immediately.

The glass fronted Regional Scientific Support Services building was modern and impressive. Mills was looking forward to seeing inside, particularly the laboratories if she was allowed to access them. She was a few minutes early so was asked to wait in reception for Dr Barnes. When she finally appeared she looked harassed.

'I'm sorry, I've only got a few minutes but we'll go back to my office. I've asked Robert to look after you while you're here.'

Mills hoped there would still be enough time to talk about her project idea. She decided to tell her as they walked but to her surprise, Ruth already knew about it.

'That's why I was delayed meeting you,' she said. 'Simon Pringle was on the phone. He mentioned his suggestion that you work something up. He said you'd given him a rough outline.'

Undeterred Mills took the paper copy from her bag and handed it over. 'I'd appreciate your comments,' she said.

'It's really up to Simon,' Ruth said dismissively. 'If he's supervising it I'm sure it will be fine.'

Her office was neat and business-like. The desk was clear and she placed the proposal carefully down on it without comment.

Mills hesitated to ask but needed to understand. 'What about the cost?' she asked. 'Are there funds available for this sort of project?'

Ruth was picking up the phone. 'I can sort that out with Simon if he's supervising you.'

Mills wanted to explain she wasn't one of Pringle's students but she was already asking Robert to come down to the office. She replaced the receiver and asked for the results Mills had brought. She handed over the memory stick, explaining how to find the data, particularly for the evidence from the Carr murder.

'DS Featherstone would like the results put on the national database as soon as possible.'

'Understood. If you like, Robert can do it now.'

A young man in jeans, trainers and a sweatshirt with a heavy metal band logo on the front was entering the room.

'Robert, this is Ms Sanderson.'

'Dr Sanderson but please call me Mills.'

Ruth looked puzzled as she took her leave of them, instructing Robert to show Mills round but first to get the DNA profiles entered on the system.

Robert was rather like Tim, Mills thought. He was polite, helpful and clever. He took her down to where they could both sit and look at the computer screen as he copied the results from her memory stick. Then he accessed the database, entered the results and closed the program. Mills sent a text to Nina to say it had been done. Relieved that the business part of her visit was over, Mills followed Robert as he began the tour of the labs. She was overwhelmed by the facilities as he explained what was going on in each laboratory. His area of expertise was DNA and they spent most time there. They were using robotics to process samples with capabilities far beyond those of Yardley Forensics. They could work on degraded material from cold cases with all the up-to-date techniques at their fingertips. She couldn't hide her envy. Finally they came to "Toxicology". Here she asked whether Professor Pringle had any involvement in the research. Her host replied diplomatically but she could sense he wasn't seen as an expert in the field by the analysts.

When they went for a coffee Mills asked Robert about how he came to be working at Calder House. His background was chemistry but he'd always wanted to work in forensics. He sounded just like Tim. When he asked what she did, she described her role at Yardley Forensics, the fire and the samples she had to hand over. He was sympathetic.

'It must be difficult competing with a big organisation like ours,' he said. 'The company is global. They have labs across the world.'

It was something that hadn't occurred to Mills before. She realised now why Brenda had found it hard to keep the company afloat when work was haemorrhaging away to Wakefield. It was obvious, even she would send work here herself if she had the choice. Perhaps there was no future for Yardley Forensics after all.

They were joined by members of Robert's team, young enthusiastic analysts just like him. He introduced them to her, explaining which parts of the labs they worked in. Mills thought it must be nice to be in a group of like-minded people. It was something she'd missed once she had finished her studies; since then she always seemed to be on the outside, never fully integrated. It was hardly surprising when she divided herself between two different university departments and a forensics lab.

The team drifted back to work leaving Mills alone with Robert, who suggested they return to the office. He clearly had things to get on with and Mills said it was time for her to go. She was collecting her jacket when Ruth arrived, out of breath.

'They said you were still here. Are you in a hurry?' Her meeting had finished early so she could spare an hour, if she would like to tell her about her research plans. Perhaps she'd finally realised that Mills was an academic not a student. She led her to a meeting room down the corridor where they could talk without interruption and pulling the proposal from her bag, asked Mills to talk her through it. When she'd finished, Ruth asked her why Simon Pringle was involved in the work. Mills explained he was at her appraisal and was acting more like a mentor, to help her formulate a career plan. Ruth seemed satisfied with the explanation.

She smiled. 'I think it would be better if the work involved someone here'.

Unsure exactly what that meant, Mills said she had no objection to that.

Ruth continued, 'I could fulfil the role of collaborator at this end. I have support for research projects and can probably find a bit of money to start you off while we wait for official approval.'

'That sounds great, thank you.' Mills couldn't have wished for more. 'Will you let Professor Pringle know?' she asked.

'Don't worry, I'll have a word with him.'

As Mills was leaving, Ruth asked what was happening to the staff now that Yardley Forensics was closed. Unsure how to respond, she mumbled something about not being sure what would happen to the lab.

'We're always looking for competent analysts. Do tell them to call me if they're interested.' She looked steadily at Mills. 'I don't suppose you need another position yourself if you're on the staff at the university.'

Mills shook her head. She was right, she didn't need another job, tempting as it sounded.

'And how is Brenda? It must have been a terrible shock, the fire, and the fatality.'

Mills nodded.

'She's a very clever lady,' Ruth said. 'There's no-one more knowledgeable when it comes to textiles. Give her my regards when you see her.'

They parted, arranging to catch up in a couple of weeks. Meanwhile Ruth would organise funding for their joint project and go through the proposal to make any tweaks to ensure it was accepted. Mills signed out of the building wondering what Simon Pringle would make of the new arrangement and hoping Ruth Barnes wouldn't take over her research in the way he had tried to do.

As soon as she was in the car she rang Brenda to tell her about her meeting with Ruth. 'She sends her regards,' Mills added.

Brenda seemed unwilling to hear about the Wakefield lab, which Mills put down to the fact it was probably the reason for her own company losing work. So Mills turned the conversation to the future of her employees and why she was asking.

'If Ruth Barnes is offering jobs at Wakefield they

should be jumping at the opportunity,' Brenda said.

'You don't think we should at least try to hang onto Donna?'

'What for?'

'In case you change your mind.'

It was her last attempt to get Brenda to admit she might be wrong but it was hopeless. The woman was adamant she was retiring from forensics all together.

'If you're so keen to see it struggle on, *you* run it,' she exclaimed before slamming the phone down.

Chapter 18

Nina had told Ruby to check FINDS for the DNA from the cigarette ends as soon as the results were on the system. It wasn't long before she reported back.

'No matches, sorry.'

'Damn. We've got no-one in the picture. It doesn't make sense. A woman in her thirties happily married with a beautiful daughter. Everyone says they were a perfect family. Which usually means it's the husband.'

'Except for the fact he was abroad at the time.' Ruby was always ready to play devil's advocate.

'...and there's no motive,' Nina continued.

'The MO was pretty violent.'

'The two cigarette ends suggest premeditation.'

'Assuming they're relevant to the case.'

'It's all we've got, Ruby.' Nina sighed. 'It's all we've got,' she repeated to no-one in particular.

She updated her files until she reached the report on the Yardley arson. 'Any luck in locating this Jordan Henderson, Ruby?'

'Nothing.'

'Let's hope Mills can help us then. We need a suspect other than Brenda Yardley. If it goes on much longer, Hazel will be getting a warrant to search her place for accelerant.'

'Are you serious?'

'I hope not but you know Hazel once she gets an idea.'

*

The cottage was chilly when Mills arrived back mid-afternoon. She grabbed her scarf and gloves before venturing out into the cold wind with Harris. Her head was full of ideas that needed sorting so she turned east at the top of the track, heading across to Gunnerside Gill. Brenda's final shot as she left had made an impression that had nagged at her all the way home. Why *did* she think she could make the lab viable when Brenda couldn't? Mills had several possible answers, including her wish to see it succeed, her better handle on finances, and her health. Even so, any competitor to the Regional Science Support Services would have to have a "unique selling point". Apart from Brenda's expertise in textiles and Tim's mass spectrometry capability, which was sadly no longer available, what did they have? Perhaps other niche areas, like Alex's digital forensics and Phil's knowledge of bones, could be built up in time.

The wind was so strong on the tops they could barely fight their way forward so Mills decided to turn back. Soon they were making their way downhill at full pelt with Harris anxious to get back for his tea. As Mills was removing his lead, she noticed a scrap of paper on the mat. It was a note from Jean Price to say that Lucy was collecting bric-a-brac for a stall in Reeth on Saturday, part of a fund-raiser for her school trip. It was the perfect opportunity to find out more about the tensions between the Prices and the Banford family, particularly between Justin and Gareth. She quickly fed Harris, microwaved a leftover portion of pizza she found in the fridge and munched it while she sorted out a few paperbacks and an ugly vase she'd had for years. She would take them down tomorrow night when she was visiting the fish and chip van. Finally she made a quick call to Donna, arranging to meet up for a coffee on Saturday morning.

It was still early and she was full of ideas for her project so she sat down with her laptop to plan the research in detail. It was going to be brilliant working with Dr Ruth Barnes. First she would contact the police, the fire investigators and the insurance company. She wanted as much information as possible about the way the fire spread, it could be important for future laboratory design. She made a list of questions for the fire service and was looking for contact details when an email pinged up. If it had been a departmental message she would've ignored it but this was from her Yardley Forensics account, a response from the DNA test customer she'd been chasing. He was asking to meet her to discuss his results. She had tutorials the next morning but suggested he came to the university in the afternoon.

The tutees were as uninspiring as usual. A couple of the students hadn't turned up, with the excuse that they had bad colds, leaving just four. The time dragged as she tried to keep their discussions going despite a lethargy that was contagious. Before the allotted time was up they'd all run out of steam so Mills suggested they went away to finish their assignments. Suddenly everyone had livened up, chattering as they left her office about what they'd planned for the weekend.

'All clear?' asked Nige as he reappeared after they'd gone.

'Yes. Friday morning is the worst time for spontaneous discussion,' complained Mills.

'I always get my students to prepare something themselves and ask them to lead the group,' said Nige airily.

'That's why you're a senior lecturer and I'm still a probationer,' Mills answered sulkily.

'Here's something to cheer you up. Nina says to come over on Sunday.'

Mills groaned. 'It's my turn to invite *you*.'

'No. "She who is to be obeyed" says Phil is coming and he's got news. He says you've got to be there.'

Mills thought of Alex with his news. Perhaps Phil is going to announce his engagement to the famous Maria.

'So shall I say you're coming?' Nige was asking.

'I wouldn't miss it for the world.'

'Well sound as though you mean it!'

Mills had suggested to Mr Henderson that he come to her office at two o' clock. It was Nige's habit to go home early on a Friday but she casually asked when he would be off.

'Why? What are you up to?'

'I've got a visitor, that's all.'

'Mysterious.' He was looking at her with a mischievous smile.

'No,' she replied, letting him think what he liked.

As soon as he went to get lunch, Mills rang the number she'd found for the fire service investigation team. It took a few minutes to locate but soon she was talking to the person who had authored the report. After she'd explained that she was researching the fire he offered to send her a copy. She thanked him but stopped him from ringing off.

'Were you by any chance involved in the investigation

of the fire at the Manor in Mossy Bank, Swaledale?' she asked.

He thought for a moment then asked her to wait while he spoke to someone at his end. Eventually he came back on, saying he was passing her over to a colleague.

'Hello,' said someone with a deeper voice.

Mills repeated her question.

'Yes, I had a quick look over it. There was little to report really, except for the empty can that had held red diesel.'

'Red diesel?'

'Yes, it's…'

Mills knew what it was, diesel sold at reduced tax and dyed red to differentiate it from normal diesel.

'The sort used in farm vehicles?' she asked.

'Exactly,' he said. 'So it could have come from anywhere round Swaledale. They might even sell it at the local garage.'

'So is there going to be any further investigation into the fire?'

He confirmed the case was closed so she thanked him for his help, making a mental note to check for red diesel at Reeth garage on the way home.

Jordan Henderson was a large man. He filled the doorway as he announced his arrival. Mills jumped up to greet him, offering him a chair next to her desk. He was wearing a bulky red padded jacket and jeans. His hair was close-shaven and he had stubble on his chin. Mills took all this in as he took his seat.

'Hi, thanks for agreeing to see me,' he said.

Mills guessed he came from somewhere round

Manchester although she'd been wrong before when it came to accents.

'It's no problem. I'm only sorry that you were misled into thinking you had an accredited DNA analysis.'

He rubbed his chin. She thought he looked nervous.

'The thing is, does the result still hold?' he asked.

'Is it a correct analysis? I would say it is very likely to be but you should have it repeated at an accredited laboratory.'

He looked confused so she spent some time explaining how certificates were only issued for accredited analyses. She offered to find him an alternative lab that was reputable but he shook his head.

As an afterthought she asked, 'Can you tell me what the analysis was for?' It was a very personal question but this was her only opportunity to talk face to face with one of Tim's clients.

He pressed his lips together. Mills thought he was refusing to answer, waiting as he rubbed his forehead. It seemed an effort for him to reply.

'I wanted to check whether she was telling me the truth.'

Mills regretted the intrusion. 'I'm sorry, I didn't mean to pry.'

He was looking at the ceiling then down at his hands. He stood up suddenly, knocking over his chair. He picked it up and thumped it down awkwardly so it fell to the ground again.

'She lied to me about the baby.'

Without another word he left, almost bumping into Simon Pringle who was standing in the doorway.

'Well, who was that?'

'Just someone,' Mills muttered, embarrassed.

Simon was on his way to the bar and wanted to know if she fancied a drink as it was Friday. She made an excuse. He lingered, asking how her visit to Wakefield had gone. It seemed Ruth hadn't been in touch with him yet so she described the revised plan.

'So Ruth is collaborating with my research. She's finding some funds for me to get started and revising the plan for a formal submission for support,' she explained.

'Really?' He appeared stunned by the news.

'Isn't that great?' added Mills with a smile, feeling more confident.

'Yes, I suppose it is. Congratulations. Ruth Barnes is a very competent lady.' He didn't sound particularly pleased. 'But just watch out, people like her can be hardnosed. You'll need to keep your wits about you.'

'Thanks for the warning.'

He left without another word. In a way Mills was sorry they wouldn't be working together; he seemed genuinely interested in her work and wanting to help her career. It would be good to continue to keep in touch with him. She packed her bags determined to carry on with her research plans over the weekend. The department had emptied and so had the car park which was why she noticed the familiar large figure in a red padded jacket sitting in a black car. When he saw her looking in his direction he flicked his cigarette away and closed the car window.

Mills was anxious to get back home early that evening. Her suspicion that Justin had started the fire at the Manor was even stronger now she'd learned about the red diesel.

Armed with the oddments for Lucy's stall, she drove down to the Price's farm. Jean seemed delighted to see her, inviting her in out of the bitter wind.

'I'm on my way to the fish and chip van,' Mills explained. 'It's just a couple of things for Lucy.'

Jean called her daughter down to thank her but when Lucy had retreated back upstairs Mills asked if Jean had time for a quick chat. She'd been rehearsing what to say, beginning with the proviso that everything was in complete confidence and wouldn't go any further. Jean looked intrigued.

'What is it?' she asked.

'It's about the fire at the Manor,' she said.

'What fire?'

Clearly Jean hadn't heard so Mills told her the details.

'…and because there were fireworks that night – it was the Saturday before Guy Fawkes Night – we all thought it was an accident but it was definitely arson.'

Jean looked appalled. 'Do they know who started it?'

'No but they used red diesel.'

Mills waited for Jean's reaction. She finally broke the silence by asking, 'Why are you telling *me* this?'

'I just thought you should know,' replied Mills, as casually as she could.

'Everyone uses red diesel round here. What exactly are you suggesting?'

'Nothing, I just thought you should know that's all.'

She turned to leave. 'I didn't mean…' she mumbled as she struggled with the doorknob.

'Thank you for Lucy's jumble,' Jean said coldly, shutting the door behind her.

*

Mills had arranged to meet Donna in Harrogate. It was surprisingly pleasant to see her again; she was so calm, quiet and self-assured. They carried their coffees to an empty table by the window and watched the shoppers hurrying past. The town was full of people enjoying a patch of good weather. Mills felt herself relaxing a little.

'I visited the Wakefield lab on Wednesday,' Mills began.

Soon she was describing all the modern technology they had for forensic investigations. Donna was leaning forward, absorbing all the details Mills was giving her.

'Dr Ruth Barnes is really dynamic,' she continued. 'She was asking about Yardley staff.'

'Was she?' Donna was definitely interested.

'Yes.' She repeated what Ruth had said about needing competent analysts.

Donna nodded. She understood what Mills was suggesting. But she also wanted to know what was happening to Yardley Forensics and Mills gave her the truth: finances were in a bad way and they couldn't compete with the big labs.

Donna leaned back in the big leather armchair. 'Are you sure there's no future for Yardley's?' she asked, clearly embarrassed. 'I mean, you aren't going to carry on, even if Brenda doesn't want to?'

That was quite a question. It put Mills on the spot but she wasn't going to give the girl hope.

'No. There's no way I could run the lab.'

'We'd all be keen to help. My dad says we could have like a management buyout where we all have a share.'

'I'm sorry Donna. I think we have to be realistic. We don't have the resources to keep going, not after this.'

The girl appeared disappointed but lifted her head,

looking Mills straight in the eyes. 'In that case I think I'll apply to Wakefield, if you'll give me a reference.'

'Of course I will and I don't think you'll regret it,' Mills replied.

She left Donna, promising to put in a good word for her with Ruth Barnes. She stopped at Reeth garage to fill up the Mini on the way back home specifically to find out if they sold red diesel.

'We do.'

'What about petrol cans?' she asked.

'We do but we're out at the moment. When we sold the last one we decided to wait until everyone had finished with bonfires. It's not wise to start them with fuel you see. We were told by the fire brigade to warn people about the dangers of explosions. Funnily enough when they came round we only had one can left. I gave the lad who bought it one of their leaflets.'

'Was that for a bonfire then?' Mills asked.

'He said not but he did fill it with fuel and it was just before Guy Fawkes Night.'

Mills could feel her pulse racing. 'So that would be Justin Price then,' she said daringly.

'You know him then? Aye it was. I told him, if you set fire to that it could cause an explosion.'

Mills left but only got as far as Healaugh before she turned round and went back to Reeth.

'Did he fill the can with red diesel?' Mills asked the man in the garage.

'Diesel? No, that wouldn't burn well, would it? He filled it with petrol, that's why I warned him about it.'

Chapter 19

Phil was already there when Mills arrived at Nina's. He was sprawled on the floor playing dominos with Tomos and Owen. Nige appeared from the kitchen with a beer bottle in each hand.

'Ignore them,' said Nina. 'I've got wine in the fridge.'

Mills followed her friend into the kitchen where a pan was rattling on the stove.

'I've just got to drain these potatoes and pop them in the oven,' Nina continued. 'Then everything is under control for a while.'

Mills offered to help but was given a glass of wine and told to relax. So she wandered into the living room and took a seat. There was much merriment and shouting as the game continued. The noise brought Rosie downstairs who was soon showing Mills her neon drawing pad. It wasn't until they were squashed together round the dining table that Mills and Phil acknowledged each other's presence by enquiring about work. This time it was her turn to enthuse about her latest research initiative, how she was being funded by the Regional Scientific Support Unit, working with Dr Ruth Barnes. Phil had heard of her and was suitably impressed.

So was Nina. 'That's great news. I heard you were in Wakefield last week.'

Mills told them about her visit and that Donna was going to apply for a job there.

'Perhaps they'll offer you a consultancy down there,'

suggested Phil.

'Would you want one?' Nina asked.

'What *is* going to happen to Yardley's?' asked Nige.

Mills shrugged. 'Brenda's retiring. No-one will take over, unless I do.'

That surprised them. It wasn't something she'd considered but she was interested in their reaction.

'That would be cool.' Typical of Nige.

Nina smiled. 'It would be an interesting challenge.'

Mills looked at Phil. He had an amused expression. Yes, it *was* a joke, thought Mills.

'Small labs can't compete with places like Wakefield,' he said after a pause.

'But they do work for the police,' Nige pointed out. 'Someone has to work for the defence.'

He's right, thought Mills but Phil was looking sceptical. Nina, who was clearing the dinner plates, called the children back to the table for pudding.

'Anyway,' said Mills, turning to Phil, 'Nige said you had some news.'

He grinned. 'I've already told these guys – I've been offered a full-time post for three years.'

'At Nottingham?' Mills asked.

'Yes and no. It's on their staff but a lot of the time I'll be working in the States. It's a joint project with the Smithsonian's Department of Anthropology in Washington.'

He looked pleased with himself.

Mills forced a smile, trying to put enthusiasm into her congratulations.

'It starts in the new year,' he added.

She wanted to ask if he'd be working with Maria but let

him carry on describing the brilliant team he'd be joining in America while she concentrated on eating her rice pudding. She was having difficulty swallowing. And guess what, he was going to be studying bones from different geographical regions to research, among other things, diet.

'Isn't that Maria's area?' Mills asked, knowing the answer.

'Yes, she's one of the main collaborators. I've got her to thank for getting me the job.'

I'm sure you have, Mills thought.

Now dinner was over the twins were demanding to play football. Rosie said it was too cold and her mother agreed. Mills was relieved to see Nige and Phil heading off to the park with the boys, leaving her to help Nina clear up after lunch.

Nina had been watching Mills; she could see that Phil's news had affected her although she'd said little. He was clearly oblivious to the impact his plans were having on her despite the fact she'd warned him as tactfully as she could. Nige would have been the same, charging in without thinking. Until now she'd thought her friend was misjudging Phil's feelings for her but it did appear that he saw Mills in the same way he thought of her and Nige – as a friend.

They had set up a rhythm together, Nina was washing plates before placing them on the draining board for Mills to dry.

Neither spoke until, finally, Nina turned to her and asked, 'What do you think about Phil's new job?'

'It sounds good, it's an interesting topic.'

'I mean what about him going to the States. We'll miss

him.'

'It's what he does, Nina. He's always going away.'

'I suppose.' She carried on washing plates. 'What about Harris?'

'He'll stay with me. He's no trouble.'

When they'd finished Nina made a cup of tea and they sat chatting about the future, if any, of Yardley Forensics. Nina thought the idea of a lab devoted to defence work was a good one but neither of them could see how it could be set up without funds. Then Nina asked if Mills had heard from the last DNA test customer.

'Yes, I have.' She sounded cagey.

'I guess that's Jordan Henderson?' Nina asked.

'Yes, he asked to meet me.'

'When?'

'I saw him on Friday.'

'What?'

'He came to uni. He wanted to know if the test was accurate.'

'Did you get his address, Mills?'

She was shaking her head.

'His phone number?'

'No.'

Nina was in work mode now, fetching a notepad to jot down any relevant details. She quizzed Mills about the man's age, appearance and attitude; what he asked and how he reacted. Her friend, looking anxious, asked why she was so interested.

'Ruby has checked out all the other names you gave us and eliminated them. He's the only contact who asked to meet Tim face to face. We can't identify him because his phone is pay-as-you-go.'

'You can email him.'

'Yes, we could, but I'd prefer to know a bit more about him first – to eliminate him if we can. Could you get an address from him somehow?'

'You think he might be…'

Nina didn't want to say too much. 'We just want to know who he is.' If he's not Jordan Henderson, she thought.

Nina was saved from further discussion by Rosie joining them. Her daughter wanted to show Mills her latest fluorescent picture. Soon they were discussing school and inevitably the conversation turned to the holidays. Mills asked Rosie if they would be at home for Christmas.

Nina answered for her. 'We'll go to my parents on Christmas Eve. They do celebrate, despite being Hindus, but they don't drink and they're vegetarian so it's a little different. We'll be back here for Christmas Day so Nige can drink and eat to excess before flopping in front of the TV. You should come.'

Her friend laughed. 'It sounds fun but I think I'll be going down to London. Dad and Fiona are keen to see me.'

Nina understood that Mills would have mixed feelings about spending time with her family. 'Shopping in London at Christmas, who wouldn't want to be there?' she said.

'Can *we* go?' Rosie asked her mother.

'I wish. I've got to go into work on Boxing Day this year.'

It wasn't long before the boys were back and Nina was busy making tea. As she moved in and out of the living room she heard Mills asking Phil what he planned to do about Harris. He was trying to abdicate responsibility, citing the fact that she'd brought Harris from the animal sanctuary without consulting him. Neither gave in to the other. After a quick cup of tea Phil announced he had to get back and said his goodbyes rather hurriedly. She felt sorry for Mills.

After Phil had gone Nina told Nige to get the boys bathed and whispered to Rosie to help him then she sat down next to Mills.

'So you get to keep the dog?' she said, giving her friend a nudge in the ribs.

Mills giggled. 'I told you it wouldn't work out. He's never going to settle in one place long enough.'

She waited to say goodnight to the boys when they came downstairs. Nina asked her to stay longer but her friend was keen to get back for Harris.

'Can *we* have a dog, Mummy?' Rosie asked when Mills had gone.

Nina always gave the same answer. 'When you're old enough to take it walks and feed it and wash its bed, then you can have a dog.'

Her daughter stomped upstairs, pushing past Nige as he was coming down.

'She's growing into a sulky teenager already,' he remarked, slumping down beside Nina. 'Has Mills gone?'

'She went just after you took the boys up.'

'Is she all right? She looked a bit, well, you know...'

'I'm surprised you noticed, but yes I think she is a bit despondent right now. Phil didn't exactly let her down gently.'

'I could never work out whether they're together or

not,' Nige said, turning on the television.

'I don't think Mills could either,' Nina commented as she got up to start ironing school uniforms.

Monday morning Mills woke with a headache. She went downstairs to let Harris out and made a mug of tea. The dog soon came back inside, his hair was wet and his paws left grubby marks on the tiles. Rain matched her mood as she rinsed out the empty wine bottle from the night before and put it in the recycling. Her feet were getting cold so she picked up her mug and a packet of paracetamols, shut Harris in the kitchen and went back to bed. She sat up with the pillows behind her, staring at the walls. It was still dark outside but soon it would be time to get up. What was the point of going in to uni when she could work just as easily at home? She considered the possibilities. She could tell Muriel not to bother – that *she* would be walking Harris in the rain. Muriel would undoubtedly bring something round for her to eat and stay chatting. On other occasions that would sound attractive but not this morning. She finished her tea and went into the bathroom to shower.

Breakfast was half a piece of toast, a crust, the other half was mouldy and had gone in the bin. A second mug of tea and she was ready to go. Harris looked up from his bed as she put her waterproof jacket on. He knew the routine.

'You're in the right place,' she told him as she pulled her hood up and went out.

The wind was blowing the rain in her face as she unlocked the car. A rivulet of water trickled down the inside of the door and dripped onto her jeans. A soft top car was fun in the summer but there was a downside. She'd known it wasn't practical when Fiona had said she no longer needed the Mini but as her Dad had said, "Don't look a gift horse in the mouth." Well this gift horse's windscreen wipers weren't too hot either, come to that.

It must have been raining steadily overnight because the road into Reeth was flooded in places and Mills had to take it slowly, praying the engine would keep going. Traffic on the main roads was busy making the journey long and tedious even for a Monday. She circled the full car park, eventually finding a space so narrow no-one else had attempted to park in it. She managed to open her door just enough to squeeze out between the cars. She anticipated a rude note on her windscreen when she returned. She went straight to the cafeteria to collect a coffee, taking one back for Nige before remembering he would already be in lectures. But it wasn't wasted. With the equivalent of four shots she was sufficiently caffeine-fuelled to face her inbox.

Simon Pringle was suggesting they meet up for a drink in the week. He certainly was persistent. Maybe, just maybe, she would take him up on the offer. After all he had good taste when it came to wining and dining. She replied that she was free on Wednesday and pressed "send" before she changed her mind. There was a message from Nina asking her to blind copy her in on the email she would be sending to Jordan Henderson. Mills wrote to him suggesting she needed his address for her records.

Her headache was almost gone; she felt quite revived now and had cleared her inbox by coffee time. After another flat white she tackled what was left and celebrated with a bowl of chips to accompany her sandwich at lunchtime. Looking forward to an entire afternoon to spend on her research, she made the mistake of checking her messages. Jordan Henderson had replied that he had no fixed address at present – sorry.

'Do you think he's got something to hide?' Mills asked Nina when she told her.

Her friend didn't answer, which meant there was something suspicious going on.

'OK,' Mills said. 'I won't ask but shall I try to meet him again? You could come along this time.'

'No, Mills. That's not a good idea.'

'I could ask him to come to discuss some more information I've found,' she suggested.

'No Mills, do not do that please.' Nina sounded adamant.

But after the call Mills was thinking about the black car Henderson was driving. If she could get the registration number the police would be able to trace him. She was a woman of action today, nothing ventured nothing gained. She typed: *Hi Jordan, I've got some further information confirming the accuracy of the DNA test. Can you come over tomorrow at 10 am? regards Dr Sanderson.* Unsure what she would tell him she sent the message off.

She needed shopping and wanted to speak to Jean Price again so she grabbed her laptop – it was easier to work at home anyway.

Mills had expected an icy reception when she knocked on the farmhouse door but Jean looked almost relieved and invited her inside. The kitchen was warm and smelt of baking. Mills started with an apology but Jean interrupted her, telling her to sit down at the large pine table. She sat opposite her with her hands clasped in her lap.

'I wanted to speak to you and this is a good time because Lucy is having tea with a friend. What you said about the Saturday before Guy Fawkes – Justin was out that night,' she coughed. 'He was out very late, which is unusual for him. He said he was at a mate's but I've spoken to the mother,' she paused. 'And he wasn't.' She looked up at Mills. 'Do you really think…?'

'Jean, he bought a petrol can at the garage in Reeth that weekend and filled it with petrol.'

She looked puzzled. 'How do you know that?'

Embarrassed, Mills answered, 'I asked.'

'But you said the fire was started with red diesel.'

'I know, that was the assumption because of the empty can in the Manor's garden but apparently it's almost impossible to start a fire with diesel, I've checked.' Mills had to be careful now. 'I think whoever set fire to the moor tried with red diesel first but failed and chucked the can away then came back with petrol for a second try.'

Mills looked across at Jean.

'It sounds as if my son has some explaining to do,' she said.

'I know things have been strained between David and the Banfords,' Mills said. 'But that appears more to do with Gareth and Justin not getting on at university. Do you know what that was about?'

'It was something to do with licensing for killing nuisance birds, I think. I'd have to ask Justin.'

Mills stood up, it was time to leave.

But Jean stopped her. 'He'll be home in half an hour,'

she said. 'Please stay. I want to get this sorted out before…' she hesitated, 'it goes any further.'

Mills didn't know whether Jean was worried about gossip or her son's actions escalating. She sat back down while Jean put the kettle on and buttered one of the scones cooling by the Aga to give to Mills. When the tea was ready to pour she brought it to the table and they sat together listening to the clock ticking. Eventually Jean asked Mills what she was doing these days. Relieved, she responded by describing the last month in detail: the fire at the lab, the discovery of Tim's body, her boss's reaction. She'd just started on how uncertain the future was when the door opened. Mills looked up and Jean turned round in her chair.

'What?' asked Justin as he came inside and stopped abruptly.

'Sit down, Justin,' his mother ordered.

He hovered, apparently deciding whether to obey but she repeated the command and he pulled a chair out at the far end of the table. He was looking over at Mills as he did so. Once he was seated, Jean began in a measured tone, calm but firm. She was treating him like a child, making Mills nervous of his reaction.

'Justin, love, we need to ask you some questions about a fire in Mossy Bank.'

Mills couldn't detect any reaction.

Jean continued. 'Someone set fire to land very close to the Banford's place.' She looked at Mills. 'It was the Saturday before Guy Fawkes night.'

They were expecting Justin to say something but he sat expressionless.

Jean carried on. 'The person who set fire to the land

used petrol.' She paused. 'We know you bought petrol in a can from Reeth garage.'

Mills could see he was becoming anxious.

'I did but that was ages ago.'

Jean looked across at her.

'I'm afraid it was that weekend,' Mills said.

'But why would I want to start a fire?' he demanded.

'You tell me Justin.' His mother had remained composed throughout. 'Millie, what was the thing about the red diesel again?'

She explained that a small can that had held red diesel had been found in the Manor's garden. 'Whoever the arsonist was threw the can over the wall when the diesel wouldn't light,' she concluded.

Jean pushed her chair back to stand up. 'Should we look for our can, Justin? Or will it be missing?'

The young man's face was a picture. He seemed almost in tears as he put his elbows on the table and held his head in his hands.

Jean sighed loudly. 'So it *was* you. What on earth were you thinking, lad?'

It was definitely time for Mills to go. 'I'm sorry Jean but I've really got to get back.'

She made for the door and Jean followed her outside, asking what Mills was going to do about Justin.

'It's up to you Jean,' she answered. 'I won't be doing anything. But you might want to sort out the rift between your family and the Banfords, particularly if you want to buy some of their land.'

Chapter 20

Mills had woken early, anxious about her impending meeting with Jordan Henderson. Uncertain what to say to him, she rehearsed various scenarios as she drove into work. So she was partly relieved when she read his latest email – at first. *We have nothing more to discuss.* It began. But then, *Keep out of my business or you will regret it.* The threatening tone of the message concerned her and she immediately rang Nina.

'That sounds rather an extreme reaction when you only asked for his address!' exclaimed her friend.

Mills was deciding whether to admit that she'd asked to meet him. 'It wasn't just that.'

'What?'

'I asked him to meet me again. I thought I could get a bit more information out of him.'

She heard Nina sigh at the other end. 'Mills, now you've frightened him off. Tell me, what was the purpose of his particular test?'

'I think it was a paternity test. He submitted two samples. We identified them by his initials.'

'Right. Get the profiles onto FINDS as soon as possible.'

'But...'

'I don't care how you do it, just do it! At least we'll see if they're on the national database.'

So instead of entertaining Jordan Henderson, Mills spent the first part of the day contacting Donna to send her the DNA profiles marked JH. Once they were in her possession she rang Robert at the Wakefield lab and asked him for a favour. Fortunately he was happy to oblige and by twelve she was able to confirm with Nina that the profiles had been entered on FINDS.

It was a relief to spend the afternoon on a practical session with the second-year students who were taking her option on forensic analysis. They were in the laboratory preparing soil samples for mineralogical examination. The ten students were working quietly in pairs; some hunched over microscopes, others sifting soil through different sized sieves. Mills had a postgraduate demonstrator to answer questions so there was little for her to do but watch. She passed the time checking the previous week's work until it was four-thirty, time to clear up and go home.

It was dark when Mills left the building. She always parked her Mini near one of the bright lights that illuminated the car park. There was no-one else about but as soon as she closed the car door a set of headlights lit up her rear view mirror. She waited, thinking the car behind would move off but after a minute she gave up and backed out carefully. She checked her mirror as she made for the exit, the car followed. She indicated left, so did the car. At every turn the headlights were behind her. At the traffic lights she could see it was a black saloon but not the driver. There are thousands of black cars on the road, she told herself but it spooked her and she decided to go via Richmond even though the traffic would be bad at that time.

She was sure it was still the same car behind her at the traffic lights as she entered the town. She took the second exit from the roundabout but only after circling it once. Then she made a detour through the market square before joining the road to Reeth. She assumed that if she was being followed they would be gone. She had no idea what sort of car was behind her now but she drove as fast as she dared until she reached Reeth, only slowing down through the village and at the turn off to Mossy Bank. When the car behind continued straight on, she breathed a sigh of relief and chided herself for being so stupid. However, she didn't feel safe until she was indoors with Harris.

She lit the fire after tea and settled down to watch TV, slowly relaxing until Harris suddenly jumped off the sofa. Then there was a knock at the door. Her heart was beating fast as she walked slowly down the hall and put the chain on the door before opening it. At first she couldn't make out the hooded figure on the doorstep.

'Justin, is that you?'

'Hello Dr Sanderson, I'm sorry to bother you.'

He stood waiting as Mills unhooked the chain and indicated for him to come inside. She told him to sit on the sofa, offering him a beer. He grinned and nodded. Once they were settled by the fire with a bottle each he began what was clearly a rehearsed speech.

'I know by rights you should report me to the police.'

'I told your mother I wouldn't.'

'Yes but I want to thank you for not telling them about me and the fire. It was a stupid thing to do and I'm really sorry.'

Seeing he had finished what he'd come to say, Mills asked him to explain to her why he'd done it. He looked sheepish, muttering something about it being a childish prank.

'Justin. I know you and Gareth Banford have history,' Mills said. 'Perhaps you could tell me what it's all about? It seems to me that the bad feeling between your families is because of you and Gareth, not your parents.'

He scratched his head before answering. 'It was at college last year. I was studying agriculture and he was doing sustainability. We kept bumping into each other at the university farm. At first it was cool, we knew each other although we didn't socialise.'

'So what went wrong?'

'I was in the bar one evening and he comes over with some mates. I was talking about our farm and somehow, I don't know why, we got onto shooting crows and rooks. One of his friends, a girl, started banging on about how it shouldn't be allowed. I told them, they can attack young lambs, we've seen it at home. It developed into a right row. After that we didn't speak and his mates shouted things at me when they saw me. It was stupid.'

'And you just turned the other cheek?'

He looked abashed. 'No, me and my mates pulled a few stunts as well.'

'So what happens now, Justin? How are you going to sort it out so your dad can expand the farm?'

He didn't know. Mills considered the options while she fetched two more bottles.

'I guess the Banford's will be down here over Christmas as usual?'

'I suppose so.'

She had been on the verge of offering to act as a kind of mediator but realised that she would probably not be in Mossy Bank at Christmas. 'Well, you've got a bit of time to think up something before then. Perhaps find some common ground away from birds.'

As he left he thanked her profusely and told her that his mother wanted to invite her for dinner on Sunday. It was nothing special just a family meal. She said she would be delighted.

Mention of the family meal reminded her of a call she had to make. But when she rang her father to say she'd love to come down for the holidays, his response was unexpected.

'Sorry Mills, we got a late booking yesterday. We left it over two weekends in case you called but when you didn't Fi said we should go for it. I was going to ring but you know Fi – she just did it.'

Mills couldn't hide her annoyance. 'That's all right, Dad, I'll probably go to Spain with Phil.'

'That'll be nice, love. Do you want to speak to Fi? She's here.'

'No, it's fine. I must go. Speak to you soon, bye.'

Well, that was a slap in the face, thought Mills, typical of Fiona. She could've rung before booking. Anyway, who goes skiing with a five year-old? They're probably taking the nanny as well.

Ruby handed Nina the test sheet as soon as she came through the door, before she'd even take off her coat.

'Result!' the researcher said. 'They've got a match, it's just come through.'

Nina was busy reading the report. One of the two DNA samples submitted by Henderson, which they called a long code number followed by an A, was a partial match to the other, called B. That wasn't unexpected, she thought. But there was more. Sample A was a perfect match to two entries on the national database; they simply gave the code numbers.

'This is no help,' said Nina. 'Why haven't they put the person's name instead of these numbers?'

'I'm just looking them up,' replied Ruby distractedly. She was peering at her computer screen and typing rapidly. 'Here they are.' There was a pause. 'Wow.'

'What? Who is it?'

'They're the cigarette ends found at the scene of Jennifer Carr's murder,' she said slowly.

'Jordan Henderson's DNA matches Jennifer Carr's killer?' Nina was stunned.

'Well technically we can't say that but he definitely smoked the cigarettes found in Jennifer's front garden.'

Nina was thinking hard. It was a worrying coincidence and she hoped it wasn't a case of cross-contamination. The samples had all been analysed at Yardley Forensics and Henderson's samples were handled by someone who wasn't properly qualified to carry out the test. Had Tim Fletcher contaminated the samples from the Carr murder? If so, he'd effectively destroyed the only evidence they had that might lead to identifying a suspect.

Mills wasn't answering her phone so Nina left a message for her to ring back *immediately*. There were two scenarios here and she wasn't happy with either of them. If Henderson was Jennifer Carr's killer, how were they going to locate him without knowing his identity? If the cigarettes were contaminated with Henderson's DNA, they had lost any chance of finding the killer.

When Hazel arrived Nina quickly updated her before they

went together to see their DI. Mitch listened patiently then told Hazel to treat the DNA match seriously. She argued furiously that it was obviously a case of contaminated evidence.

'That laboratory tested the DNA samples from the crime scene, from the victim and the suspect. Now it appears in samples analysed by some maverick analyst who was running an amateur DNA testing scam at night. What d'you expect?'

Nina offered to speak to Mills, who would be able to tell them exactly where such cross-contamination could occur.

'If you ask me it's a good thing the laboratory has closed down,' commented her colleague.

'Hazel, I need you to find out if there's any connection between this Jordan Henderson and Jennifer Carr,' Mitch ordered.

'We're pretty sure it's a pseudonym,' Nina said.

'That does make it difficult unless someone has seen the guy.'

Nina hesitated before admitting that Dr Sanderson had met him. Hazel was suitably incensed.

'What's she been meddling in it for?'

Nina scowled at her colleague. 'She contacted all the people who sent DNA samples to Tim Fletcher. As it happened she met up with Henderson at the university.'

Fortunately Mitch didn't want to know more. He asked Hazel to go over the details of the Carr case again to see whether any names had cropped up that they hadn't been able to check. Nina offered to contact Mills so she could give a full description of the man calling himself Henderson.

It was late when Mills woke. She pushed Harris outside although he wasn't keen to spend long in the frosty air.

'Don't worry,' she told him. 'Muriel won't take you far in this.'

She dressed in her warmest sweater, the one with only a little hole in the elbow, and her baggy woollen trousers. They didn't really go together but she would be warm. Grabbing a slice of toast she ran for the door, knowing it would take ages to scrape the windscreen. It was only as she was driving and thinking about what the day would bring that she remembered with horror that she was meeting Simon Pringle for lunch. She thought about going home to change but she was over halfway to uni and it was already late. As it was she'd only just make it in time for her ten o'clock lecture.

She read her messages as she made her way to the lecture hall. Nina wanted to speak to her urgently – it would have to wait, the students were lined up in rows expecting her to entertain them for the next hour. Fortunately she had some interesting case studies that included a couple of murder investigations.

Nige was on the phone when she got back to the office at the end of the session.

'Nina's been trying to contact you – here.'

He handed her his landline so she had to stand in front of his desk while his wife explained the curious results obtained from Jordan Henderson's samples.

'Hazel is convinced it's a mix-up at the lab. Could it really be contamination?'

Mills was thinking fast. Tim was a professional analyst, she was sure he wouldn't have messed things up but if he had, the reputation of the lab would be in ruins. She would have to investigate, and fast. 'I guess it will depend a lot on the dates the various samples were tested,' she said. 'Donna will know.'

'Please ask her, it's really important.'

'I'll get back to you this afternoon.'

'Yes you will. I need you over here to provide a full description of the man we know as Henderson. What time can you be here?'

It was the perfect excuse not to meet Simon in her old clothes. 'I'll come over as soon as I've spoken to Donna.'

When Mills got through, Donna told her excitedly that she had an interview at Wakefield. Then she asked after Brenda, leaving Mills feeling bad because she had no idea. She promised to find out.

'Listen Donna, the police have come up with some confusing results from our DNA samples. They're saying Tim may have contaminated their forensic evidence. Is that possible?'

Donna wasn't sure without knowing the details.

'First tell me when you tested the cigarettes,' suggested Mills.

'It was a few days before the fire wasn't it? I can look it up now.'

'Wait. There's another one: when did Tim test the samples with the initials JH?'

'Hold on, I can do all this now if you like. The info is on my laptop.'

Mills waited. She could hear the clicking as Donna typed. A few minutes later she was back on the phone.

'He tested the two JH swabs over a couple of days in the week commencing the fifteenth of October.'

'Is there any possibility that DNA from those samples could have contaminated the evidence from the Carr murder?'

There was silence at the other end. Finally she said, 'Absolutely not. Tim's work was finished in October. We didn't receive the police evidence until November. They weren't in the lab at the same time.'

'Are you sure? What about the equipment? Could he have contaminated it somehow?'

'Well if he did, it would have shown up sooner. Other samples would have been affected. Everything is done to avoid contamination, it's really quite impossible.' She began to sound upset.

'OK, that's fine then but I had to ask to confirm it.'

Mills wished her luck with her interview and said goodbye but Donna had a question.

'Should I have received my salary for November by now?'

Of course, that's why the girl was asking after Brenda. Mills promised to sort it out and put the phone down. It was nearly noon so Simon would be coming to meet her any minute. She grabbed her jacket and bag.

'If Professor Pringle is looking for me, can you tell him I had to go to Northallerton on a police matter?' she asked Nige.

There was a departmental tour in the afternoon and a large number of teenagers were milling about in reception. She struggled to get past the queue waiting to sign the visitors book. The car park had been gritted but there were still patches of ice where puddles had formed and frozen. She rang Nina before setting off to tell her she'd be less than an hour. Once she was out on the road it was fine and there was little traffic, she reached Northallerton in half an hour and after finding somewhere to park she was in Nina's office in the police headquarters by ten to one.

Ruby was sitting at her desk eating a wrap. Nina offered Mills a coffee and passed her one of her own sandwiches. While they ate Mills explained why there couldn't have been any contamination of the cigarette ends.

'...and anyway, if the DNA was contaminated it wouldn't be such a clean match,' she concluded.

That seemed to satisfy them both but Nina told her to send a report for Hazel, who was certain the samples had been mixed up. Then Nina asked Mills to describe Henderson in as much detail as possible. She did her best but there seemed little to remember. She described his clothing, the distinctive red padded jacket, but apart from the fact he was white, clean-shaven with short hair she remembered nothing distinctive about him. What age was he? Maybe thirty-five or forty years old? Mills was unsure about his accent but still thought he was from Manchester. And he drives a black car. If only she had the registration, they agreed.

Mills left Northallerton on the Thirsk road. She would visit Brenda to sort out why the staff had not been paid but on the way she wanted to take another look at the lab. It was a sorry sight, boarded up and padlocked, with graffiti on the plywood covering the windows. No wonder Donna wanted to move on. And once the staff disappeared it would be hard to give it a new lease of life. She started the engine, pleased to leave it behind.

Her boss was surprised to see her. She switched off the

television, offering her a cup of tea. Mills followed her into the kitchen, which was reasonably tidy. Perhaps Brenda was finally recovering from the trauma of Tim's death.

'I had another visit from that insurance woman last week,' she said, filling the kettle. 'She's still investigating me.'

'Oh dear. Can I ask how bad it is?' Mills ventured. 'Only I was speaking to Donna…'

'Oh and she's been on to me.'

That was quick, thought Mills. 'Was it about her November salary?'

'No, pet, she's got an interview. They're going to send me a request for a reference and she wants to be sure I'll respond promptly.'

'Did she not ask about her pay?'

Brenda looked puzzled. 'Why?'

'No-one's been paid for last month, Brenda.'

She was surprised, had no idea why not, and would get in touch with the bank immediately. She disappeared into the dining room, which served as her study and Mills heard her talking animatedly for some time. Then there was silence. Eventually she finished the call, reappearing to announce that there were no funds to pay the salary bill.

'Didn't they let you know?' Mills asked.

'The book-keeper did call a little while ago to say it might be a problem but there were some outstanding payments. I assumed they would cover it.'

Mills sighed. 'Shall we ring to find out what to do?'

She followed Brenda into the dining room where the table was covered in papers and sat opposite her while she rang the book-keeper. As soon as there was an answer she told Mills to take the phone. After explaining who she was, she asked to know what the current financial position was regarding Yardley Forensics. The man was polite and sympathetic as he described the situation as "dire". The only advice he could offer was if Brenda was willing to cover the salaries herself, nearly eight thousand pounds.

Her boss offered to transfer the money straight away.

'Donna, Glyn and the others will be paid by the end of the week,' she said as she put the phone down. 'If you tell me how many hours you did last month…'

'There's no need for that, it was only a few,' Mills said and changed the subject. 'I've just come from talking to Nina Featherstone.'

'Your policewoman friend?'

'Yes, she was quizzing me about possible cross-contamination between their DNA evidence and a set of the samples Tim was doing out of hours.'

She waited for Brenda's response.

'Is that possible?'

'Donna says not but Hazel Fuller is making an issue out of it. I've got to give them a report explaining why it's not possible. If there was contamination their samples from the Carr murder would be completely compromised.'

'I'm sure Donna will be right in her evaluation.'

'If she is, I'm guessing this guy is somehow connected with the murder.'

'Really?'

'So I'm thinking he might also be a potential suspect for torching the lab.'

Brenda seemed to be digesting the information. 'If

that's true, and they can prove it, it will be a great weight off my mind.'

Mills assumed she meant the suspicion hanging over her that she'd started the fire herself. 'So have you thought any more about selling the business?'

Brenda snorted. 'Selling what? There's nothing left!'

'You know that's not true.' Her boss started to raise objections but Mills persisted. 'I know it's a mess but it's still a piece of commercial land in the middle of Harrogate, which must be worth something. But more importantly it was a forensics laboratory doing work for the police.'

'Might I remind you it was a business that was losing money.'

'But in the right hands, maybe someone with a niche set of tests could turn it round. Nina suggested specialising in defence work.'

'No-one's going to get rich working for the defence. Would *you* risk it?'

'If I had the money,' Mills responded. 'It would be fun trying.'

Chapter 21

Ruby was looking through the CCTV from the car park at the University of North Yorkshire. Their security guy had been happy to provide it and she'd downloaded the file expecting to identify Henderson arriving in his black car. However, the quality of the picture was appalling.

'Either it was raining or they need to clean their camera glass,' she told Nina. 'I can hardly make out the cars never mind their number plates. The people are just dark shadows, it's useless.'

Nina had been just as disappointed with the description of Henderson provided by Mills.

'Have *you* found anything?' she asked Hazel, who'd spent the morning trawling through the details of Jennifer Carr's murder.

'Nothing,' she replied, slamming the file shut. 'The woman was a paragon. The only man in her life was her husband. I'm going over to see him now.'

She picked up the file and struggled into her coat. She was convinced it would be a waste of time but Mitch had insisted she speak to him face to face about Henderson, in case he was an acquaintance, despite the possibility that he was using a pseudonym. All the Sanderson woman knew about him was that he might have a Manchester accent. What a nightmare.

'Would *you* like to go instead?' she asked Nina, who was much better with bereaved partners.

'Sorry, I've got to finish the report on the DNA profile

matches,' Nina replied.

Ruby was smirking and Hazel told her to get lost before slamming the door behind her. At least she'd be able to have a cigarette on the way. The chat with Mr Carr would take no more than fifteen minutes so she could take a detour into town on the way back to get the shopping, to save doing it on the way home.

The Carr's house was an older property, terraced but with a decent front garden. It was in the shrubbery to the left of the front door that the two cigarette ends had been found. The smoker must have been waiting some time for Jennifer. Why she came outside that night wasn't established, possibly to answer the door, maybe to put out the empty milk bottle that was still standing on the doorstep in the morning. It didn't mean the person waiting for her was the killer, although everyone now assumed it was. Hazel was still of the view that you were most likely to be murdered by a member of your family so she was distrustful of the husband when he answered the door.

He led her into the sitting room, offered tea and when she refused took a seat opposite her. He looked about fifty although Hazel knew he was only forty-two. He was dressed in a suit and tie so she assumed he'd come straight from the travel agency he owned.

'Just a couple of quick questions, Mr Carr,' she began.

'Has there been a development?' he asked anxiously. 'When you rang I assumed it was to give me some news.'

'We're not sure, that's why I wanted to speak to you. You see we've come across someone who might, just might, be of interest to us.'

He leaned forward, concentrating on her every word. It

was extremely irritating.

'Does the name Jordan Henderson mean anything to you?'

He frowned. 'Yes of course. Why?'

'How do you know him?'

'I don't *know* him exactly. Why would I? He's a footballer.'

Hazel sighed. 'So you don't know anyone else called Jordan Henderson?'

He shook his head. 'No.'

'Thank you. What about someone with a Manchester accent?' This is ridiculous, she told herself.

He was looking even more bemused. 'You mean acquaintances?'

Well I didn't mean celebrities, she thought, but smiled and nodded. 'Or friends of your wife.'

Now he straightened up in his chair. 'Do you mean "men friends"?'

Hazel shrugged. 'I mean men who were friends of your wife.'

He thought about it for a while. 'All her male friends are my friends and none of them are from Manchester as far as I know. What is this all about?'

'I can't really say at present. It may be nothing at all, in fact it probably is, but I had to check.'

She got up to leave and he followed her. As he went to open the front door Hazel feared he was going to cry. No, please no, she thought. He stood holding the door handle, trapping her in the hall.

'I know I should want to find out who killed Jenny,' he said with a tremor in his voice, 'but it won't bring her back. Harriet will still grow up without her mummy.'

'I understand but we should try to get justice for Jennifer, shouldn't we?'

Hazel couldn't get out of there quick enough. She should've forced Nina to go instead – she was good at that sort of thing. It just gave her the creeps. As expected the trip was a waste of time, except for the fact that she could now get tonight's tea and have a quick look in the shops. She simply had to get a new top before the night out with the girls on Friday.

Simon had messaged Mills, asking if everything was all right. Apparently he'd got the impression she was in trouble with the law.

'I told him it was a police matter,' Nige said with a grin when she asked him what he'd been saying.

'I know you don't like him but he's been really supportive,' Mills said.

Nige's response was to tell her to be careful.

'Anyway, I'm going to have lunch with him today so I can tell him what I was doing myself.'

She'd chosen her outfit carefully. Jeans for a casual look, although they were the ones she kept for best. Her sweater was fairly new, in a green-blue that she thought matched her eyes. She'd washed her hair in the morning so it stayed straight and she'd used some make-up.

'I wondered why you were all tarted up,' Nige said.

'Behave,' she replied with a smile, 'or I'll report you for lewd comments.'

Simon arrived in the reception area apologising, although he was only a few minutes late.

'Third year toxicology,' he said. 'Always overruns. They ask too many questions, little swots,' he joked. 'So where would you like to go?'

Mills thought he would suggest somewhere.

'It's your turn, Mills. I'm not sure you enjoyed my last choice so I think you should decide.'

Embarrassed, Mills said she was happy to go down the road. There was a pub within walking distance popular with staff and students alike. Simon agreed it was a good idea and they set off. Fortunately although the bar was crowded they managed to find a small rickety table by the fire. Mills soon discovered why it was empty as she warmed up. She asked for a coke and Simon came back with a beer for himself. Mills chose a chicken pie off the specials board that came with chips and peas. Simon thought it a good choice and went to order two. When he returned he asked why she'd had to rush off the day before.

'It was just something to do with the lab burning down,' she said keeping it vague. 'The police wanted to know about someone I'd seen.'

'Well that's a relief, your colleague had me worried. And what's happening to the lab? When will they start rebuilding?'

Mills took a sip of her drink. 'I don't think they will. I was talking to the owner and she has no intention of starting again. I told her she should sell the business.'

Simon agreed. 'So how come you were working as a consultant there?'

'It's a long story but basically I met Brenda through an osteoarchaeologist I worked with. She bought the lab as a going concern from Bishop Laboratories about ten years ago. I used to work there part-time until I was taken on as a full-time lecturer.'

He asked what sort of forensic investigations the lab used to do.

'It was mainly police work, lots of routine DNA and fingerprints but we had elemental techniques for matching glasses, paints, that sort of thing. We even had digital forensics for a while. Getting rid of that was the start of the financial downturn.'

He asked if they covered forensic toxicology and it was her turn to ask about his work. He trained as a chemist, before moving into toxicological analysis when he graduated.

'I went to the States to do my postgrad work,' he said. 'That's where I met my wife. I spent six years over there all together.'

'What research did you do?' Mills asked.

'Developing ways of identifying what in those days were referred to as "legal highs". It was a race to keep up with the different forms of psychoactive substances coming onto the market each week. They result in ten thousand deaths a year in America.'

'Seriously? And is that what you do now?'

'Yes and no. I'm still working on psychoactive substances but now I'm researching how to identify them in combination with other drugs such as opioids and tranquillisers.'

Mills listened to him as he described the array of techniques he'd had at his disposal in the States. Eventually she asked him why he decided to return to England when clearly the university over here was less well equipped. He explained he much preferred the British way of life but his wife had found it difficult to settle here. She missed her family, travelling back frequently until one time she decided to stay. Mills didn't know what to say and was saved by their food arriving.

'Anyway, she's met some chap now, according to my son.'

'You have a son. How old is he?'

'Arnie's nine. He's great. He lives with his mother but spends time in the holidays over here.'

'You must miss him.'

'Yes.'

They ate in silence.

'So what do you like to do in the evenings Mills?' asked Simon after a while.

She shrugged. 'The usual things I suppose, although at the moment I tend to stay in with Harris.'

'Is Harris your partner?'

Mills laughed. 'Harris is my dog. He's a lurcher. I got him from a rescue centre a few months ago.'

She had to explain what a lurcher looked like and ended up showing him photos on her phone. She told him how Muriel acted like a child minder for him.

'So you live alone?'

'Yes I do.'

'Is that why you got the dog?'

'No, not at all, Harris really belongs to Phil, the osteoarchaeologist I mentioned. He'd had a dog before he went away. When he came back he was ill with post-traumatic stress disorder. I stupidly thought it would be good for him to have a dog.'

'That must've been hard, the PTSD I mean.'

Mills agreed. She found herself telling him how difficult it was to get Phil to accept medical help.

'Anyway he's better since he went to Nottingham so

I'm left with Harris.' She stopped, embarrassed that she'd said so much. 'I'm sorry, I didn't mean to go on about it.'

'Don't worry. So will you keep Harris?'

'Oh yes I couldn't take him back, he's far too attached to me.'

'And you to him?'

Mills laughed. 'You could say that.'

'So this guy is in Nottingham?'

She nodded.

'Well, that's not so far away.'

'Yes but funnily enough he's going to work in Washington after Christmas.'

'I guess that's something we have in common then. Would you like another drink?'

Mills asked for a coffee and watched as he stood waiting to order. A man who'd been sitting at a table joined him, slapping him on the back and they seemed to be sharing a joke. She hoped it wasn't at her expense. She'd recognised a couple of people from the department and assumed he was from uni. When he'd been served Simon left him at the bar.

'A colleague of yours?' she asked as he put the coffees down.

'Don't you know Gordon? He looks after forward planning. Been here years I believe. He was telling me how jammy I am.'

Mills feared she'd been the subject of their merriment.

'Yes,' he continued, 'he'd just heard about the million pound grant I've got for equipment.'

'Wow.'

'Yes, I'm very excited. It includes money for a technician who will spend a hundred percent of their time on the project. Of course it means I'll take on several research students as well.'

Finally it was time to leave the warmth of the fire and get back to work. Simon helped her on with her jacket and held the door as they emerged into the cold. It wasn't late but already it was growing gloomy and they hurried up the road to the departmental building. They entered the reception area one by one through the revolving door and Mills emerged first, so it was her that the suited man approached.

'I've got an appointment with Professor Cole,' he said. 'Do you know where I can find him?'

There was no-one at the reception desk; Mills peered into the little room behind it but it was empty. The usual procedure was for the visitor to sign in to receive a badge; the receptionist would then ring the office of the person they wanted to see and they would come down to escort them. Mills asked the visitor to sign in the book while she found someone to give him a visitor's badge.

'I'll let Professor Cole know you're here,' Simon offered. 'I'm on the same floor.'

He disappeared towards the lifts. Mills peered down the corridor hoping that someone would appear. Suddenly the receptionist emerged from the ladies cloakroom, walked quickly round to her position on the desk and asked for the visitor's name. Mills explained that Professor Cole had been informed, leaving her with nothing else to do. She wanted to say thank you for lunch – Simon had insisted on paying – but it was awkward hanging around for him to return so she walked back to the office to send a message thanking him.

Nige looked up when she walked in. 'Nice lunch? I

heard you were down the pub.'

So tongues were wagging already. She pulled a face. 'Yes it was a very nice lunch, so you can tell Nina I enjoyed it too.'

'Actually she wanted to speak to you.' He consulted a scrap of paper. 'She says can you remember anything else about Mr Henderson? She asked me but I wasn't here when he came to see you.'

'No you weren't.' But it occurred to her that someone else had been. 'Simon came in just as he was leaving,' she said. 'He might have noticed something.'

When she rang he offered to come down but Mills said she would come to his room, not wishing to have Nige listening in. She ran up the stairs and straight into his office.

'Hi Mills, I just wanted to say how much I enjoyed...'

'Yes, so did I. My treat next time though.'

'Next time?'

'Oh, I didn't mean... I...'

'I'll look forward to it. Actually, I wanted to ask you something.'

'Yes?'

'Prof Cole is having his usual Christmas drinks party on Saturday, I wondered if you were going?'

She shook her head. 'No I wasn't invited.'

'You could come as my plus one, if you wanted.'

Without a thought she nodded. She knew she would probably regret it later but it would be one in the eye for Prof Cole. There was a pause and she was reminded why she'd come to see him. 'I needed to speak to you urgently,' she began, trying to cover her embarrassment, 'because I had a visitor last Friday. He was just leaving when you came into the office.'

'Big chap, red jacket, stubbly beard.'

'You remember him? Was there anything else? I've been asked for a full description.'

He looked amused. 'Really? Well let me think.' He pondered. 'He was shouting as he pushed past me... something about a baby. "She'd lied about the baby." That's what he said. Which was why I was intrigued but you wouldn't enlighten me.'

'She lied about the baby?' she repeated.

'Yes, definitely, all very "EastEnders" I thought.'

Chapter 22

Nina couldn't contain her excitement when Mills reported what Simon had said. She told her friend to repeat it word for word.

'He actually said that?' Nina questioned her twice.

But when Mills asked her why it was so important, she refused to answer. 'Sorry, can't say any more at this stage.'

Nina passed the news onto Hazel and Ruby, who started making notes immediately.

'So Henderson, or whatever he is really called, had a DNA test showing that *she* – whoever *she* is – lied to him about a baby,' Ruby reflected back to her.

'Correct,' Nina replied. 'And, if the match between Henderson and the cigarettes is correct – and Mills assures me that cross-contamination is impossible – then there is a connection between him and Jennifer Carr.'

'I've read the report and I still don't believe contamination is absolutely one hundred percent impossible,' retorted Hazel.

'But any connection between the cigarettes and Jennifer Carr's killer is…'

'Circumstantial,' said Hazel.

'Are you suggesting that Henderson stood in the garden smoking two cigarettes that night and then walked away?' Nina countered.

Her fellow sergeant was looking irritated. 'We still can't guarantee the connection between Henderson and the cigarettes is valid.'

Nina looked at her. 'Let's assume, just for a minute, that the DNA profiles are correct, shall we? That Henderson smoked the cigarettes in the garden, agreed?'

'It's possible,' Ruby acknowledged

Hazel remained silent. She was playing with a paperweight on her desk.

Nina continued. 'He said to Mills "she lied to me". What if it was a paternity test and he was referring to Jennifer Carr? That sounds like a motive to me.'

'She only had one baby,' said Ruby.

'That's right,' said Hazel crossly. 'If he meant the daughter it was a very long time ago.'

'Ten years,' said Nina.

She looked across at Hazel, who was still fiddling with the paperweight. 'I think we should find Henderson as a matter of urgency.'

'Ruby, have we checked every single Jordan Henderson in the UK?' Hazel asked with a sigh.

The researcher nodded. 'It didn't take long. None meet the description Mills gave, even vaguely. Just one was slightly possible but wasn't anywhere near the university on the day Mills met him.'

Hazel sighed. 'I'll go and see what Mitch wants to do but I'm not happy. It'll be a complete waste of time if that laboratory has muddled everything up.'

It had certainly got Mills thinking. If Nina considered what Henderson had said to be important he must be something to do with the arson attack. So that evening she sat down with a blank sheet of paper and made a list of everything she could remember about their conversation. It wasn't easy. She'd been worried about the meeting and had been concentrating on what she was saying to him. She was nervous when she asked him why he'd wanted the DNA test. She hadn't recalled him saying anything about someone lying. When she shut her eyes she could see him sitting opposite her, his red jacket, the stubble on his chin. Then he knocked over the chair and stormed out.

But he was in the car park when she left so he must have gone out to his vehicle and waited – except he would have had to hand in his visitor's pass at reception. That's it! He must've signed in before he came to see her. So why didn't they ring her to say her visitor had arrived?

And that was why Mills was waiting in reception at eight the next morning, long before the desk was manned. Members of staff were arriving and so were visitors, who were beginning to form a queue. Consequently it was well after nine before Mills could quietly ask if she could look at the Visitors' Book. The girl behind the desk shrugged and pushed it towards her.

Her heart was racing as she flicked back to the previous Friday. He'd turned up on time wearing a visitor's pass so he must have signed the book. Eventually she found it. His signature was illegible but he'd printed his name – Jordan Henderson. More importantly he'd completed the final column. Now she had something she could give Nina. She scribbled it down on the back of her hand and rushed back to the office to call her.

'Nina? I've got something for you.'

Ruby could hear her colleague talking excitedly to her friend. After a few minutes she put down the phone, beaming.

'Finally we've got something on Jordan Henderson!'

she called across to Ruby. 'Mills has found his car registration number.'

She repeated it to Ruby, instructing her to check ownership immediately. She knew it would take a little while to gather all the information but she couldn't settle to anything while she waited.

'Coffee?' she asked.

By the time she came back with two mugs Ruby had a name.

'So the car is owned by a Michael Johnson.'

'Address?'

'Preston. Do you think it's him?'

'Whoever Michael Johnson is, Henderson is driving his car so we should interview him.'

'Right I'll get the local force to pick him up.'

While Nina waited anxiously for a result she went to give Mitch the good news. Her DI suggested another visit to Mr Carr to see if the name jogged his memory. In Hazel's absence, Nina offered to go and she had an idea, although she didn't share it with her boss.

Back at her desk she called Mills. 'Are you free to come with me to visit someone? We've got a name from the registration number you gave me and I want to run it past him. If he knows this man it will be useful to have someone who has seen Henderson to confirm they are the same person.'

As expected, her friend agreed enthusiastically and Nina said she would pick her up in half an hour. On the way Mills was curious about who they were going to meet, assuming it was to do with the arson attack. But Nina would say nothing, leaving her believing it related to the fire. She instructed Mills to keep quiet throughout the interview unless specifically asked to speak.

'Yes ma'am,' Mills promised with a mock salute.

They parked in front of the house and Mills followed Nina to the front door, standing behind her as they waited to be admitted. The owner, dressed in suit and tie, led them into the sitting room where she sat obediently next to her friend. Nina explained that she had someone they wanted to speak to about his wife's death. He was watching her steadily.

'Does the name Michael Johnson mean anything to you?' she asked.

He considered for a moment before leaning forward. 'I worked with a Mike Johnson years ago but it's quite a common name.'

'Where was that?' Nina asked, taking out a notebook.

'At a travel agency.'

'Go on.'

'It was my first job after I left university. He was already there. It was where I met Jenny.'

'So they would know each other?'

'Yes. At one stage we were all working there at the same time but I left about six months after Jenny arrived. I took a better paid job in another branch.'

'So did you keep in touch with this Mike Johnson?'

He shook his head.

'What about Jenny?'

'No. She left when she was expecting Harriet.'

Nina looked up and asked if by any chance he had a photograph of Mike Johnson.

'No.' He looked almost indignant. 'Why would I?'

'Would he have come to your wedding, for example?'

'I really can't remember.'

Nina sat waiting, pen poised. 'Do you have any wedding photos?' she asked eventually.

'Of course I do.'

'Perhaps we could have a quick look?'

He seemed irritated by her request but disappeared upstairs. They could hear him rummaging about above them.

Nina smiled at Mills. 'Do you think you'd recognise your Jordan Henderson if he was ten years younger?' she asked.

Mills shrugged.

He finally returned with a large photo album.

'Would you recognise Mr Johnson, if he's in any of the photos?' Nina asked.

'Oh yes,' he replied as he began turning the pages. Nina could see the early photos were of the happy couple and close relatives. Carr was looking tight-lipped and she guessed it was hard for him to confront the images. The rate at which he turned the pages slowed as he reached the guests lined up. He was scanning the rows, running his finger across them until at last he stopped and turned the album round to show them.

'That could be him,' he said.

Nina passed it across to Mills, pointing to the face at the end of the back row. She looked questioningly at her.

'Yes,' said Mills. 'It could be.'

Nina asked if he had a digital version of the photograph. He went off to download it from his computer and came back with a memory stick. It had clearly given him time to think and now he had questions.

'Is Mike a suspect?' he asked.

Nina avoided the question by asking what the man was

like.

'That's just it. He was a nice bloke. We all used to go to the pub on a Friday evening after work and he was a good mate at the time. That's why he was at our wedding. I'd forgotten all about him. I don't think he would've harmed Jenny. No, you're wrong there.'

'We just need to talk to him, that's all,' Nina said as she put the memory stick in her bag and was getting up to leave. 'We'll speak to you again soon.'

In the car Nina said Ruby would send the photograph over urgently so Mills could enlarge it on her monitor to confirm whether the man calling himself Henderson was Michael Johnson. Mills tried once again to quiz her about their visit now she'd worked out it wasn't about the fire at all.

'He called his wife Jenny,' Mills said. 'Was that Jennifer Carr's husband?'

'I said I wasn't going to discuss the case,' she told her friend, knowing Mills would put two and two together fairly quickly.

She dropped Mills back at the university and went straight to the office.

'Here you are, Ruby,' she said, almost throwing the memory stick onto her desk. 'There's a photo on there that needs to go over to Mills for identification purposes.'

The researcher put it in her computer. 'Wow that's a large file!' she exclaimed.

'Good, that means we'll get high definition on it. Let me see.'

She looked over Ruby's shoulder at the crowd of guests and indicated the man they wanted to interview.

'That's him.' Ruby enlarged the picture until the face

was clearly visible. 'I reckon she should be able to recognise him from that, don't you?'

'I don't see why not,' Ruby answered as she opened her email, typed a brief message and attached the photograph. 'By the way, he's not living at the Preston address any more. Apparently he moved out of the flat last year.'

'In that case, Ruby, we need to search ANPR data.'

Five minutes later Nina's phone rang. It was Mills sounding excited. 'Yes, it's him. I'm pretty certain.'

'Exactly how certain are you?'

'I'm ninety percent sure, no maybe eighty-five percent.'

Nina smiled. 'That's good enough for now. Thanks, Mills.'

'No problem. Nina, I was thinking if there was no contamination issue, Jordan Henderson's DNA really does match the cigarette profile. Have you considered that?'

'Yes,' Nina replied.

'Yes it does or yes you've considered it?'

'You know I can't discuss details of the case.'

'I'm only trying to help.' Her friend sounded offended.

Nina sighed. 'I'm sorry, I'm sure we'll be able to discuss it all when it's sorted. Meanwhile, please send Ruby a message confirming exactly which of the wedding guests you're identifying as Jordan Henderson.'

'Not Michael Johnson?'

'No, you don't know his real name.'

'Really?' Mills gave a mischievous laugh before finishing the call.

'Trouble with your inquisitive friend?' asked Ruby with a grin.

'She's already deduced that we've got a match with Jordan Henderson's DNA sample and the cigarette ends from the murder scene.'

Nina went straight to see her DI. She told him about her meeting with Carr, how he had known a Mike Johnson who'd worked with him and later with Jennifer Carr. He'd even been invited to their wedding. Mitch was quick to pick up the possibility that the other DNA sample submitted by Henderson could have belonged to Jennifer Carr's daughter, Harriet.

'Get a sample from her and fast track it,' he ordered.

'Surely her DNA was put on the database when forensics did a sweep of the Carr house, for elimination purposes?' Nina asked.

'It might be there unless the assumption was that her DNA would match the parents so it wasn't necessary. I think she went to stay with an aunt in Devon immediately after her mother was killed. Hazel will have all the details, ask her.'

Nina wandered slowly back to the office. There was no sign of Hazel and Ruby confirmed she wasn't expected back in that day.

'Ruby, can you look at the details of forensics taken from the scene of Jennifer Carr's murder? Specifically what DNA was taken?'

After ten minutes of silence except for the sound of typing, Ruby summarised the report, saying that forensics focussed on the garden and front door. Fingerprints and DNA found belonged to Mr and Mrs Carr apart from the cigarette ends, which have subsequently been matched to the samples associated to a Jordan Henderson, no address or details.

'They took DNA from the Carr family for elimination then?'

'Yes.'

'But not from Harriet Carr?'

Ruby scrolled through a few pages then shook her head. 'Doesn't look like it.'

Nina sighed. 'So I'd better go and get a sample then.'

'There is something we can try before you do that, if you're suggesting that this Michael Johnson is the father of Jennifer Carr's daughter.'

'What?'

'The second sample Henderson submitted for testing should be a mixture of his DNA and Jennifer Carr's. I could ask FINDS and see if it comes up with anything. It will take a while.'

'Good but Mitch wants me to get a sample as soon as possible so I'm going to organise that anyway.'

Later that day, when Nina was putting on her coat and was wrapping her scarf round tightly, Ruby let out a squeal.

'There's been a sighting of Johnson's vehicle!'

Nina went over to Ruby's desk. 'Where?'

'Preston.'

Nina went to give Mitch the news. He said he would contact the local force to inform them and see whether they had any intel.

'They'll soon pick him up if he's in the area,' he said.

Nina had arranged to collect the DNA sample from Harriet Carr at six o'clock, after she returned from her swimming lesson. The girl was still in her school uniform but her father had changed into a pair of jeans and a sweater. The house smelt of cooking, reminding Nina of how little food she'd had that day. Harriet was a petite little thing with dark hair still wet from the pool. She sat bolt upright on the sofa beside her father. Nina took out the kit and began to explain what she was going to do, showing her the swab she would be using, describing how she would take a sample from inside her cheek.

'Oh I've done that before,' she said airily.

Nina looked at her father who expressed surprise. 'When was that, love?' He was glaring at Nina.

'It hasn't been part of the investigation to date,' she assured him. Turning to Harriet, she asked, 'So when was that?'

'It was to check I'm cleaning my teeth properly, that's what Mummy said.'

'She swabbed your mouth? Are you sure darling?'

Nina didn't know what to think. Harriet was opening her mouth so she took the girl's sample and placed it in a labelled evidence bag.

Then she asked, 'Can you remember when that was, Harriet?'

'Just after we went back to school I think.'

Carr asked his daughter to check on the vegetables and as soon as she was out of earshot he apologised to Nina for thinking the police had gone to Devon to get a sample from his daughter. He'd known nothing about any dental swab being taken. His wife hadn't told him about that. Nina reassured him it wasn't a problem but as she drove back she wondered if it was Jennifer who had taken the swab from her daughter to give to Henderson. But why would she do that if it was going to prove that *he* was Harriet's father?

Chapter 23

Mills was in panic mode. She went all the way to Darlington on Saturday morning to find a dress after discovering she had nothing suitable to wear to the party. Normally she wouldn't be too concerned but this was special – it was the Head of Department's do for a start and it was a sort of date with Simon. Harris was unhappy that she was going out, he knew when it was the weekend he would finally spend the day with her, often getting a really long walk.

'I'll make it up to you I promise,' she said as she left.

Of course it was a nightmare trawling the rails. She had no idea what she wanted but didn't want to spend much. In her experience she'd rarely find an opportunity to wear it again whatever it was. A small boutique came to her rescue when the girl asked if she would consider a tunic top rather than a dress. Once Mills had decided she could wear it with her best black jeans, the choice became simpler and more economical. She left town with a rather dressy top that hadn't cost "an arm and a leg" as Gran used to say.

She was back in Mossy Bank by mid-afternoon but despite feeling worn out she quickly walked Harris down to Muker and back. After washing his muddy paws and leaving him in the kitchen, she went upstairs to shower and change. At the back of the wardrobe was a pair of tan strappy sandals she'd bought for a wedding. It was the only pair of shoes she owned with a heel and although it would be chilly, she thought she would take them to change into once she arrived at the party. She put them beside the bed and laid out the new tunic and black jeans feeling satisfied with her purchase.

The shower was tepid – the hot water wasn't timed to heat up until five she remembered too late. She used a new conditioner and found it made her hair look shiny but rather lank. The time was getting on so there was no possibility of correcting it. She regarded her reflection in the mirror deciding it would have to do. Her outfit met with her approval so she changed out of the sandals into socks and boots for the drive and went downstairs to give Harris his tea.

At exactly six o'clock she said goodbye to the lurcher, promising she wouldn't be late. The dog always slept after his dinner and would be fine but she hated leaving him for too long. If she was delayed she would message Muriel to pop round to check on him. It was only after she was on the A1M that she remembered her sandals, which were still beside the bed at home. It was far too late to go back, she decided, so her scruffy old boots would have to do but she felt hot at the thought of how unsophisticated she would now appear.

As it turned out she needn't have worried. Once she'd been admitted into the large Georgian house, Simon rushed over to greet her, saying how "cool" she looked. On another occasion she might have felt the comment was a bit creepy coming from a man in his, she considered for a moment, forties? But in this particular situation it made her feel considerably more relaxed.

'Drink?' he asked.

She stuck to soft drinks as she was driving but it didn't

stop him taking a glass of red wine before steering her over to meet Mrs Cole, the Head's wife. They chatted politely for a while about what Mills was doing at the university before escaping to the conservatory where some of Simon's colleagues were congregating round the food. Mills recognised them and they acknowledged her while eyeing Simon expectantly. He ignored their questioning looks and began loading a plate with party nibbles before steering Mills over to a window seat.

'I can't believe this is the first of Cole's parties you've attended,' he began. 'Does that mean you haven't experienced the Head and his wife singing karaoke?'

'What!'

'Oh well, in that case you've got a treat in store.' He was laughing so much he nearly spilled his wine. 'But of course we're all expected to do our bit. I hope you've got a party piece?'

Mills was horrified. 'You mean we're expected to sing?'

He was still laughing. 'Not if you really don't want to but it's quite good fun and it's worth a few brownie points.'

Mills looked to see if he was serious.

'Honestly, if you want to get on his good side a rendition of "I will survive" or "Wind beneath my wings" could make all the difference.'

'You're not joking, are you?'

He shook his head. Taking her hand, he said, 'Of course we could do a duet.'

'I'll need a glass of something stronger than orange juice.'

'No problem. White wine all right?'

She smiled, he was good fun after dealing with Phil's

269

moodiness. It wasn't Phil's fault but last year had been a struggle and she felt she deserved to have a laugh.

'Here you are,' Simon handed her a glass. 'Apparently the fun starts at nine, so we can enjoy the next hour choosing our song.'

He was brandishing a printed list. Mills quickly realised that the lyrics of duets between men and women were generally about breaking up. The time went quickly. Their discussions over songs were interrupted as various colleagues came to chat with them, including a couple of lecturers that Mills also knew. It was strange being perceived as a couple. Eventually Prof Cole clapped his hands, requesting loudly that everyone congregate in the library where there was a professional karaoke system set up. There was no shortage of volunteers to start the proceedings but it was the prerogative of the hosts, Prof Cole reminded them. He'd clearly had quite a lot to drink and his wife nearly fell over as he helped her onto the makeshift stage. It was difficult to keep a straight face as they launched into a very serious rendering of Elton John and Kiki Dee's "Don't go breaking my heart".

Mills looked at Simon. It had been their selection, based mainly on the fact that Mills thought it could be done in a light hearted way. Unfortunately the duets they were now left with were rather sugary, except for Alicia Keys and Jay Z's "Empire state of mind".

'Are you sure?' Mills asked when Simon suggested it.

'Why not, I'm happy to try a bit of rapping.'

She couldn't stop giggling, possibly due to the wine on her empty stomach – she'd had little to eat all day apart from the party bits and pieces.

Simon took her hand and squeezed it. 'We'll blow their

socks off,' he said.

The party became more raucous as normally staid academics took their turns on the rickety platform. When Prof Cole announced they would have just one more turn, Mills was thinking she wouldn't have to perform but Simon dragged her onto the stage, holding her hand tightly as the intro began. She took a deep breath and as soon as she began "Ooooh, New York!" everyone was cheering. Simon was such an impressive rapper Mills nearly forgot to join in when it was her turn. They were both laughing so much at the end that they nearly fell off the stage. Everyone was clapping, stamping and shouting for more.

'That was fun!' Simon shouted to her above the noise.

She agreed. It was a long time since she'd enjoyed herself so much. Simon's arm was still round her waist and it stayed there as they danced.

'I'd better go soon,' she told him at half past ten.

He persuaded her to stay a little longer but by eleven she insisted she must get back for the dog.

'What are you doing tomorrow?' he asked as they searched for her coat. 'Perhaps we could take Harris for a walk.'

'That would be nice,' she began but then remembered Jean's invitation. 'Oh, I can't, I've been invited to dinner by a neighbour.'

'What time?'

She had no idea. 'I assume it's for Sunday lunch,' she said.

'Shame, I'll have to wait until Monday to see you again then.'

He accompanied Mills to her car and kissed her. And it

271

was a proper kiss. They hugged before she climbed into her seat and he closed the door carefully. She drove off thinking that it really had been a super evening. Her mood continued as she drove home, smiling as she recollected their duet together and Prof Cole's reaction to it. As Simon had indicated, her performance had raised her profile in the eyes of her Head of Department, in a good way.

Muriel, bless her, had left a note to say she'd popped in to check on Harris and had taken him into the garden last thing. Her neighbour constantly made Mills feel guilty about leaving him, although he didn't seem concerned. He was already in his basket in the kitchen, lifting a weary head in acknowledgement before returning to his slumbers. She turned out the lights taking a glass of water upstairs with her. She threw the posh sandals back into the wardrobe, put her new top on a hanger and the rest of her clothes in the wash basket. She was quite exhausted; being with Simon was going to be quite exciting, she decided.

Mills woke in an unusually optimistic mood. It was a bright day with a blue sky devoid of cloud. Outside it was freezing cold but she wrapped up well and sprinted up the track with Harris in tow. After toast and tea she went next door. She had an ulterior motive for popping round to see Muriel; she wanted to thank her for checking on Harris but mainly it was because her neighbour would know Jean Price's phone number.

Later she apologised to Jean for ringing to ask what time she should come for dinner but it was fine because apparently Justin should have told her. Sunday dinner was served at one o'clock in the Price household, otherwise David moans, Jean explained.

'I'm really pleased you're coming,' she added, 'because we've got a surprise for you.'

Mills couldn't think what it could be but Jean wasn't giving anything away. She just told her to come along by one, adding that she'd be very welcome any time after noon.

At eleven-thirty there was a fine layer of white covering the ground and Mills decided to walk over to the farm. She was glad she did. Now the snow was blowing down the dale and settling in the cracks of the stone walls. If it carried on all afternoon she might not have got the Mini back up the hill to Mossy Bank. She carried on along the track, enjoying the first proper snowfall of the year. Her jacket was turning white and she was conscious that, under her hood, her hair was getting damp.

'Millie, look at you, covered in snow!'

Jean flung the door open and ushered her into the hall. As soon as she was inside Jean helped Mills struggle out of her jacket but they didn't go straight into the kitchen.

'Gareth Banford's here with his girlfriend,' Jean whispered excitedly. 'Guess who it is!'

Mills smiled politely, she had no idea.

'Frances Cartwright, she was the head girl at school with Justin. They were good friends before he went to university. Justin found out on Facebook that she was dating Gareth and when he told me I suggested getting back in touch with her. I said to invite her round and it worked!'

She smiled, straightening her apron. 'Anyway, Millie, come through.'

The youngsters were seated at the table playing a board game. She remembered Gareth but hardly recognised him.

'You know Justin and Lucy,' Jean said. 'I think you've met Gareth?'

They nodded.

'And Frances, this is Dr Sanderson. She's a forensic archaeologist.'

The girl with long blonde hair gave a little wave before they all returned to their game.

'You'll have to clear out in...' she referred to the clock. '...thirty minutes, so I can lay the table.'

There followed some good-humoured groaning and objections as the game continued.

Mills offered to help Jean but was given a glass of wine and told to relax. So she sat on a stool and chatted to her hostess as she dealt with the roast dinner. She was describing last night's karaoke when there was a blast of cold air from the back door, announcing David's arrival. He washed his hands at the kitchen sink before greeting Mills.

'Well it's a long time since you've come to see us,' he said with a grin.

Mills was embarrassed.

'David, get changed, and tell Justin to clear up.'

Her son and his friends took their game and disappeared. Mills helped set the table.

Finally, when the meal was ready, the kitchen was empty except for Mills and Jean, who summoned the family by shouting loudly up the stairs. Feet thundered down and soon they were crammed round the pine table, chatting, laughing, a relaxed family lunch. Mills listened to

Justin and Gareth joking about lecturers they'd both had at university. Frances was quiet but seemed to be enjoying the apparent camaraderie between the two young men. Lucy was asking Frances about her university course – she was still studying physics at Newcastle.

The young people dominated the conversation but Jean and David seemed happy to sit back and let them have their say. It suited Mills; the wine was making her feel quite sleepy after her late night. Apple pie followed the roast beef then the youngsters were excused to finish their game in Justin's room. Mills helped clear the dishes and David made coffee while Jean finally relaxed.

'Well, Justin and Gareth seem to be getting on very well,' Mills said as they sat down together.

David grinned. 'Like a house on fire?'

Jean slapped his arm. 'I told you not to say that.'

He feigned sheepishness.

'So are the boys friends again?' Mills asked.

'I think Frances has told them to grow up,' Jean said. 'And they've agreed to disagree.'

'Then let's hope that means Gareth will talk to his folks about the land,' added David. 'We really need to take on some more pasture if we want to increase the flock.'

Jean nodded. 'I think he will – he's a nice lad.'

'I think it's wonderful that Frances got the lads together like that,' said Mills. 'It shows a maturity I rarely see in my students.'

'She did take a bit of persuading,' Jean admitted. 'When Justin said she'd mentioned Gareth on Facebook I knew it was the way in. I didn't tell Justin but I contacted her directly and asked for her help. So it all worked out in the end. Another coffee for anyone?' Jean asked with a grin.

Chapter 24

Ruby was in the office first on Tuesday morning so she'd opened the report on Harriet Carr's DNA, knowing it would be an opportunity to update her colleagues and she could hardly wait for them to arrive. Her expectation, based on experience, was that Nina would be in first but she was wrong.

'God it's cold out there!' DS Fuller exclaimed as she entered the office, pulling off her gloves and hat. She removed her coat to expose a thick mohair jumper over her jeans.

Ruby waited until Hazel returned with a coffee before giving her the news. 'Harriet Carr's DNA is a familial match to Johnson. He's definitely her father.'

Hazel absorbed this information while she took small sips from her mug. 'And Jennifer is still her mother, yes?'

Ruby nodded.

'So how did they know each other?'

'They worked in the same travel agent's.'

Hazel rested her elbows on the desk and rubbed her eyes.

Ruby waited for her to say something but eventually risked stating the obvious. 'So when he said "she lied about the baby" he was meaning that Jennifer had said it *wasn't* his.'

'I *do* understand that, Ruby. Have we located him yet?' Hazel asked.

'No but ANPR has picked him up a couple of times on

the same route at the same time of day. Preston traffic is alerted to watch out for him.'

'Where's he going?'

'We think he's visiting the supermarket. It might be shopping or he may be working there. They're checking the shop's personnel for him.'

'Let me know if and when they pick up Johnson,' Hazel instructed her. 'I'm just popping out for a minute.'

She picked up her bag and disappeared. For a cigarette, Ruby supposed.

It was actually quite a bit later, almost lunchtime, when Ruby heard that Johnson's car had been spotted pulling off the M6 motorway into Lancaster Services. They had picked him up as he was filling the car with petrol. He didn't struggle but walked quietly away with the arresting officers and answered questions at the station politely and without prevarication. He was now in custody and either Hazel or Nina would be going with their DI to Lancaster to interview him.

It was the talk of petrol that suddenly got Nina thinking. 'Ruby, can you run a check on the ANPR for Johnson's car on the night of the fire at Yardley Forensics? See if he was seen in Harrogate please. Phone me if you get a hit, I might not be back in tonight if I go to Lancaster with Mitch.'

Nina was sent the police photograph of Johnson to confirm urgently that he was "Jordan Henderson". She emailed it straight off to Mills and rang the university a few minutes later. Her friend picked up immediately and, after a short pause identified the photograph as Jordan Henderson. Although Nina was in a hurry, she just had to ask about something else.

'Did you do anything exciting over the weekend, Mills?'

Her friend said she'd had Sunday dinner with the family that owned a nearby farm.

'That's nice but what about Saturday?'

'What about it?'

'I heard you were at the Forensics Department's Christmas bash with a professor no less.'

'Who told you that? As if I couldn't guess. Nige!'

Mills had guessed correctly, her husband had heard reports of the karaoke on the grapevine.

'So who is he?'

'Simon Pringle.'

'Are you seeing him again?'

'Yes, we're going out tonight as it happens.'

'That's great, Mills.'

'Yes, it is.'

Hazel accompanied Mitch to Lancaster for the interview. In fact she offered to take the wheel because she'd experienced his erratic driving in the past. It was foggy across the Pennines and wagons were travelling too fast for her comfort. She had to concentrate hard as Mitch droned on about his interview plan. It was getting dark as they joined the motorway, the evening traffic was building up as they approached Lancaster.

Nina contacted Mitch just as Hazel was parking the car. She reported that Mills had confirmed Johnson was definitely the man she'd met calling himself Henderson.

'Leave the talking to me,' Mitch instructed Hazel as they entered the building.

That was no problem for her, the less she had to do the better. They sought out the officer responsible for the arrest and soon they were following him to the room where Johnson was already waiting. He was a big man, clean-shaven and neatly dressed in a navy pullover. Beside him sat a very smart young woman who they'd been informed was his solicitor. After the introductions Mitch began his rehearsed interrogation.

Johnson admitted he'd used a false name when he'd approached Tim Fletcher to carry out DNA testing for him. It was because he wanted to protect his anonymity. When asked the reason, he responded that it was a very personal matter that he was pursuing.

'Was it a paternity case, Mr Johnson?' Mitch asked.

'Yes it was.'

Mitch asked him to describe the circumstances that led to his request for a paternity test but he refused, at which point the DI asked if it concerned his daughter. The man nodded reluctantly. At first, when asked for the name of his daughter he refused to answer but eventually, as Mitch made it clear they already had that information, he confirmed it was Harriet Carr. Mitch then changed tack completely, turning to ask about his visit to see Dr Sanderson.

'When you visited her place of work you became rather distraught.' He paused dramatically. 'Do you remember what you said to her as you left?'

Johnson looked anxiously at his solicitor who smiled encouragingly. He shrugged.

'No?' asked Mitch. 'Well you were heard to say "she lied about the baby". What did you mean by that?'

He was looking down at his hands clasped on his lap.

'Did you mean your baby, Harriet Carr?' Mitch asked.

He nodded.

'So did you mean the baby's mother had lied?'

He didn't respond.

'Did you mean Jennifer Carr had lied?'

No response.

'Did Jennifer Carr take the DNA swab from her daughter so you could have it tested?'

Henderson's demeanour changed. Once more he appeared anxious to help them. 'Yes. I gave her one of the kits and she returned it to me for the test.'

'Why would she do that for you?'

'Because she said I wasn't the father. She was certain I wasn't so, she said she was happy to take the swab.'

Mitch asked how he could be sure the sample was genuine and he was at pains to explain how he'd watched her take the swab through the window.

Over the next hour they covered the testing at Yardley Forensics, how he'd been told to order the kit from a reputable supplier then he'd sent the samples to somewhere in Harrogate. Johnson couldn't remember exactly where. Hazel assumed it was Tim Fletcher's home. The results were transmitted by email. Mitch questioned him over the request to meet Tim after the results had been received but, despite several challenges, Johnson simply replied that they'd never actually met because the analyst had refused his request.

It was time for a break. Johnson and his solicitor were offered tea while Hazel and her boss withdrew to join the officers for a brew. Mitch immediately turned to Hazel and asked why they hadn't picked up earlier that the girl's sample, submitted by Johnson under his assumed name, matched DNA from Jennifer Carr, their murder victim.

'There was no reason to look for a match,' she

explained. 'There was no reason to think there was a link between him and Jennifer Carr.'

She warned him that if Johnson was watching Jennifer Carr take Harriet's DNA swab from outside the house he could claim that he smoked the two cigarettes on that occasion. However, in her opinion the cigarette butts were in such good condition they could not have lain in the garden for more than a few days, certainly not for over a month.

Mitch agreed but said he intended to leave the forensic evidence of the cigarette ends until the interview was nearly over, which meant he wanted to tackle the fire at the lab next. She went back through her notes while they drank tea and she took the opportunity to point out that if Tim Fletcher really had refused to meet him, Johnson still could have gone to the laboratory the night it was burned down with the analyst inside. Mitch nodded in agreement once more.

She added, 'I'd like to ask him about his relationship with Jennifer and why he waited ten years to check Harriet's parentage.'

Mitch told her she could ask Johnson herself, finishing his drink, ready to continue the interview. Johnson, who was chatting to his solicitor when they entered the room, looked relaxed. Mitch began going over the night of the fire but Johnson continued to insist he never went to the laboratory and didn't even know where it was. Soon the DI indicated to Hazel that she could start her questioning.

'Obviously you had reason to believe that Jennifer Carr might have had your baby. So presumably you had a relationship with her at some stage. Was that before or after she was married?'

He seemed composed. 'We were at university together and went out a few times. It was a surprise when she came to work in the same office. There were quite a few of us used to go out drinking and clubbing together. She got engaged to a guy who I worked with, Derek Carr.'

'You went to their wedding,' Hazel said.

He was taken aback and appeared surprised that she would know something like that about him.

'Yes,' he replied, regaining his composure. 'Derek went to another branch soon after that, which was when it started. We had the odd drink. It didn't last very long.'

Hazel could tell he was almost enjoying telling the story and pursued it. 'Why did the affair end? Did she finish it or did you?'

He frowned, leaning forward. 'She fell pregnant. I said she should leave him. I wanted her to live with me and our baby.'

'You knew it was yours?'

'She said she thought it was. Derek had been away a lot.'

'But she chose to stay with her husband?'

'It wasn't like that.' He raised his voice. 'She said she was going to get rid of it; she was only a few weeks gone. I pleaded with her but she was adamant. She just wanted it to go away. I was gutted. I knew she couldn't do that if she loved me. I couldn't bear to think of it so I asked for a transfer.' He paused. 'I hadn't seen her since that night more than ten years ago.'

Hazel was puzzled. She looked at Mitch who nodded encouragingly.

'So tell me Michael, why did you get in touch with her

after all that time?'

He wore an anguished expression. 'I saw her Facebook page. She had a ten-year-old daughter, Harriet. I realised that she'd lied to me. She kept *my* baby without telling me. She brought her up with a man who wasn't her father.'

'Surely it was still possible that Harriet was Derek Carr's child though?'

'That's what she said. She tried to bluff me but I proved her wrong.'

Mitch made a slight movement with his hand indicating to Hazel that he wished to speak. 'Is that why you killed her, Michael? Why you stabbed her in the heart – to punish her?'

His reaction was to scream at them that he was innocent. He loved her and he wouldn't ever have hurt her. He became hysterical and they called a halt to the interview to allow him to calm down.

Hazel checked her phone as they left the room to find a message from Nina. It said that ANPR had located Johnson's car in Harrogate close to Yardley Forensics on the night of the twenty-eighth of October.

'Yes!' she cried. 'We've got him near the lab on the night it burned down. We can have him for arson and at least one count of murder.'

They left him for a couple of hours while Mitch dealt with the CPS. Then they resumed the interview. Johnson's solicitor said he was fine but would not be answering any more questions. Hazel confronted him with the news that his car had been seen in the vicinity of the forensic lab on the night of the twenty-eighth of October, when it was deliberately set on fire, resulting in the death of a member of staff.

Despite the advice he'd been given, he spoke out. 'It wasn't me, I've never been to Harrogate,' he said sullenly.

Hazel grinned. 'I thought you said you didn't know where the laboratory was.'

After that he refused to comment except to say he knew nothing about the fire. They charged him with arson, leaving him in the custody suite at Lancaster. As Hazel drove him back to Northallerton Mitch went through the events of the day, concluding that the only motive Johnson could have for setting fire to the lab was to destroy evidence of his DNA enquiry. Surely the assumption was therefore that he'd murdered Jennifer Carr and was hiding the evidence of his relationship with her.

Hazel laughed. 'Ironically, if he hadn't set fire to the lab we may not have ever discovered that Fletcher was moonlighting. But investigating Henderson led us to Johnson and his link with Jennifer Carr. You know I'm really looking forward to tomorrow,' she informed her DI.

Back in the office she had a request for Ruby. 'Good work locating Johnson in Harrogate. Can you look for him at the Carr's place on the night of Jennifer's murder?'

Nina was at home when she called Mills. She wanted to give her the news straight away.

'Tell Brenda she can stop worrying.'

'What d'you mean?' Mills was in the middle of cleaning up a spill in the kitchen.

'Hazel rang. They've just charged someone for the fire.'

'Who? Was it Henderson, I mean Johnson. I bet it was!'

'I can't say.'

'Really? What if I say it was him and you say nothing if I'm right?'

'Mills, stop it. You know I can't say a word and that doesn't mean I'm saying yes. It just means don't ask me.'

'OK but thanks for letting me know. I'll call Brenda now. She'll be relieved. I was almost suspecting her myself.'

'Before you go, how was your date with Simon?'

'Fine. We had a meal in a really nice Italian restaurant and went back to his place for coffee.'

Nina wanted details but it was her friend's turn to refuse to say more, except that they were going to another party on Saturday.

They ended the call so she could ring Brenda. She sounded fine but Mills knew her boss had been worried.

'Good news,' she began.

When their conversation was over, Mills was smiling to herself. The news had been a much bigger relief to her boss than she had predicted. Brenda had obviously been in tears at the other end of the phone; her voice had gone all emotional in a way she'd never heard before. She had thanked Mills maybe five or six times despite the fact she'd insisted it had nothing to do with her. However, it hadn't changed Brenda's plans, she would still be selling the building as a shell, pay redundancy to the staff and retire on the insurance payout.

Mills sighed as she put the phone down. What a waste of the effort they had all put into the business. If she had the money she would save it herself but that was just wishful thinking. She had enough difficulty keeping her two Heads of Departments at the university happy. She wished she could find someone with money who would be willing to take over the business from Brenda.

Michael Johnson had had a bad night. The duty officer informed Hazel that he'd been creating pandemonium most of the evening and in the end the doctor had been called. Now the man was subdued but fit to interview, apparently. She told Mitch, who said they should "crack on".

Subdued was one word for it, Hazel thought, when Johnson arrived. He looked rough, that's how she would describe it. He seemed to have aged ten years overnight. She wondered if it was caused by a guilty conscience or from the stress of being wrongly accused. They would find out this morning, she was certain of that. She didn't feel that chipper herself. Her son had come home late stinking of booze so she'd laid into him for keeping her awake and he was still asleep when she'd left the house today.

'Shall we begin?' Mitch was asking Johnson's solicitor.

She looked at her client and nodded uncertainly.

When the DI asked him how he was feeling, he was rewarded with a grunt.

'So, Michael, we've established that you tried to destroy the laboratory that analysed your DNA sample and that of your daughter, Harriet.'

Johnson objected but Mitch ignored him and continued. 'So, this morning I want to establish why you wanted to destroy the evidence. Was it because you knew that it would connect you to Jennifer Carr?'

His composure was almost eerie. 'No comment,' he muttered.

Hazel hated it when they did that. It wasted valuable time.

Mitch frowned. 'You told us that you had arranged with Jennifer to have Harriet's DNA tested. So what did you do when you received the results proving she was your daughter and not Derek's?'

There was no response.

'Did you arrange to meet her?'

Johnson looked up. 'Yes of course I did,' he said softly. 'I was entitled to meet my daughter, wasn't I?'

'So you went to her house. When was that?'

'I don't remember.'

'We have your car passing the end of her road on the night she died.'

'I don't remember when it was.'

Mitch looked at Hazel, this was it. 'We found cigarette ends containing your DNA in her front garden.'

He came back quickly. 'I smoked while I waited for her to collect the DNA swab.' He looked slightly pleased with himself, not arrogant but quietly confident.

Nina was surprised he could think straight, he looked so ill. She told him forensics had shown they were too fresh to be from the visit he made to collect Harriet's swab. 'Tell me exactly what happened from when you got the positive DNA test results.'

Unexpectedly that started a long description of how he'd rung Jennifer to give her the news, asking to meet to discuss the positive result. Her husband was in Dubai so she said he could come over but only after Harriet was asleep.

'She made me wait outside until my daughter was in bed. She said ten o'clock but it was much later. It was cold waiting out there. I could see them through the window, she wasn't hurrying. Eventually she comes out and pulls the door behind her, there's no way she's letting me in the house.'

'That must have annoyed you,' suggested Mitch.

Johnson ignored him. It was as if he was re-enacting the night. Hazel hoped it would cause him to admit his part in it. 'What did you say to her?' she asked.

'I told her I'd like to meet my daughter,' he replied.

She tried to keep her voice low and sympathetic. 'And how did she respond to that?'

He shuddered. 'She said "Over my..." His voice faltered. 'She said no.'

Over my dead body, thought Hazel. That's what she said, poor woman. 'What happened then?' she asked softly.

He sat up, suddenly full of life. 'She produced this knife and waved it at me. She told me to go away. "Stay away!" she screamed at me.' They all waited for him to continue. 'I went to take it off her but she flew at me. I don't know exactly what happened but we fell over and there was blood, a lot of blood.' He ran his hand through his hair. 'I just ran.'

'What did you do with the knife?' Mitch asked.

Johnson appeared irritated by the question. 'I just threw it in the river later.'

He was staring at them as if challenging them to do something about what he'd just said. Mitch looked at Hazel, his solicitor watched Johnson. Three hours later he was charged with Jennifer Carr's murder.

Chapter 25

There was a party atmosphere in the office next morning. Mitch had bought doughnuts and Ruby made real coffee for the four of them. The morning meeting had gone well but it remained for Nina to visit Derek Carr to give him the news. It wouldn't be easy, she would not only be telling him that his wife had been unfaithful but Harriet was not his daughter. It was unavoidable because it would all come out in court when the entire world would know. It was not something she would want her own daughter to learn from the press.

But before she left, she asked Hazel to ring Brenda Yardley's insurance company to tell them they had charged the arsonist. 'Then you can tell Brenda yourself,' she instructed her colleague.

Hazel immediately passed the message on to her researcher and she left the office. That's typical of DS Fuller, thought Ruby, as she looked up the phone number, no emotional intelligence. The loss adjuster wanted an official letter on headed paper before she was satisfied but seemed pleased she could proceed with the claim. Not as pleased as Dr Yardley sounded when Ruby spoke to her.

'Of course, Mills told me last night,' she confided but Ruby pretended she hadn't heard.

Nina was on the phone to Derek Carr. He was at work and it took some persuasion to convince him to see her somewhere private. Nina reluctantly agreed to meet him in his lunch break near his office in Darlington.

She left town at half-eleven and took it slowly, parking in a multi-storey and having a quick look at the shops before making for the park where he said he would meet her. It wasn't an ideal spot for the conversation they were due to have so when he arrived she suggested they might go back to his house. Instead he sat on a bench, producing a pack of sandwiches which he proceeded to open while asking her to "spill the beans". She tried to present her explanation of events in as matter of fact way as possible. She told him they had Michael Johnson in custody for Jennifer's murder.

'Mike Johnson - the one in the wedding photo? But we haven't seen him for years.' He continued to shake his head and deny it could be him. Having finished one sandwich he automatically began the second.

Nina kept her voice down as she told him that Johnson had been to see Jennifer recently.

'She didn't tell me,' he muttered, replacing the half-eaten sandwich in its packet.

'There is a reason for that.' Nina tried to keep any emotion out of her voice as she described why Johnson contacted his wife. Carr was looking at the ground but he was listening intently. His chest was moving in and out as if he was short of breath.

'…so she agreed to take a DNA sample from Harriet for testing.' Nina paused.

'So it wasn't for the dentist.'

'No.'

She knew what he would ask next.

'What was the result?'

'He is her biological father.'

Nina gave him time to digest the information. He stood up and walked off, stopping a few yards away, turning as if to ask something then moving away again without speaking. He had his back to her but Nina could see he was wiping his eyes with the back of his hand. She waited until he returned and sat down.

'Is that why he killed her?' he asked quietly.

'He says it was an accident.'

'An accident!' he repeated angrily.

'He came back to see your wife after he received the DNA results. She told him to leave, threatening him with a knife. When he tried to take it they fell. That's what he says.'

'Do you think it's true?' he asked.

Nina considered her answer. 'I don't know. That's something for the jury to decide.'

They sat side by side for a while until Carr thanked her for coming to see him. He told her she must be busy and she sensed he wanted to be left alone. He said he'd be fine but would stay there for a while to think about what to tell Harriet. Nina walked away thinking it was the worst part of her job. She would keep in touch with the Carr family when the case was due in court, particularly if Harriet was required to give evidence about having the swab taken. She was just a year older than Rosie and Nina couldn't imagine how her daughter would cope with the ordeal the poor girl has been through already. She really hoped Derek Carr had a supportive family to help them get through the trial.

She drove back to the office in a sombre mood that wasn't easily dispelled despite the festive atmosphere at work. It was the office Christmas dinner that evening and she'd brought a sparkly dress to change into for the evening. Nige had been visibly relieved that they couldn't find a babysitter free that night as he didn't enjoy being one of only a few partners that attended each year. Hazel always refused to bring her current date along and Ruby was single at the moment. One or two of their colleagues brought partners, including Mitch whose wife appeared to scarcely endure the experience. Hazel and Ruby had suggested they hire an escape room in Darlington but were outvoted and, once again, it was dinner in a hotel outside Northallerton despite the pair's protestations that it was going to be boring. Nina just braced herself for the usual questions about whether Hindus celebrated Christmas.

Mills left work early before the build-up of Friday night traffic. She needed to do a big shop at the supermarket on the way home if Simon was going to be coming over. He said he wanted to see where she lived and meet Harris. The party was in Richmond so he offered to pick her up and bring her back home, so she thought it would only be polite to offer for him to stay over. That way they'd have Sunday together. He'd agreed. But now she would have to tidy the cottage and cook before Saturday evening.

She was packing away the groceries when the phone rang. She rushed to answer, hoping it was Simon but it was Fiona and she sounded excited.

'Mills, it's me. I told your dad *I'd* ring because I can explain it better. It's about the skiing thing. Hugh told me how disappointed you were that we'd gone ahead and booked. I'm really sorry. Anyway, that's irrelevant now.'

Mills was irritated by her chattering. 'What is it you want?'

'We've got you a ticket! It was rather complicated but we managed to change the flights so we can all go. The chalet's huge so that's not an issue. Isn't that wonderful?'

'Yes, it is.' Mills tried to sound pleased while she was considering what to do about Harris. She wanted to think it over but they'd already bought the ticket so it was all arranged. She sighed. 'Yes it really is great. Thank you for doing that, it's brilliant.'

Fiona gave a long string of instructions, dates, and logistics. She didn't need ski equipment or clothing, it would all be there. Her friend who owned the chalet had loads of things to spare. Mills should come down for Christmas Eve and they'd leave on Boxing Day. There was no more to be said.

Her head was reeling when she came off the phone. There was no way she was sending Harris down to Phil for Christmas. Nina and Nige already had a house full with the children so they wouldn't want a dog to deal with. She would have to ask Muriel.

In the morning she popped next door to see her neighbour, who was on her way out to the shops.

'Hi, Muriel, how are you? Busy? I just wanted to say I'm out this evening but Harris will be fine, I won't be too late.'

Her neighbour said she'd always pop in if needed.

'Actually I wondered what you were doing for Christmas this year.'

'Scotland, we're off to Edinburgh. My cousin invited us to stay until Hogmanay. It'll be a real holiday for us.'

'That sounds lovely.'

'Sorry, I must dash. I've got a fruitcake in the oven so there's just time to get to Reeth and back.'

She was gone, leaving Mills feeling unsettled by the dilemma of possibly having to ask Phil to do his duty and look after Harris.

Simon arrived promptly at six reporting that he'd found the last part of the journey quite challenging.

'I nearly missed your turning,' he admitted.

He was through the door before Mills could warn him that Harris was rather boisterous. The dog jumped up, nearly knocking him over but Simon wasn't daunted, he was down on his knees making a fuss of the lurcher.

'What a great dog,' he said, standing up and brushing hairs off his jeans.

'He's certainly taken a shine to you.'

She'd lit a fire in the sitting room and told him to take a seat while she made tea. She could hear Simon playing with Harris while she boiled the kettle.

'Have you eaten?' she called. 'Would you like a sandwich?'

It was good to just sit in front of the fire, eating and drinking tea together. It had been a long time since she'd felt as comfortable with someone as she was with Simon. She told him she was going to be with her family for the holidays.

'Skiing? That sounds great. Although I'm disappointed you won't meet Arnie.'

'Your son is coming over for the holidays?'

'Yes, just for a few days. He's staying with me for Christmas then going back to be with his mother's family for New Year.'

'I'm sorry to miss him, he sounds great.'

They were so comfortable that it was an effort to leave the fireside. Mills got changed while Simon and Harris remained on the sofa. Eventually they had to venture out into the cold, dark night. The heater in Simon's car was fairly ineffective but he had bought a brand-new wool rug for Mills to wrap herself in. Very considerate, she thought.

The party was being held by an older colleague of Simon's but it wasn't in the same league as Professor Cole's bash. There was gentle music playing quietly in the background, canapés being passed round and small talk, lots of small talk. Many of the guests were older, closer to the age of the host and his partner, and Simon admitted he knew very few people. They were introduced to neighbours who told them at length about their house renovations until Simon looked at his watch in an exaggerated fashion declaring they really should be going. When their host's wife came down with their jackets, they thanked her profusely, explaining they had a long journey.

Harris was certainly pleased to see them back so early. Mills poured two glasses of wine while Simon got the fire going again. They sat in its glow with the dog stretched across their feet.

'I've been thinking,' said Simon. 'What's happening to Harris while you're away? Do you have to put him in kennels?'

'I don't want to but the only alternative is to make Phil take him.'

'I see. That's a shame.' After a pause he said, 'Arnie loves dogs.'

Nothing more was said until Sunday evening when

Simon was getting ready to leave. They'd wrapped up well and walked to Muker for a pub lunch, returning the long way round high up on the tops. Simon had put Harris on the lead for them to cross where there were sheep about and Mills commented that she hadn't seen the dog so well behaved.

Simon put his arm around her and gave her a hug. 'You know, we make a good team,' he said, 'me and Harris. Why don't you let me look after him over Christmas, I'd really like to.'